FISH OUT OF WATER

FISH OUT OF WATER

A GIRL WITHOUT A PHONE/LITTLE MERMAID STORY

JENNIFER SOMMERSBY

BE WHO YOU WERE BORN TO BE

Marina Andersen's structured life is ruled by the Three S's: Swim. Study. Succeed. But all this routine and order leaves little time for what she *really* wants to do: SING. Try telling that to her overbearing father, a former rock legend whose personal demons keep Marina's extraordinary musical talents behind closed doors.

After a chance performance at school drops a once-in-a-lifetime opportunity—and a gorgeous young rocker—at Marina's feet, she'll have to decide what lengths she's willing to go to in pursuit of the one thing that reminds her heart to beat.

While navigating the rough seas of managing her father's expectations and finding her own voice, will Marina summon the courage to show her dad who she really is inside before their family is dashed like a galleon in a storm?

Brought to you by the hugely popular YouTube series, *The Girl Without A Phone,* from the Young Actors Project, in collaboration with YA novelist Jennifer Sommersby, *Fish Out of Water* is a timeless, heartwarming tale inspired by the beloved *Little Mermaid.* Join Marina—alongside friends Lily and Sierra—in this fresh new adventure meant to inspire the reader to find their own song.

Sleight
The Undoing / Scheme

For all the Marinas out there, trying to find their song.

CHAPTER 1

JUST AN ILLUSION

Sometimes I swear I see her sitting in the bleachers.

When my goggles are fogged or when the seal against my face has broken and water has seeped in and the chlorine stings my eyes. You'd think I'd have a resistance to that sting after all these years. I don't.

It's those moments when I think I see her sitting there, cheering me on, that steal my breath.

The eighth anniversary has just passed. Seeing her—or thinking I see her—happens more often around this time of year, when the leaves change and the air has a bite to it, reminding you to take a heavier coat and not just a cute sweatshirt or cardigan, or you'll shiver through all your classes.

But then I blink my stinging eyes a few times, readjust my goggles against my face, look back to the bleachers, and it's not *my* mom sitting there but someone else's. It's those moments I feel most alone in the world. My father is usually there, but instead of cheering, he's hunched over his silver clipboard, a stopwatch in his hand. I can tell what the rest of the day will be like with a single glance at the shape of his mouth.

Parents sit in groups, high-fiving and hollering. She used to high-five and holler too. The stakes were a lot lower then. A meet, good or bad, meant a trip to the ice cream shop after. Nowadays, a bad performance in the pool means hours more in the pool.

I blink again. The mirage fades. Again, someone else's mom.

The squeeze of grief, like a hand wrapped around my heart—it never goes away. Well-meaning folks say it gets better with time, and maybe with a hundred more years, it will.

Then the start beep goes off, and I hit the water, racing against the dolphin-like bodies on either side of me, and she floats out of my mind as quickly as she floated in.

CHAPTER 2

SONGBIRD

The acoustics in the locker room showers are surprisingly good. That's why so many people think they can sing. Everybody sounds good in the shower, lathering up with their perfumey soaps, belting out tunes from their favorite pop stars. Pull them out of the shower and put a mic in their hands? The magic of the shower disappears like suds down the drain.

I'm working out the kinks on a new song. My song, an original, again. Always. Easier that way. I don't like being compared to other singers, but people like their comparisons. "You sound like P!nk." "You sound like early Gaga, but not as deep." "You sound like that girl who was on *America's Got Talent* a few years ago. The one who plays the ukulele?"

I think I sound like me. My friends Lily and Sierra think I sound like me too.

The choir director at school likes pushing her singers, but she's also obsessed with Stevie Nicks and Chrissie Hynde and Debbie Harry from Blondie and other performers from a million years ago that my Uncle Tim listens to. Ms. Amberly is careful with my voice, though. A former opera singer herself, she developed nodes on her vocal cords from pushing herself and her voice too hard while she toured. She had surgery, the surgeon cut too much—same thing that happened to Julie Andrews, apparently—and now singing is in her rearview mirror.

It's really sad, actually. The damage forced her off the international stage and into the classroom and while we're glad to have her—and her crazy-cool handmade wardrobe full of custom dresses and skirts that look like they belong in a movie from the 1950s—every once in a while, I see her face as she watches us sing. I think I wear that same face sometimes. Regardless, she's taught me a lot about my body's role in making music and when not to push, that I sit firmly in mezzo-soprano with a three octave-range.

Bottom line, I can sing.

My dad, former heartthrob rocker Trent Andersen, doesn't want me to sing. He wants me to swim. His house rules: *Swim. Study. Succeed.*

You can see maybe why I like to sing.

My swim-team sisters? They're standing around the outside of my shower stall, clapping and whooping, throwing out requests like I'm on stage at karaoke night.

I turn off the shower, still singing (I'm just at the good part), and flap the curtain open, my towel wrapped around my goosebump-covered body. Goosebumps not from the cold, but from the feeling I get when I make these sounds come out of my throat and face.

I finish the song.

The applause and hollers bounce off the tiled ceiling, walls, and floors. Like I said, good acoustics.

Coach Tosto barrels into the locker room as she always does, a hurricane in Spandex and expensive foam flip-flops. "I think some of you are supposed to be in the pool?" My audience breaks up, tossing sideways glances at Coach's back, glances of solidarity at me.

"Songbird," she starts. It's not a compliment the way she

says it. "If you spent as much time focused on your split times as you spend on your nursery rhymes, you'd be more than ready for districts."

I want to tell her she has a good start of a song there: *split times and nursery rhymes.* I don't tell her that.

"I am ready for districts."

She hoists her clipboard between us and gives it a wiggle. "The clock says differently."

"It's five thirty on a Thursday afternoon. It's been a long week, and my body is tired."

Coach Tosto mimes a talking mouth with her hand, like she's animating an invisible puppet. "I'm hearing a lot of excuses. *Wahw wahw wahw.*"

I pull my towel tighter and reach for my dripping suit hanging from the hook next to me. "I have an Advanced Biology test tomorrow. May I be excused?"

"Your dad is out front. I talked to him about the butterfly mini workshop on Sunday. He wants you here. Those butterfly times are not going to get you into the regional meet."

"Can we focus on districts first?" I try to move past her but Coach Tosto is built like a fortress. All muscle and close gray curls against her head, a mouth that looks painted on with an old pink crayon.

Her office is decorated with the medals and trophies that qualify her to be an elite swim coach, which is why I'm standing here, dripping and covered in goosebumps that are now truly from the cold, waiting for the lecture to end. My father sought her out and moved us here when I was eight just so I could train with the esteemed Coach Maria Tosto.

"But I don't want to be a swimmer," I told him as he pulled into the parking lot of the swim club, the best on the West Coast. "I want to be a singer. Like Mom. Like you."

He laughed, but it wasn't because he thought it was funny. Sadness—not humor—sat heavily in his eyes.

I started swimming the next day, before the movers had even finished carrying the boxes into our new house.

I've been swimming ever since. I am the living embodiment of the silly blue-tang fish from that Pixar film—"Just keep swimming! Just keep swimming!"—minus the short-term memory loss, of course. Though my dad may argue with that …

Coach Tosto lifts her penciled-on left eyebrow at me. It's always the left eyebrow. We joke that she should just draw it that way instead of wasting the muscle energy to lift it.

"I'll see you at Saturday practice at eight." She spun and left a whiff of chlorine and bargain-brand women's deodorant in her wake.

I'm dressed and pulling on my second shoe, grumbling in my head about how cold the water is at eight in the morning, how sore I will be after two hours of butterfly practice, how really I just want to hang out with my friends, when the main locker room screeches open. They really need to fix that.

"Ah! You're still here!" Lily bounds toward me, outfitted in the beige pants and turquoise-blue uniform required by the swim club management, her hair a little messy from pulling off her hairnet. She works in the concession stand three days a week after school and says the hairnet will be the thing that makes her quit. Not the crabby parents or little kids begging for free cookies—the hairnets.

I thought she got the job because she wanted to hang out with me, but then I realized that her adorable boyfriend, Steve, is on the water polo team—and all the local high school teams use our pool for their year-round practices. It makes sense that Lily would want to be there as much as possible to hang out with him.

And most of my other friends who apply for jobs at the swim club? You guessed it: water polo guys.

Truth? Lily and Sierra and I have spent many nights sitting on the cold metal bleachers watching the water polo practices. It's a ritual: I finish swimming; Lily gets off work but before doing so, she makes us each hot cocoa with extra whipped cream dusted with chocolate powder; Sierra shows up after she finishes her babysitting job; and then we perch on the highest bleacher and cheer whenever Steve's team does something amazing. We pretend we're quizzing each other with whatever flashcards we've got in our bags that week as cover. It's the only way my dad will let me stay out for anything after swim practice—if I'm studying.

Let's just say we know a lot more about water polo than we do about mitosis and meiosis.

"Your dad is out front," Lily says. "Talking to your swim coach." She slides my wet towel over and sits.

"Of course. They're planning new ways to torture me."

"Which is why I had to run in here before you left. He heard you singing."

"And …?"

"Nothing. We all heard it. The parents all love it—but they know better than to say anything to your dad."

"Trent Andersen, former rock star, refuses to let his daughter sing in public."

Lily twists her lips to the side for a beat. "I'm sorry, Mar. I know this is a thing between you guys, so I just wanted to let you know so he didn't get in your face about it in the car or whatever."

"Yeah. Thank you." I'd tell Lily that I don't know why my dad is so weird about me singing, but we both know why my dad is weird about me singing. No one on the outside could possibly understand why Trent Andersen wouldn't want his daughter to follow in his footsteps. Rock-and-roll worked out well for him. He cut some great records. He hit the Billboard charts a few times. He toured the world and fell in love. He made a lot of money for a while. From the outside, everything looks so pretty and perfect.

No one really knows why my dad still wears his wedding

band, even though the woman who gave it to him has been gone for half my life now.

"We're still on for karaoke this weekend? Sierra texted and she's in. Doesn't have to babysit," Lily says. Her smile is like a warm blanket.

"Can't wait."

"I *may* have something cooler than karaoke for us to do," Lily says, trying to smooth wayward strands in her long blond hair, "but I don't want to jinx it yet." She stands and grabs my wet towel, rolling my swimsuit into it for me.

"Something cooler than karaoke?"

"Seriously cooler." She hands me the towel roll.

"What is cooler than karaoke? A hint? Just one?"

She slides onto the bench again, her hand soft and warm on top of my wrist. She's done her nails again—I love the color. I never do my nails because the chlorine from the pool water makes the polish brittle.

"One hint: it involves music."

"Oh, come on! Another hint! Please?"

Lily throws her head back in an exaggerated evil laugh. "Okay, only one more hint: it involves LIVE music."

"Are you serious?" She knows how much I love live music.

My phone vibrates against the metal bench, startling us both. I hold it up for her to see, the giddiness evaporating in my chest. Text from my dad: **Get a move on. We need dinner. Talked to Coach about [butterfly emoji].**

"Your dad uses emojis to talk about swimming?"

"Rarely. The family counselor said emojis could be a 'fun' way for us to communicate."

"My mom discovered the poop emoji and she thinks it's funny to use all the time. For everything," Lily says.

"Trent Andersen would be mortified if I sent him a poop emoji," I say.

"You could try it. Maybe when he's being a jerk about not

giving you any days off." Her phone timer chimes. "My break's over so call me later, after you talk to your dad about butterflies or whatever." She backs toward the door, talking in a loud whisper. "And don't despair, Songbird! Saturday night is only forty-eight hours from now!"

"Don't call me 'songbird'!" I yell after her, but the screaming locker room door drowns me out.

Forty-eight hours to ace an Advanced Bio exam, get through swim practice tomorrow and first thing Saturday morning—and, of course, survive my dad's inquisition.

Ironically, it's Coach Tosto's voice I hear in my head: *"One stroke at a time, songbird. One stroke at a time."*

CHAPTER 3

HEY, MOM ...

Dad barely waits for me to get my seat belt on.

"You looked tired out there today," he says. I'd think he was concerned about the fact that his child is tired, but it's not that. He's concerned that I won't hit the times I need to place at the upcoming district meet, which means I won't qualify for the regional meet, which means university scouts won't pick me out of the lineup of dozens of other swimmers competing for the same scholarships and early acceptance offers.

"I *am* tired, Dad. It's been a long week." I reach over and turn on the radio. Maybe he'll get the hint.

He lowers the volume using the button on the steering wheel. "'Never make excuses. Your friends don't need them and your foes won't believe them.' John Wooden said that."

I don't want to know who John Wooden is. My dad is obsessed with self-help books and people who proclaim to be success gurus. Right now, I'm so tired, I could fall asleep sitting up. I wonder if John Wooden has a quote about that.

"Talked to Coach—she told you about the butterfly workshop on Saturday?"

I nod.

"Honestly, Marina, if you want these scouts to take you seriously—just because you're a junior doesn't mean you have loads of time to get this right. You're sitting at the bottom of the top ten swimmers in your division right now—as an eleventh grader—but you're just barely there. Even with the seniors graduating next spring, it doesn't mean you stay on that list. New kids start in the swim program every fall—you know that. One slow heat and you're out of the top ten."

"Would that be such a bad thing?" I say under my breath.

"I know what you're capable of. So does Coach. You just need to get your head in the game and push a little harder."

I close my eyes and put my head back against the headrest. He continues talking. It's a buzz in my waterlogged ears.

"Marina, are you listening?"

I pop my eyes open, my vision a bit fuzzy for a few blinks. "Dad, full disclosure: I am not listening because I have an exam tomorrow on cellular energetics, so my brain isn't concerned about how fast I swam across the pool today."

His hands tighten on the steering wheel and his jaw clenches. He reaches for the pocket in the dashboard and grabs a piece of gum from the plastic tub he keeps there. The car fills with the scent of spearmint. He chews to the count of ten, takes a deep breath, and loosens his grip on the wheel.

"Swim. Study. *Succeed*. Remember? I just want the best for you, Marina."

"I know. And I'm trying as hard as I can to make it all work." I prop my head in my palm against the closed window. I brave a look over at my dad to see if he is actually listening to me or if he's still wound up. Seeing the wedding band on his finger squeezes my heart for a single beat. I don't know how he can keep wearing it.

Man, I miss Mom.

"Just let me get through the exam tomorrow and I promise to be faster on Saturday." On the radio, one of my dad's songs starts up, introduced by the DJ as "an oldie but a goodie." I like this song—he and my mom used to dance around the kitchen singing it, not hard and loud like the rock version but soft and romantic, like he wrote the song just for her. I think he probably did. He'd sing, she'd sing, they'd duet, then they'd kiss and I'd giggle and slam into their legs because when you're five, seeing your parents sing and dance and kiss meant that all was right with the world.

With one long, guitar-calloused finger, he silences the radio, leaving only the sound of his aggressive gum chewing and our separate breaths behind.

～

EVEN THOUGH I showered at the pool, I have a chill I can't get rid of, so I stand under the hot water, steaming up the mirror, coating my hair in a deep conditioner. I have my mother's hair—thick and dark with a natural wave—and I've managed to keep it long and relatively healthy by doing a long conditioning treatment every week. Once that's done for tonight, I slide into my cozy bathrobe and warm socks. I'll make peppermint tea, and I throw my biology textbook onto my bed—because nothing says relaxation like memorizing the steps in aerobic oxidation of glucose.

My dad is preoccupied in his study—a podcast blares through speakers, muffled by the closed door and underscored by the *clack-whirr-clack* of his elliptical—so I make tea and tiptoe back upstairs before he decides to rush out and start a new lecture on whatever self-help genius is filling his head with inspiration.

I set my steaming-hot mug on the nightstand and slide my books aside on the duvet.

"Neptune, how was your day?" My goldfish thinks he's a puppy—I've trained him to jump through these tiny little hoops Sierra found on the internet after we watched a video of a guy training his own goldfish. Neptune took to it, well, like a fish takes to water.

What started out as a carnival prize in a plastic bag seven years ago has become a fish the size of my palm with a tank big enough to accommodate. He knows he's beautiful, which is why it's so appropriate that Uncle Tim and I named him after the Roman god of water.

I tap flakes and some freeze-dried treats into his tank; he offers his thanks with a quick hop just barely above the water's surface. "I love you too, buddy."

I close the tank lid and grab my earbuds, but before stuffing them into my ears, I pause and rest a gentle hand on my mother's guitar—a Martin HD-35 Nancy Wilson Dread-nought acoustic, named after the vocalist, songwriter, and guitarist from the band Heart, my mom's favorite growing up and the reason she got into music in the first place. This guitar was one of the last gifts my dad got for her before she died.

Now it's mine.

"Hey, Mom …," I say. The guitar sits quietly.

I know how to play it. They put a guitar in my hands before I could talk, but after Mom died, Dad stopped with the music. It's as if it was surgically carved out of him. Like one day, music was everything to him, and the next day, it was all about finding something better for my future, something better than music. Music is bad. It tears families apart. It makes you crazy. The industry is full of lies. They will chew you up and spit you out.

His favorite refrain that usually ends whatever argument we're having about why I can't take voice or guitar instead of swimming all the stupid time: "Look what it did to your mother!"

We sold the house—the house with the pool I was attached to from the age of two, the custom-built recording studio and "jam hut" where Dad and Mom and their respective bandmates and friends would come and practice before stepping foot into the proper recording studio. They'd hang out and have long nights of playing music and trying out new stuff. My childhood was loud and percussive and filled with faces of people important to my parents, people who became my "aunts" and "uncles."

When it wasn't Mom's turn to rehearse, I would sit on her lap as she swayed and hummed along with whomever was playing. She'd gently rub my hair back from my forehead, me nestled in this fuzzy green blanket with my beloved stuffed goldfish, still so new the orange fabric was practically neon. I'd catalogue the faces on the jam hut walls, the framed, signed photos of my parents' favorite rockers from the 1970s and '80s, the years when Trent and Calla were just kids learning how to play music themselves. Joan Jett, Fleetwood Mac, Bruce Springsteen, the Rolling Stones, Debbie Harry, Pat Benatar, the Go-Go's, Annie Lennox, and of course, Ann and Nancy Wilson from Heart, who my mom actually got to meet once.

I'd scroll through those faces, comparing which of them looked like my mom or dad or my dad's brother, Uncle Tim, as I listened to my mom's voice against my ear, lulling me to sleep, inhaling the smell of her perfume and shampoo with every breath. All that noise around me in the jam hut, and I would sleep like a stone, safe in her arms.

She was studying to be a music teacher when she married Trent Andersen. But when people in my dad's world heard what Calla Stone Andersen could do, a lot of doors opened for her. Man, could she sing … my dad always knew her talents were far greater than his. Sure, he can shred on a guitar, his vocals are decent enough, and he can certainly write songs. But my mom—she was a rare talent. And the studio executives were starting to figure that out.

One night not long after she died, I heard Dad talking to Uncle Tim, my dad's words slurred because he'd had a lot to drink. He said, "My Calla was so big. Her voice, her talent was so big. On her worst day in the studio, she was better than my best day. This business … it killed her … Marina can never know this kind of pain. I won't let it happen."

Within a week, our house went on the market. The jam hut was disassembled, the parts carried off by friends who maybe sold the stuff, maybe kept it. I don't know. I was eight. The last time I saw the jam hut, it had been turned into a guest house with a tiny bedroom and kitchen and the walls were a boring white. The acoustic tiles and framed signed photos had been replaced with ugly pictures of seashells and beaches.

The chair we snuggled in was gone; even the fuzzy green blanket disappeared.

That's how I knew my mom was really dead. She was never coming back, no matter how many promises I made to be good and do my homework and try extra hard at swim practice and brush my teeth and get As on my spelling tests.

Eight years later, and I can't help but wonder if, wherever she is, she's watching me, wanting me to do what Dad says and study hard and get swimming scholarships, or if she wants me to be playing music, like she did. If she wants me to use the voice she gave me.

From my perch on the side of my bed, I watch the guitar. I *will* it to respond to me. "Mom, give me a sign … play a single note."

The guitar, of course, remains silent. Because this is reality. If ghosts are real, they certainly don't play guitars.

Life would be so much better if it were a fairy tale.

CHAPTER 4

THE THREE S'S

My phone buzzes against my cheek. I've fallen asleep, a bit of slobber on the open page of my biology textbook. I sit up, disoriented, and wipe my face, surprised to see it's only 9:38 p.m. when it feels like it should be tomorrow already.

It's Lily, texting both Sierra and me in our group chat: **OK, so that thing I mentioned earlier, Mar? It's happening! Instead of karaoke, there's a band playing at the Coffee Beanery. My mom got us tickets from a lady she works with because it's her kid's band and anyway, it's totally sold out so you know it's gonna be AWESOME!**

Sierra: **And I don't have to babysit! One of the kids has chicken pox so boo for them, yay for me! What are we wearing? Lily, you have to dress me. Mar, what are you wearing?**

Marina: *My dad won't let me go listen to a band.*

Lily: **He'll let you karaoke but he won't let you go listen to a band?**

Sierra: **So don't tell him.**

Lily: **Yeah, it's sleepover night. He won't know if we're at karaoke or at the concert.**

Sierra: **Unless he has one of those stalker tracker apps on your phone. Does he?**

Marina: *Not that I know of. Please don't tell him about those or he'll download one.*

Lily: **My mom tried to do that to my phone and I told her I'd just go buy a new phone. LOL ...**

Sierra: **WHAT ARE WE WEARING, you guys?**

Marina: *I don't know if I can sleep over. Swim practice Sunday morning.*

Sierra: **Mar, you seriously need a day off. You're going to turn into a fish.**

I put my hands against my neck and laugh. *I think I'm already sprouting gills.*

The bubbles bounce on the screen indicating an incoming response. **Tomorrow, lunch, we strategize and coordinate our fashions,** Lily says. **GTG. I'm watching a livestream and don't want to miss it.**

Sierra responds with a line of kissy-face emojis.

See you beauties tomorrow! xoxoxox, I type.

My dad doesn't need to know anything more than the basics: I am going to Sierra's for our usual sleepover, I will be at the pool by eight on Sunday morning, and yes, I promise to text if I need a ride.

While brushing my teeth, I smile at my sudsy reflection. A concert! Live music! A local band! With actual outside people not in bathing suits!

FREEDOM!

Finally, something to look forward to.

~

"MARINA ... TIME TO WAKE UP." My dad nudges my shoulder. I don't want to know what time it is—one eye cracked open reveals that it's still dark outside.

I groan. "Please ... sleep ..."

"It's a gorgeous morning and no rain so come on. Let's run. Two miles before school is the best way to start your day!"

"The sun isn't even up," I murmur into my pillow.

He yanks my comforter off. I guess that settles it.

"Downstairs in five!" he throws over his shoulder on his way out of my room.

I yank on a pair of Spandex running pants and a tank top and zip-up sweatshirt. I can hardly see my laces to tie them. How can a human person be this tired and still be alive?

Moving down the stairs, I'm more blob than feet and legs taking steps. Dad hands me a glass of fresh juice from his latest overpriced juicer—I think we now have four in the cupboard? The green goo tastes like he mowed the lawn, shook out the trimmings, and added an apple to mask the earthy flavor. I pinch my nose to swallow, trying not to imagine ground-up worms and bugs in this latest concoction.

I'd normally be at the pool this morning, but every fourth Friday, they do a maintenance thing where we can't swim until noon. What a pity. Every fourth Friday is basically my favorite day of the month. Except when it's not raining and my dad makes me run instead of swim.

After a few stretches on the porch, Dad sets the pace. My uncle Tim teases his brother now about how fit he is, how important nutrition and wellness has become to him. He stopped drinking alcohol completely, though Tim still gives him a hard time about his rocker days, how my dad didn't even know the food groups existed and how he single-hand-edly kept all the local takeout restaurants in business. The more grease, the better.

Not anymore.

We're a few blocks from the house and I'm falling into my breathing pattern that ensures I'll be able to run as long as he wants, despite the lawn trimmings bouncing around in my belly. Though it's not raining, it is late October and fall is well underway, the early air bitingly cold. We live in a suburban neighborhood filled with families with little kids, so just about every house we pass has their Halloween decorations on full display. Pumpkins and skeletons and witches, oh my!

"So," Dad says, eyes forward as he pounds the pavement, "I heard you last night. In the locker room. Everyone did."

I don't say anything. It's too early to get into an argument about me singing. It's *singing*, Dad, not grand larceny.

"You sounded good. Really good," he says. I jerk my head at him for a few steps.

"Thank you?"

He smiles at me but I'm not sure if I should take the bait.

We get through the first mile and stop at our usual turnaround spot to swallow some water. My dad sips carefully—he says if you gulp water during your run, it will give you a stomachache when you need to burp. I've never found this to be true, but he can do what he wants as the self-appointed expert. I gulp my water heartily.

He tightens the lid on his bottle, his eyes on me. "It's not that I don't want you singing. You know that, right?"

I almost choke but swallow without spraying a mouthful of water all over him. "It sorta seems like you don't want me singing."

"It's just—I—"

"I know. The music industry is toxic and terrible and they will ruin my life. I get it."

His face is so sad as he looks away, off into the distance. "I'm just trying to protect you. You can sing all you want—at home. You've got an incredible voice. Like your mom's. Beautiful and full and your range is something most singers can only dream about."

"But …?"

"I just need you to focus. Swimming doesn't have to be your life—you don't have to grow up and be Coach Tosto or anything."

"Seriously, that is *not* going to happen."

"And I know that." He flexes his back, wincing. Probably a tight muscle from an old injury sustained when he was a wild skateboarding, rock-playing teenager—the complete opposite of me. "The three S's: swim, study, succeed, right? It's important that you focus now. College is expensive. Scholarships are only available to the best of the best. It's not that I didn't plan for your college expenses—we can manage it, though it'll be tight—but you are too skilled a swimmer to let this opportunity get away from you. Universities across the country are going to be fighting to get you to sign with them IF you can improve these heat times. IF you win at districts so you can go into the regional meet at the top of the rankings list—"

"DAD, I know all this. Can we just run? I don't want to be late for school."

The light in his eyes, the one he gets when he starts dreaming about what *my* future will look like, dims a little. "I just want you to know that I'm pushing you so hard because I love you. I want what's best for you."

It's too early for a heart-to-heart. "Thanks." I step off the curb and start toward home, my dad falling into step beside me.

"I'll do the butterfly clinic Sunday morning, but I'm going to Sierra's for a sleepover tomorrow night. That's cool, yeah?"

"Aren't you supposed to be at the pool at eight on Sunday?"

"A day off would be nice," I say, hoping he'll agree. His jaw tenses again. "Yeah, Dad, I can get to the pool at eight."

"Does it have to be a sleepover? I can come pick you up whenever you guys are done … doing whatever it is teenage girls do on a Saturday night. No boys, right?"

"Daaaaad," I growl. "It's Lily and Sierra. We will probably go to a movie or karaoke or get sushi or something completely benign and boring and boy-free." I hope he doesn't see my fingers crossed in my fist. It's not my fault if Charlie shows up to see Sierra, or if Steve magically appears to see Lily. He doesn't need to know anything about my friends having boyfriends, or then he'll get all weird about them possibly trying to find *me* one too. (As if that would be the most terrible thing in the world … ugh.)

He doesn't say anything; I can see I'm on the verge of Saturday night not happening at all.

"It's Sierra's birthday," I lie. "She'd be super sad if I missed it. We're just going to do something quiet. No party or anything. You know we're not like that."

"Didn't Sierra just have a birthday?"

I don't answer.

We finish our run in silence, which is preferred as the way home is uphill and talking is too hard. I wait for Dad to unlock the front door and then follow him into the kitchen, noting that I have just enough time for a quick shower and to toast a bagel.

I stop on the bottom stair. I'm not leaving this morning without a solid answer that I can go out this weekend.

"So, yeah? Saturday is cool?"

Dad is stuffing more celery and twigs into his juicer. "As long as you can be at the pool at eight on Sunday morning, I don't see a problem."

I fly up the stairs on winged feet before he can change his mind, flopping my sweaty butt onto my bed and grabbing my phone.

I can go! I can GO! He said yes! I type into the group chat, followed almost immediately by celebratory emojis and GIFs from my two friends.

Okay, Friday. Let's do this.

CHAPTER 5

LET IT GO!

"**S**it still! This cat-eye isn't going to look very catlike if you keep wiggling," Sierra says, eyeliner posed in hand, ready to strike.

"Where did you learn how to do this?" I ask.

"YouTube. I learn everything on YouTube."

"I learned how to make my famous fudge from YouTube!" Lily yells from the bathroom, flatiron in hand. Sierra's room smells like a mix of heat-protection spray, perfume, and her latest scented candle. It's quite the contrast from my room that chronically smells like a swimming pool.

"I thought her secret fudge recipe was from her grandma or something," I ask. Sierra gives me a stern look. I'm wiggling again. "Sorry."

"Who cares where the recipe is from as long as she keeps making it for us," she says, pausing for a high five. Sierra then resumes running the eyeliner along my closed lid. She leans back to admire her handiwork. "You have the most gorgeous eyes, Mar."

Lily's newly ironed blond hair shines like its lit from within. "Use the blue eye shadow on her. It matches her eyes so well." She moves to her bed and digs through my bag to

22

see what I've brought. My fashion choices are somewhat limited because I spend so much time in a swimsuit.

"Okay, none of this is going to work." Lily rests a hand on her popped-out hip.

"I haven't gone back-to-school shopping yet," I say. I had a growth spurt last spring that carried on through summer, adding three inches to my height, so my current wardrobe choices are the total opposite of fashion. It's just easier to live in my Adidas track pants for school and my favorite sweats every other time.

"Marina, it's almost November! When do you think's a good time to go back-to-school shopping?" Sierra says, laughing. "You could just wait until Christmas and let Santa bring you a new wardrobe."

"Oh, man, no. Santa will only buy me shirts that button up to my neck and pants that are three sizes too big so no one can see I have a figure under all that denim."

"It is so weird that your former-rock-star dad is *so* old-fashioned," Lily says. She's not wrong. It's because he knows all the trouble I could be getting into if I wanted—trouble he got into as a teenager and young adult.

"I have the perfect thing." Lily empties her backpack onto Sierra's bed, pulling free a soft, lavender T-shirt with a screen-printed white rose on the front.

"Lil, no. This is your favorite shirt."

"It's perfect for you. This is definitely your color."

I slide off my ratty tank top and pull on the shirt, the cotton so soft and the rose just the right amount of faded. Sierra grabs my upper arms and steers me in front of her full-length mirror, stepping around me as I'm now the tallest amongst my friends, thanks to that aforementioned growth spurt. She fluffs my wavy hair around my shoulders.

"Gorgeous. I am very good at my job," Sierra says, winking. "Now get out of the bathroom, Lily! It's MY turn!"

~

THE COFFEE BEANERY and Art Studio is a local hangout in a repurposed warehouse. Apparently, it sat vacant for years, a collection place for graffiti and troublemakers, until some successful tech start-up group bought and renovated it into a coffee house-slash-art-gallery-slash-performance-venue.

Bottom line, it's amazing. And it's all ages—they only serve coffee and food—so concert nights are open to everyone. I've only been here for one concert before, thanks to my dad's tight leash, but Lily and Sierra and I have easily spent a year's allowance each on extra-foam vanilla lattes and their world-famous cookies during our frequent daytime visits.

It's close enough that we can take one bus from our neighborhood and then walk to it, but Sierra's mom offered to drop us off, which is even better because then I don't have to explain to my dad why my transit pass reloaded at the bus station when I'm supposed to be at Sierra's birthday party, watching cheesy romcoms and doing our nails. I swear my dad thinks girls nowadays are straight out of an '80s movie where all we care about is our fingernails and if a certain boy likes us.

Parents, right?

Sierra's mom pulls up in front of the Beanery, and we're surprised to see the lineup to get in already winding down the block. Mrs. Schmidt is still dressed in her scrubs from work—she's an ER nurse—but she reaches into her purse and pulls out three ten-dollar bills, handing one to each of us. It's what she does every time she takes us somewhere, even though Lily and I are not her daughters.

"You've got the tickets?" she asks. Sierra fans the paper stubs in front of her face. "Okay, I'll pick you guys up out here when the show's over. Text me when you're ready. I have episodes of *The Bachelor* to catch up on." She puckers her lips at her daughter, who stretches across the console between the two front seats and plants a kiss on her mom's cheek. My dad is not an affectionate guy, so I'm always a little envious of Sierra's warm relationship with her mom.

As we're climbing out of the car, the line starts moving. "Hurry up! They opened the doors!" Lily squeals. She grabs our hands and pulls us down the sidewalk to the line's end; we wave at Sierra's mom as she drives off.

It doesn't take long to get inside, and even though the exterior lineup looked like the place would be filled to capacity, we find a decent table along the left side of the stage. Our view will be partially blocked by one of the huge speakers, but we're here! I'm out of the house! We're about to listen to some live music!

Sierra agrees to watch the table while Lily and I weave through the crowd to get our drinks. A few people smile as we pass, and for five minutes, I feel like I'm part of the In Crowd rather than the nerdy swimmer girl whose dad used to be someone a lifetime ago.

We queue up to get our coffees right as the emcee takes the stage, and it gets so loud in here that the barista can hardly hear our orders. By the time we get back to the table, I realize she really didn't hear us because I ended up with some weird fruit-flavored coffee instead of the vanilla latte I asked for, but I don't even care. The first licks out of the guitar through the massive speakers make everything else fade away.

And no one stays in their seats for long. After three songs, we abandon our coffees and squish into the table-free pit at the front, bouncing and screaming and singing along with everyone else. I close my eyes and feel the beat pounding through the floor, through the air, and for a brief second, I'm back on my mom's lap at the jam hut while their friends ripped through one of their loudest songs, the ones that would make the neighbors yell at us over the fence. *Hazards of living next door to rock stars! At least you get a free concert!* my dad would yell back. The next day, my mom would bake one of her incredible pies and leave it on the neighbor's porch as a thank-you.

This band—they're young and pretty good, mostly doing covers of other bands with a few original songs thrown into the mix. Their lead singer is decent enough, a little screechy now and again, but I'm not here to be a rock critic.

I'm here to dance.

And dance we do.

Until our legs give out and the second encore is done and our shirts are soaked and we've high-fived and/or hugged everyone around us because it's just been the perfect night.

By the time we get back to our table, our unfinished coffees are long gone, cleared by the industrious serving staff who are eager to be out of here when the last patron picks up their stuff from the coat check. I don't want to look at my phone for messages or for the time because that means the night is over, and I'm not ready to go home, even if home tonight is Sierra's house.

Because that means we have to take off our fancy makeup and put on our pajamas and go to sleep and then I have to set my alarm and sneak out of the house long before Lily and Sierra wake, just so I can take my tired body to the swim club and jump into the freezing cold water and listen to Coach Tosto yell at me for two hours.

"I should not have worn these heels," Lily says, rubbing her temporarily shoeless foot.

"These guys were so good!" Sierra says, sprawled on her seat. "I want to keep dancing!"

"Wait—do we have to go home now?" I ask, an idea bursting bright in my head. "Can we go out still? Karaoke! Please?"

My friends laugh and check their phones. "It's eleven. If your dad finds out you're out much later than this, he's gonna ground you. And you do you even have energy for anything else?" Sierra says. Always the voice of reason.

"I always have energy for karaoke. That's what caffeine is for," I say, nodding toward the still-open coffee bar. "Call your mom, ask if we can take the bus to karaoke, and then we'll be close enough to walk home after."

Lily looks worried. "Sierra's right, though—what if your dad finds out?"

"I don't care!" I yell, throwing my hands in the air and my head back. "I wanna have some fun! I'm out with you both and I'm so amped up after hearing those guys play and now I want to sing my heart out!" I drop my hands, slapping them on the tabletop. "If he grounds me, he grounds me. Small price to pay for an awesome night."

Sierra's face cracks in half with her smile. She picks up her phone, thumbs flying as she texts her mom. Within three minutes, it's decided.

Karaoke it is.

THE KARAOKE PLACE IS BUSY, as per usual on a Saturday night, so we have to wait about fifteen minutes to get a room. Even then, we end up sharing with another group of girls our age who are out celebrating one of their birthdays. I'd ordinarily be nervous about singing in front of strangers, but I'm so hyped up after listening to the band, I don't care who listens in. Invite the whole world!

Even though Lily and Sierra are in our school's choir too, they don't love singing the way I do. But because they're amazing friends, they humor me on my rare nights out and let me pick what we're going to do, knowing full well it's going to be karaoke. We usually go ice skating or to the trampoline park on Sierra's Choice nights, and to the movies on

Lily's Choice nights, especially when the cheap theater is playing classics or anything remotely related to fairy tales.

With me, there's little variety: *Let's sing, my sisters!*

The girls we share the room with end up being super cool —they're actually choir kids from another local high school. It only takes a few minutes for us to realize we kind of know each other from choir competitions over the last couple of years.

We take turns picking songs, everything from schmaltzy Celine Dion classics to a Beatles tune, some Gaga and Ed Sheeran, followed by Ariana Grande, U2, Alanis Morrisette, Adele, Katy Perry, Florence + the Machine, Queen, Beyoncé, Jimmy Eat World, Taylor Swift, One Direction—and yes, no karaoke night would be complete without a few Disney classics, including "Part of Your World" from *The Little Mermaid*.

It's our turn to pick, so we flip through the options, everyone else laughing and talking and taking selfies on the couches behind us. Lily pulls up "Let It Go" from *Frozen* on the screen and hands me the mic. Within just a few bars, the room gets very quiet.

And then by the time I'm rounding the bend on the last verse, our room door is open and we have a crowd in the hallway.

Song finished, the gathering erupts.

It's not the first time that's happened.

I laugh and take a wide bow and blush against the applause. There is nothing like this feeling. I don't get it when I win in the pool—there aren't enough useless ribbons, medals, or trophies to give me the feeling I am bathing in right this second.

Sierra grabs her phone and snaps a shot of me and Lily and the people gathered behind us.

I swear, this will be my favorite picture forever.

CHAPTER 6

BEWARE OF WOMP RATS

I slide into English right as the bell goes. Sierra's saved me a seat—her cheeks are so red from smiling so hard, it looks like her face might catch fire.

"Have you checked my Instagram account this morning?"

"What? No. I barely got to school on time." Yesterday after the eight o'clock practice—that I made it to, even though I'd had about four hours' sleep after my INCREDIBLE Saturday night out with my girls—my dad and Coach Tosto agreed that for the next few weeks leading up to districts, before-school sessions will be forty-five minutes longer. That puts me at the pool at 6:00 a.m. every weekday. This also means I'm not riding my bike to the pool and then to school every day—my dad is chauffeuring me, which provides even more opportunity for him to grill me about Life & Related Topics I Might Be Lying About.

So, no, I haven't checked Instagram yet this morning.

"I texted you last night! Did you not see it?"

"I fell asleep on the couch watching some *National Geographic* show with my dad. Woke up long enough to brush my teeth and fall face-first into my pillow."

The English teacher, Mr. Brody, is a short, bald man whose

beard nearly reaches his sternum and who has an impressive collection of *Star Wars* posters and fan art decorating this classroom. He starts in about the *Midsummer Night's Dream* essays due by Friday, met with groans from his Shakespeare-averse students. Which is pretty much everyone. I listen through one ear but slide my phone out of my bag so I can see what's got Sierra grinning so enthusiastically.

It's video from Saturday night of me singing, as well as the shot of Lily and Sierra and me and everyone else in the background. It has nearly a thousand likes on it—!!—and comments from all the girls who shared our karaoke room. "BEST NIGHT EVER!" "Marina KILLED it!" "Let it GO, Elsa! Marina's coming for your castle!" The comments go on and on, and I laugh to myself when I see more than a few marriage proposals from people who were allegedly there.

"Marina, unless you have a womp rat on your lap, I'd appreciate eyes forward, thank you very much," Mr. Brody says. He's taken off his tweed suit coat to reveal his round belly wrapped tightly in a faded *Empire Strikes Back* T-shirt.

I slide my phone into my bag before he confiscates it and it gets lost on some distant planet.

"What the heck is a womp rat?" Sierra whispers. The kid in front of her turns around.

"It's a pest on the planet Tatooine. Duh," he says, flashing us both a dirty look before spinning forward again.

"Yeah, Sierra, *duh*," I say. She buries her face in her bent elbow atop her desk to stifle her laugh.

We survive Mr. Brody's lecture about Oberon and Titania (he got a little sidetracked and tried to compare them to Han Solo and Princess Leia, which was kinda weird), and as we're filing out after the bell, Lily bounds down the corridor toward us, a yellow flyer in her hand.

"Hey! You didn't answer our texts last night. I was worried!"

"Sorry. Exhausted," I say.

"Did you see Instagram?"

"I showed her," Sierra says. "Mr. Brody almost took her phone and fed it to his womp rats."

Lily's eyes grow large. "Do I want to know what that means?" Before I can answer, she shoves the yellow flyer into my hand.

"What's this?"

"Rock school. Mr. Malcolm's program—he's recruiting musicians. YOU should go talk to him!"

I look at the cheesy handmade flyer that some freshman probably threw together with markers and scotch tape. "My dad would very much not agree to this."

Lily drapes a hand on my shoulder. "It's a class. At school."

"Yeah, and my schedule is packed already. I'm barely allowed to take choir as it is. I can't just go in and ask the guidance counselor to trade Advanced Bio for rock school."

Sierra giggles. "Can you imagine the look on your dad's face if you did?"

"I'm glad you think it's funny," I say, not meaning my words to sound as harsh as they do. "Sorry, Sierra. I just ..." I thrust the flyer back at Lily. She puts her hands in the air, refusing to take it, like the paper is coated in plague.

"We were there on Saturday night. Half the school has seen the video of you singing—"

"That someone posted without me knowing," I add.

"So? It's amazing! Think about all the choir nerds who would give up limbs to be able to sing like you. It's also why you're Ms. Amberly's favorite," Lily adds. It's true. I am Ms. Amberly's favorite. But it's nice to have an adult in my corner, and sometimes she's more like a friend than a teacher.

When the warning bell goes for our next class, we're still standing outside Mr. Brody's class arguing about the merits of me joining rock school.

"Please? Just go talk to Mr. Malcolm. See what he says."

Sierra moves in shoulder to shoulder with Lily and they put their hands together like they're praying. "Don't make us beg." And then the two of them drop to their knees, hands still clasped in front of them, eyes wide, cheesy grins in place.

"FINE. I'll go talk to him."

My crazy friends jump to their feet and bounce and hug me, like I just agreed to take them with me to the International Space Station.

"Girls! Get to class!" Mr. Brody yells from inside his room.

"May the Force be with you, Mr. Brody!" Lily hollers back.

"Meet by the tiger statue at lunch," Sierra says, Lily dragging her down the hall. "Don't be late!"

I watch them slide around the corner toward their next classes, waiting until they're out of sight before I let the sly smile crawl across my face.

CHAPTER 7

LUNCH AND A SHOW!

Lily, Sierra, and I launch ourselves into the auditorium like we're strolling the catwalk at Fashion Week. The seating area is darkened, but the stage is flooded with light, a collection of musicians from every grade and every skill level, their instruments draped around necks and over shoulders and in hands, drumsticks clutched in fists, as they listen to Mr. Malcolm, the band and rock school teacher.

Everyone likes Mr. Malcolm. He looks like my dad's old friends. Dark hair reaching the middle of his back striped with gray, a matching goatee, black, worn-out Levi's and a rock band T-shirt, his keys on a lanyard around his neck, phone in a leather case on his studded black leather belt. I can't see which band shirt he's got on today, but he's spawned a fashion craze without even trying. Every time he wears a T-shirt from some old band, the rock kids head online and buy their own. You can always tell a rock school kid just by their outfit.

Then again, I guess you could say that about the drama kids and the athletes and the rich kids and the gamers and the academic decathlon kids and even the kids who don't seem to fit anywhere. Uncle Tim says we're all just trying to find our place in the world. He would know—he's a high school guidance counselor, and a former teenager. He doesn't work here, thankfully. One overprotective family member in my everyday life is enough, thanks.

We slide quietly into the front row, though as my eyes adjust to the light, a quick look behind reveals we're not the only people hanging out for a free lunchtime show. Other students sit in small clusters throughout the auditorium, talking quietly amongst themselves or hunched over phones, the screens lighting their faces. A few nibble on sandwiches or from plastic containers cupped in hands while they spoon lunch into their faces.

"Seems like we've been spending our lunch breaks in the wrong place," Sierra says, pulling her lunch box from her backpack. She gets to eat whatever she wants, which is usually peanut butter and jelly on her mom's incredible homemade, fluffy white bread. Simple, and yet so tasty. Her mom could open a bakery.

My lunch, though? Usually made up of whatever my dad and Coach Tosto have agreed is the appropriate caloric, fat, protein, and carb content for this week. I sound like a brat complaining that my meals are customized to support top athletic performance, but honestly, some days I'd sell my soul for one of Sierra's sandwiches and a bag of barbecue potato chips.

Half of a chocolate-dipped pretzel protrudes from Lily's mouth, her eyes and thumbs busy on her phone. "You guys, this post is going nuts." She scrolls, reading the best comments as she pauses to chew the rest of her bite.

Sierra offers her a couple of baby carrots. "You need to eat something other than chocolate and salt for lunch." Lily pops one of the carrots into her mouth, still scrolling.

"I have chicken, rice, and cherry tomatoes here," I say. "Lil, eat some of this."

She puts her phone down. "I have lunch in my bag but I'm a little busy trying to figure out how to make you famous, Marina Andersen."

I almost choke on a mouthful of rice. "Yeah, no. Let's work on something more meaningful, like a fundraiser for the local animal shelter or replacing the lead pipes in our school."

"Or climate change," Sierra adds, head bobbing. "Except Lily's right. You should so be famous."

I shake my head, my face warming at the thought of being up on stage again. What would it feel like to have a crowd like the one at karaoke, only times a hundred? I think my heart would explode before I finished the last song.

Talking is curtailed by the crashing start of rehearsal—and I'm grateful. In the middle of their first song, a bark of laughter echoes from the seats behind us. I turn and give my meanest glare; making fun of people learning their instruments or how to control their voices isn't funny. The offending jokesters see that I'm staring at them—they're younger than we are and thus easy to intimidate. Their laughs die in their throats and they sit up straighter in their seats.

By the time the song is over, I glance quickly over my shoulder and see the little punks have left. Good.

The performers meander through their next song—I *think* it's supposed to be a number from Van Halen. Sierra and Lily are huddled together whispering about something on one of their phones, but I'm glued to what's happening onstage. I don't cringe in embarrassment when they hit a sour note or miss a cue; instead, I'm flooded with envy that these kids get to be up there and their parents *let* them.

Maybe if I just talked to Dad again, if I told him what this means to me ...

"You okay?" Lily says. "You look like you're about to cry."

I sniff, careful to not let my emotions get away from me, and grab a Red Vine from the baggie on Sierra's lap.

When the song ends, I kind of feel sorry for it—not the musicians but the actual song—for surviving what it just endured in the last five minutes. One of the mics screeches with feedback as Mr. Malcolm steps to the front of the stage, squinting into the dark seating area.

"Do I see yellow flyers out there in the audience? Now's your chance. Come on up and show us what you've got!"

Lily thrusts her arm into the air, the yellow paper in her fist. "Marina Andersen is here! She wants to sing!"

Now would be a really great time for one of Mr. Brody's *Star Wars* aliens to come in and suck my brains out of my skull.

"Marina, come on up."

I'm frozen. Sierra plops her lunch onto the floor and my friends stand and drag me from my seat. I cannot believe this is happening.

"Don't be shy, and don't take too long. Lunch is almost over," Mr. Malcolm says. "Everyone give Marina a round of applause."

The people gathered in the auditorium, spectators and musicians alike, put their hands together. The only way I'm getting out of this is to run, but I'm not a coward.

"Fine. Also, I'm going to maim you when this is over," I say to my friends. They smile wickedly as they shove me up the stage steps.

Mr. Malcolm offers me the mic instead of a handshake. "I've been trying to get Ms. Amberly to share you. Glad to see you in here today." He smiles. "So, what's your poison? Remember, these guys are still learning."

I turn and look at the musicians behind me. "Do they know 'Chandelier' by Sia?"

"You guys okay to play that one?" A round of yeses. "Cool. Let's hear it, then."

After a false start, the collection of musicians gets themselves musically organized enough to follow me into the song. At first, I feel like I should go easy, not overpower the music playing around me since a lot of them are still learning their instruments, but then something weird happens—the stronger I sing and the more power I put behind my voice, the stronger the other kids get too. Two guitarists aren't fighting for the front anymore; they're playing as one. The keyboardist finds the right synth sound. One bassist plays (two others stand on the sidelines watching). As for the drummers—there are three drum kits set up but only one girl plays—and she's killing it.

We sound amazing!

I'm grinning so hard as I turn back to the audience, throwing my voice through the microphone, feeling the sound waves sail from the speakers and bounce off the rear walls and back into my chest, like some invisible force that lights me up from the inside. I wouldn't be surprised if I were actually glowing right now.

I push everything into that last line, followed by an improvised clash of cymbals, and the students who witnessed our performance are on their feet, yelling and clapping, phones and lunches forgotten for a moment.

Mr. Malcolm applauds as he walks across the stage toward me. I hand him the mic, not at all shying away from the warmth that radiates like a bonfire burning behind my sternum.

"Oh, man, Marina, that was killer." He switches off the microphone and slides it back into its stand. "So now I really am going to the teachers' lounge to brawl with Ms. Amberly. Aren't you so bored with choir? You're a rocker!"

I laugh. "Thanks, Mr. M."

"Tell me you'll join us."

My smile dims. "My schedule is packed right now. And my dad would flip *out* if I dropped another class to replace it with rock school—I mean, I'd freaking *love* to, but my dad ..."

Mr. Malcolm bobs his head. "I know your dad, kid," he

says, pinching his goatee with long fingers. It doesn't surprise me that he knows my dad. Everyone seems to. Which makes it risky for me to do anything that could potentially get me in trouble. "But what if you didn't have to drop a class? What if you joined us during lunch hours, like today? I could talk to the music department head and the principal about extra credit. Surely your dad wouldn't say no to extra credit," he says.

I like the mischief in his eyes—it's the same look Uncle Tim gets on those rare occasions when he picks me up from swimming and we go out for ice cream before I've had dinner.

"That might work," I say. He grins and nods and then spins on one booted heel and strides across the stage, gesturing for me to follow.

From the small desk just behind one of the leg curtains, he pulls out a well-loved, blue three-ring binder. "These are the songs we're going to be workshopping during lunch rehearsals." He hands it to me. "You can hear for yourself that some kids are pretty new, but everyone is learning. It's a very supportive environment," he says.

"Thank you so much for inviting me."

"Hey, you don't need anything from me—your vocals are far beyond what I can help you with. We'll leave that to Ms. Amberly and your vocal coach. You do have one, yeah?"

I look away and shake my head. "My dad … he's really focused on my swimming."

Mr. Malcolm crosses his arms over his chest and nods. "Well, I'm not your dad so I don't know what his plans are, but I think it's a crying shame if you're not working with a vocal coach." The wheels are spinning behind his eyes again. "Let me see what I can do. I have a few friends …"

"No, seriously, don't go to any trouble. Singing with your group here would be amazing."

Mr. Malcolm smiles again and this time, he does offer his

hand. "Then we shall see you tomorrow, Ms. Andersen." We shake on it, and I fly off the side stage steps, not even sure when my feet touch the ground again.

Lily and Sierra loop their arms in mine as we jog out of the auditorium in unison with the bell signaling the end of lunch, and I'm again so grateful to have friends like these two, not only because they keep me from floating away on my current post-performance euphoria but also because they believe in me, even when I don't believe in myself.

We stop in front of our lockers, the two of them talking excitedly over one another about what just happened, about the adorable sophomore playing bass and how much he looks like Harry Styles, about how we should start charging admission to our karaoke rooms so we can finance our eventual move to Los Angeles where Lily will become a movie star, I will become a famous singer, and Sierra will become a world-renowned environmental scientist who will save the world just in the nick of time so Lily and I can go on entertaining everyone.

Lily slams her locker shut, her math book tucked against her chest. "You still gonna maim us, Mar?"

"Maybe sleep with one eye open," I tease, tucking my biology textbook into my bag. How I'm going to concentrate on anything for the next two hours is a mystery.

My friends, finished at their lockers, turn and head down the hall toward their next classes.

"Text you later, songbird!" Lily calls over her shoulder.

It's a good thing she's cute.

CHAPTER 8

ELEPHANTS IN TUTUS

Who knew that something as simple as going into an auditorium with a bunch of other kids could make such a huge difference in my outlook on *everything*? After only three days of rock school lunchtimes, I had Coach Tosto shaking her head, asking if I'd changed something in my diet or sleep schedule. My split times and overall lap times were better, and she gleefully (well, as gleeful as Coach Tosto can make herself) announced that if I keep up this pace for the district meet, I'll easily pull myself from tenth to at least sixth or seventh in the overall standings heading into the regional meet.

I don't dare tell her what's going on. And thankfully, no one on my swim team goes to my school, which means no one here will blab to her about me singing my heart out at lunch to an ever-growing crowd.

By Tuesday of the next week, even the upper sections of the auditorium are full during lunch-hour rehearsals. And Ms. Amberly has offered extra credit to any of the choir students who spend lunch in the auditorium and can name three songs we've performed. She told me it's her way of supporting the team—followed by a short lecture on how I am to protect my voice.

Mr. Malcolm chucks me on the shoulder as we stand just off stage. "Man, if I'd known you were the secret to filling seats, I would've sold tickets." Of course, with that many rowdy high school students in the audience, his job becomes a little more burdensome—rather than just tending to his musicians, he's reminding people to stay quiet and clean up their lunch messes too. Only once has he had to ask a couple to leave because they were making out and causing a distraction.

I've started to think of the other musicians as my bandmates, which is beyond cool. For years, walking down the halls at school (without Sierra and Lily, of course) meant the occasional hello to a friend from some class or someone I'd done a project with. Otherwise I'm kind of known as Lily's quiet friend who swims a lot and dresses like a jock.

But this—this is a whole new thing. It's like everyone all of a sudden knows my name, and even the mean girls who refused to acknowledge my existence before now say hello and tell me what song they liked most from that day.

And then it doesn't take long after that for people to start talking about my dad—I don't know how they found them, but two of the rock school kids show up wearing T-shirts from Hidden Villains, my dad's old band.

I don't think I even have one of those anymore. They all disappeared when we moved, after Mom.

By Thursday, I'm exhausted from the week of before- and after-school swim practices and the heavy homework load—and still one more weekday to get through—but walking through the doors of the auditorium at 12:25 p.m. with my Ms. Amberly-approved thermos of steaming, honey-lemon tea in hand makes all that other stuff dissolve.

Today we're working on an original song that one of the other vocalists—a senior named Tandy—wrote. She emailed me the lyrics weekend before last, and we've been workshopping it behind the scenes a bit here while the other musicians practiced. I tend to be a bit sloppy with my enunciation, and Tandy is really good at hitting the consonants and with breathing techniques, which is cool. She's an alto with a grittier sound than I have—sometimes she sounds a bit like Amy Winehouse, but she can smooth it out like Lana Del Rey too.

When I properly met Tandy last week—we've passed one another in the hall a hundred times before—I was worried she would think I was swooping in to steal her stage, but she's a senior, only here at school three days a week anyway, the other two days spent at an offsite internship arranged through her civics class for college credit. "I love songwriting more than the performance, but my parents want me to be a lawyer. 'Art and music are great, Tandy, but you need job security,'" she said, wagging a finger and changing her voice to mimic who I assume is her dad. "Singing is fun, but it's not *in* me—not like it is in you," she said.

I blushed from her compliment, wishing I could spill the truth about how it *is* in me, even if my dad won't let it out. Even if my dad is saying the same thing as Tandy's parents about being realistic and job security.

So today we're gonna try her song together, for real, with the mics, in front of everyone. A duet. Super scary. I've not done a real duet outside of the choir room or karaoke club, not with an audience of my peers watching. People talk about butterflies before performances, but my stomach is host to full-grown nervous elephants in scratchy tutus.

I gulp my tea, and then follow Tandy out on stage, her long, blue hair flapping against her back as she walks. As soon as they see us, the audience cheers and hollers. Sierra and Lily are front row, as always—this time with Charlie and Steve in tow—the foursome on their feet clapping with hands above their heads, getting the crowd riled up for what's about to come. Ms. Amberly is along the wall—she says she's been coming in to help Mr. Malcolm with crowd control, but I think she really just likes rockin' out.

I try not to think about how the auditorium is nearly filled to capacity, or how even though I truly love singing, any time you're working out a new song, it's kind of like taking off all your clothes in front of everyone.

Performance is exposure. Even hard-core rockers like my parents and their friends would talk about how terrifying it is to open your chest and hope the audience is gentle with your heart. They aren't always.

When I was younger, I'd be on the starting block, waiting for the beep, and I'd yell at my coach that I thought I was gonna throw up. "Coach! I'm gonna barf!" I'd yell. And instead of pausing the heat to let me off the block, Coach Tosto would laugh and yell back, "USE IT!"

She meant the nervous energy, of course. I never did barf in the pool.

I close my eyes and think about the tutu-clad elephants pirouetting in my midsection, the feeling I'm going to lose my lunch. "Use it, Marina," I say under my breath.

Tandy signals the band, again a mixture of skill levels and age groups, but they manage to find a happy medium and get through the song's intro, leaving the door open for her to start. She eases into the first verse, nodding her head when it's my turn to join. The mixture of our voices—hers is throaty and low and almost like she's catching cold, but rich and beautiful—so I go to the higher reaches of my range, harmonizing with what she's doing. Even when the drummer misfires, we keep singing, the two of us locked on one another, then out to the crowd, then back to each other.

I only ever want to do this. Forever.

The last line of the song is me only, and I hold it until my voice cracks with the exertion.

Before the bassist has pulled the last note from his guitar, the audience is on their feet. Even Ms. Amberly is jumping up and down cheering, the curls of her bright red hair and the skirt of her Miss Frizzle-inspired, music-print dress bouncing as she cheers.

Tandy and I fist-bump, and I clip my mic into the stand to offer my own applause for her amazing song.

"Lyrics and music by Tandy Monroe, ladies and gentlemen."

Tandy bows, flipping her hair forward and then over her shoulder, her grin so wide I can see her back molars. Then she grabs my hand and we bow together once, both of us laughing as she pulls me into a hug.

"You sure you want to be a lawyer?" I ask, stepping back.

"Hey, you're going to need someone to handle all your contracts when you hit the big time, right?"

I laugh. The big time. If it's anything like this, count me in.

CHAPTER 9

THE CHOICE IS YOURS

The screeching metal locker room door draws the attention of everyone in the concession area. Same thing every time it opens. No one ever gets used to that awful sound. I wave goodbye to Lily behind the food counter, nodding as she makes the sign for *call me*.

My dad sits out front, the car off, but I can hear the low bass of a voice speaking from within. His eyes are distant, his left hand resting against the side of his face. A pronounced V creases the skin between his eyebrows. Deep in thought. Must be whatever self-help audiobook he's listening to.

Or something's wrong.

I throw my bag into the back and climb into the passenger seat. "Hey," I say, testing the waters.

"Hey."

One-word answers from my dad … I quickly scroll through the last week in my head to see where I could've slipped up. I got an A on that Advanced Bio exam; my in-pool times this week have been amazing, and I know Coach emails my dad regularly with updates; I've not broken curfew or gotten in trouble at school.

He pulls out of the swim club parking lot and heads for

home. It'll be a short trip—no more than ten minutes. Everything's close in the suburbs. He remains quiet during the drive, not even the confident tones of whatever self-help guy he's listening to at the moment to serenade us.

My mouth twitches with unanswered questions as my brain switches into panic mode—do I ask him what's wrong? How do I say it? Did I screw up? Is it about something adult I'm not a part of, like taxes or money issues? Uncle Tim said Dad's been dealing with some financial stuff lately but that I shouldn't worry, he's got it all worked out. I don't know anything about our financial situation—my dad doesn't ever talk to me about anything like that, other than to harp that I have to swim harder and faster to get scholarships. Maybe he's broke. Maybe the rest of the rock star money is finally gone. And that's why I need scholarships.

Oh no, are we going to lose our house? Is he going to tell me something really bad has happened and we have to leave? Or wait—no—is Dad sick? He's lost a lot of weight these last couple years but I thought it was just because of his new obsession with raw food and exercise.

The family therapist we talked to after my mom died called these catastrophizing thoughts. Losing a parent is one of the biggest traumas a child can experience, so sometimes our young brains will develop irrational thoughts that make us believe something is far worse than it is. I can take something really simple and imagine it into a catastrophe faster than I can do a flip turn in the pool.

I know that's what I'm doing right now—but I also know that the chilly vibe coming off my dad means something is definitely not right.

He pulls into the garage, turns off the car, slides his phone from the pocket in the dashboard. He doesn't even remind me to grab my pool bag—"The towel will mildew if you leave it overnight"—the same line he's been using for eight years. I follow him inside, waiting for him to key in the numbers to turn off the alarm.

So he's been gone for more than long enough to pick me up. He wouldn't turn on the alarm if it was just a quick trip out. Did he spend the day at the bank? At the doctor's?

"Any ideas for dinner?" I ask. "I'll just hang my towel and suit and then I can cook something for us."

He's now standing on the opposite side of the marble island, leaning against the far counter, arms crossed over his chest. He points at one of the bar stools.

I drop my bag on the first step of the staircase and take a seat as ordered.

"Dad, the suspense here—is something wrong with you? Are you okay? Is Uncle Tim okay?"

A flash of surprise registers on my dad's face. "Yeah. I'm fine. Tim's fine. It's nothing like that."

"Then why the drama? The last ten minutes have felt like an eternity."

He stands straight and pulls his phone out of his back pocket. A few quick swipes on the screen and my voice, tangled with Tandy's, echoes in the spacious kitchen. He turns the phone so I can see it.

It's video of the performance today in the auditorium.

My stomach falls into my feet. I try to act cool. "And?"

"This was at school?"

"Why are you asking me? You know that it is. How did you get that video?"

He watches the video for another few seconds before closing the screen and putting his phone aside. "Marina, we've talked about this."

The happy wave I've been riding all day since the lunchtime performance crashes angrily onto the beach. "No, Dad, you have talked *at* me about why you don't want me singing in public. You have talked *at* me about why you think the music scene is bad for me, how my future can't include anything like this. But you don't understand how I FEEL when I'm on that stage—"

He strides forward and slams his hands onto the countertop. "Are you kidding me? Of COURSE I know how it feels! It's like an addiction, Marina! It's the biggest rush a person can get without putting poison into their bodies. It's like the whole room fills with the magic and you are the magician!"

I stand and push my bar stool back so hard with my legs, it tips over onto the hardwood floor, the smack making me jump in the quiet space. "Then WHY are you acting so weird about this? It's just *singing*, Dad. It's singing! And we sound amazing, don't we?"

My dad shakes his head and looks down. "You know how important it is for you to stay focused."

"I AM focused." I yank my braid around over my shoulder, demonstrating that my hair's still wet. "I spend hours in the pool. I am getting straight As in all my classes. I have more volunteer hours than anyone in my leadership class. I don't drink, I don't vape, I don't talk back to my teachers, I don't do anything bad or illegal. I'm trying everything I can to be a good person—to make you proud. And you're angry at me for singing some dumb song?"

My father looks up at me again, flames in his eyes. "This isn't just you singing a song. This is you performing for a crowd, the crowd eating it up, you getting a taste of that feeling that comes with performance. It's an *addiction*, Marina. It's a dangerous first step when you start looking to outsiders for validation."

"I was not looking for validation." But as soon as I say it, I know it's a lie. Of course I was. I love singing not only because I feel free when I'm doing it, more like my real self, but because I love the way it feels when the audience loves me right back. "You still didn't tell me where you got the video."

"Does it matter?"

"What, so now you have people spying on me? Because that's really weird, Dad."

He exhales heavily. "I don't have spies. I got it from a friend who saw it in his kid's social media feed. He sent it to ask if it was you." He pushes the phone farther away, as if it will bite him. "If you wanted to keep this a secret, singing in front of an auditorium full of people probably wasn't the best choice."

"It's ridiculous I even feel like I *have* to keep this a secret. You're a musician too, Dad—how can you turn your back on something that is so much a part of you?"

"BECAUSE IT TOOK HER FROM US. Your mother is gone because of the music!" His voice bellows loud enough to vibrate under my feet.

I'm scared quiet for the count of five. "Geez, stop with this already, please? Can you even hear yourself? A drunk driver killed Mom. She left the house, she drove in her car, and some drunken jerk plowed into her. Music did not kill Mom. STOP SAYING THAT IT DID!" Hot tears burn down my face; my throat aches from yelling and holding back the emotion. It's like I'm choking on all these memories.

"We were fighting—because of the music, because the record company wanted her to go on tour and I didn't want her to because that meant she'd be away from us, away from you. And I didn't want you living in hotel rooms for an entire year, doing schoolwork with tutors who were more starstruck than interested in teaching. We were fighting about a career that means nothing now—"

"It *doesn't* mean nothing. I hear her in my head every day. I have her guitar. They still play her music—they play the music you did together—on the radio and online music networks. Your joint music, and the stuff she did on her own —it touched people."

"Marina … it's my fault," he says, his eyes off me, staring at nothing on the countertop. When he exhales, it feels like part of his soul goes with it. "I told her to leave. We were talking about divorce," he says.

The room is deathly quiet. I've never heard this part before.

"I told her if the music was more important than our family, she should go. When she left that night, she wasn't just going out for a drive to cool off."

"She … she was leaving us?" My heart pounds so hard in my chest, it hurts.

"Not us—me. Just for a few days. So we could figure out the way ahead—the best path for *you*. She was convinced you'd thrive on the road; I was convinced it would destroy our family. I'd had enough of touring. I needed to put down roots. She didn't agree."

"You were going to get a divorce?" My voice squeaks on the last word. Just the concept paints everything in a new light. It means your parents don't love each other enough to stay together anymore. This has never been the picture in my head, the memories I have of my parents dancing in the kitchen with me squeezed between them, stepping on their feet as they kissed and laughed and sang to each other.

I'm bordering on dizzy.

"Why have you never told me this?"

"You're just a kid. What good would it have done other than to make you sadder than you already were?"

"But why? I just remember you guys being so happy."

He nods. "We were. Mostly … until it came to our careers. I'd been in the business longer than Calla. I knew what it could do to families—most of my bandmates went through girlfriends and wives like they went through beer bottles. They had kids they never saw and exes they only talked to when the child support checks were late. I didn't want that.

"But Calla's star was just beginning to rise. She was still in the honeymoon stage, in love with the possibilities that music producers and record labels were promising. It's a slippery slope, Marina … I didn't want our family to suffer. I didn't want you to grow up without her here."

I swipe at the tears coursing down my blazing cheeks. "And yet, I did. I have grown up without her here." I'm angry that he's never told me any of this. Angry that he tried to control what she did with her career. Angry that she may have loved the idea of performing for strangers more than she loved the idea of being home to raise her daughter.

Angry the family I've always idealized, that I've always envisioned as this perfect thing—me, my mom, my dad— wasn't at all perfect. It had warts and scabs like other people's families.

I was just too young to see it.

"Maybe if I hadn't talked about divorce—maybe if I'd just agreed that she go on tour, that you and I could handle things while she was gone—maybe if we hadn't been fighting around the clock, she wouldn't have left that night. If we could've just gotten through that night and made a different decision the next morning …"

"I don't remember you guys fighting around the clock," I say.

"Your mom grew up in a household where the adults fought openly and constantly," he says. "She insisted all our arguments were to be quiet and behind closed doors."

"Explains why I thought I had the perfect life … until she died."

My father looks like he's shrunk. "Nothing's perfect, Marina. Not ever," he says. "If I had just listened, she wouldn't have been in the car when that guy drove into her."

"You can't blame yourself for that, Dad."

His short laugh is bitter. "I will never stop blaming myself." When he finally looks up at me, his eyes are cold. "I don't want you singing because I want you to have a life separate from this madness. Away from the spotlight, the lure of celebrity, the siren song of sudden wealth you don't know how to handle, the temptation of fleeting romance, and the aftermath of a broken heart."

"Mom wasn't a fleeting romance," I say. "You loved her. Didn't you?"

"More than my own life." He hiccups with emotion, but the hard shell doesn't crack.

"You just said that if you'd listened to her, things may have turned out differently. Have you not learned anything? Why won't you listen to *me*, right now?"

"Because you're sixteen. You don't know what's best for you. Not yet, at least."

"I know that *singing* is what's best for me. And you keeping me from doing something that is part of my DNA—something Mom gave to me—isn't going to bring her back. It doesn't make any sense for you to deny this part of who I am."

My father leans on his fingertips atop the counter, his voice lower but bordering on threatening. "When you are older and no longer reliant on me to safeguard your health and well-being, then you can make that decision for yourself. But until then, I will do everything I can to protect you from the addiction of celebrity and the rock star lifestyle that clouded her judgment. To an extent, it clouded mine too, and it took Calla's death to wake me up. I won't have the same thing for my daughter."

"Do you ever stop to think what it's been like for me? Growing up without her? All you care about is me being the best at everything—you wrap it in this package that makes it look like you're protecting me, like you're some mythical Super Dad. But sometimes it feels like you want me to be the best just so *you* can look good. So you can show the world that Trent Andersen isn't a has-been, that he didn't walk away at the pinnacle of his fame because he fell apart. That he instead devoted his life to raising this perfect daughter—"

"Stop talking before you say something you regret."

I grab a napkin from the countertop basket and wipe my tears and snot. "Mom's death wasn't your fault, divorce or no divorce. It wasn't mine either. It just happened. And I will continue to sing every chance I get as my way of honoring the gift she gave to me with this voice. And until you start *listening* to the things the important people in your life are telling you, you have no right to tell me otherwise."

"While I'm paying for the roof over your head, I have every right."

We stare hard at each other, my head pounding with fury and fatigue, but I won't look away. I won't give him the satisfaction of breaking first.

"You're grounded. Go upstairs and get changed. I'll order something for dinner."

I square my shoulders against my father. "I'm not hungry." Another lie—I'm starving—but I have a stash of granola bars in my room I can use to tide me over until he goes to bed.

"Suit yourself," he says. "No more rock school. If you have time to stand on stage, you have time to spend in the library studying." He moves to the fridge and opens it, scanning the contents.

"And if I disobey?"

His head whips in my direction. "Then I will pull you out of school and hire a tutor and you'll spend your mornings at the kitchen table and your afternoons at the pool. Coach Tosto would be thrilled with such a scenario, I can tell you."

My chest squeezes for a breath. My dad and Coach have talked about this before, mostly when I was younger and she was trying to talk my father into grooming me for the Olympics. But I thought I'd gotten too old for such lofty dreams (theirs, not mine).

And the last thing in the world I want is to be home-schooled, away from Lily and Sierra and my new music friends.

One truth I know about my father: he does not make idle threats. If I disobey and he finds out, he will follow through, and the next year and a half will be like living in a prison of my own making.

"The choice is yours, Marina."

He slams the fridge closed, grabs his phone, and disappears into his study, the pocket door sliding closed and definitively ending our argument.

Defeated, I climb the stairs, throw my pool bag—wet towel and suit still inside—into my bathroom, and crawl into bed. When my phone buzzes on the duvet, I turn it off.

I would give anything in the world, even my voice, for just one more day with Mom. To ask her about everything Dad just said, to tell her it's okay for her to go on tour as long as she promises to come back to me when she's done, to tell her I love her and I'm proud of her, and I'm sorry she and Dad were having a rough time but maybe they could work it out if they just talked.

Just one more day for her to reassure Dad that allowing me to be who I truly am will not make the world implode.

"Mom, if you can hear me," I whisper to my quiet room, "just tell him to let me *be*."

CHAPTER 10

FRIENDS ARE LIFE

This morning, I'm back to my sluggish lap times of a week ago. When Coach Tosto nags me, I attribute it to my monthly cramps. Over the years, I've learned that Coach hates excuses, but she's also female—cramps are a part of life. Telling her much else, like that I'm slow because I had a terrible night's sleep, I'm still hungry from missing dinner last night, and I wish I had Hermione's time turner so I could undo the past and make my dad less of a bear to live with, will do nothing except end up with her emailing him about everything I've said.

Sierra and Lily are waiting for me at my locker when I arrive, taking turns asking me what's wrong, why I didn't answer last night, why do I look so tired. I wait until their barrage of questions is over before answering.

"My dad and I had a fight. I'm not allowed to sing with the rock school anymore." When the tears come, I let them, because if you can't cry to your closest friends, who can you cry to? They drag me into the bathroom so I'm not in the middle of the hall making a scene.

Sierra checks under the stalls—we're seemingly alone—and then nods. I tell them what my dad said, how I'm not allowed to practice or perform with the rock school kids anymore.

Their faces reflect the sadness inside me. Lily pauses to unspool toilet paper for me to wipe my nose on; Sierra wraps a supportive arm around my shoulders.

"We can still do karaoke, though, right?" she asks. "He can't stop you from living your life, Mar."

"Apparently he can," I say. "He threatened to homeschool me if I screw up again."

"Whoa. The big guns," Lily says. "Been a while since he's used that one."

"I just don't get why he is so angry about you singing." Sierra moves to lean against the wall. Just over her left shoulder is a crudely drawn picture of a Simpsons' character, making a rude joke about one of the math teachers. "If I had the talent you do, my mom would start a YouTube channel."

Lily and I laugh quietly. Sierra's mom is a reality TV fanatic. She'd love it if her daughter had some crazy talent she could post online.

"Is this still about your mom?" Lily asks, voice barely above her whisper. I nod.

"Last night he finally told me that they'd been fighting about her going on tour. Her record company wanted her to go, and my dad didn't want her to. They were talking about divorce—when she left the house that night, it wasn't just to go for a drive to cool off. She was actually leaving for a break from their marriage."

"Whoa." Lily flattens a hand over her heart.

"And then the accident happened," Sierra says quietly.

I sniff, eyes downcast. You'd think after eight years, I'd be used to this. But last night was the first time my dad actually elaborated on the whole story. I've always known it was a drunk who slammed into her, that my mom was just driving down the street, not far from our house, and the guy blew the stop sign and hit the driver's side of her car at full speed. The doctors at the hospital said she'd died on impact, that she didn't suffer, which was supposed to make us feel better somehow? I remember the doctor who told us, her voice soft and the white of her hospital coat so bright, it hurt my eyes, how we sat in that little beige room and listened to her say the words no little kid should ever have to hear.

But all that other stuff just adds new layers to my grief. It makes me question what else I don't know about my parents, about my own life.

"He's afraid that if I sing, I'll fall into the vicious arms of the music business and it'll hurt me the way it hurt his and my mom's relationship. And I'm so sorry for him, that he feels that way, that he's so sad. But singing makes me feel closer to her," I whisper. "I just wish he would see past himself, past his own pain, to understand that I'm not trying to get a record deal. I'm not going to start hanging out with bad influences or doing terrible things if I am just allowed to *sing*. I'm not going to stop studying or trying to get into a good college … I just don't know how he will ever see me for who I really am, for me, that I'm not some creature he's sculpted out of clay and can now control."

We're interrupted by a flock of girls coming in just as the first bell of the morning rings, signaling we have eight minutes to get to class.

"So, you're not going to the auditorium at lunch today?" Sierra asks. "We can go to the library if you want. You name the place, we're there."

"Nah, we can go listen. We should still support the band. Those kids are trying just as hard as I did," I say.

"Only if it's not too hard for you to be in there," Lily adds.

"I should go talk to Mr. Malcolm. Maybe tell him I have a cold or something, that I can't sing."

"Or, you could try the truth. Maybe if he talked to your dad …"

I look at Sierra's kind face, and I know she means well, but she didn't see my dad's fury last night. "Probably best I don't tell him too much. Last thing I want is for him to overstep. Then I really will be homeschooled."

My friends nod their agreement. I hazard a look into the wide mirror that stretches across almost the entire rear wall—I look as terrible as I feel.

"Let's splash cold water on your face," Sierra says, cranking free more paper towels, moving into what we call Mom Mode. That's Sierra—if you have a sore throat, she magically finds chicken soup. If you get a paper cut, she's got a Band-Aid. Headache? Sierra has Tylenol and a cool compress for your neck!

The water, though cold, is soothing on my puffy, stinging eyes. I dab with the towels Sierra offers; Lily's gentle hand on my upper arm turns me to face her. She has a powder compact ready with a brush.

"A little powder will take down the red and keep people from asking stupid questions you don't feel like answering," she says. She's got a point—in the days since the lunchtime concerts started, people pay more mind to me in the halls. Today, I'd like to just blend in, fade into the background. At least until lunch when I can sit in the back of the auditorium with Sierra and Lily and nibble on my sandwich and pretend that watching my "bandmates" on stage isn't tearing out my heart, one strip at a time.

CHAPTER 11

JOAN OF ARC SAVES THE DAY

"Where's Lily?" I ask.

Sierra holds the auditorium door open for me. "She screwed up her history test, so she's talking to Ms. Derricks about extra credit. She'll be here soon."

I walk in and take a seat along the back wall, trying to shrink into the hard, wooden fold-down chair so no one sees me. Maybe I should've just gone to the library …

"Did you talk to Mr. Malcolm yet?" Sierra asks.

"I emailed him during English. Brody was on some tear about the complex relationship between Darth Vader and Luke Skywalker, so I sent it then."

"What did you tell him?"

"That I have to take a break for personal reasons. I didn't want to lie to him, but I also don't want to get into the details. Like I said, last thing I need is a well-intentioned teacher locking horns with Trent Andersen."

Sierra peels her banana and pushes her glasses up her nose. "I just don't get your dad."

I don't feel like talking about it anymore. I'm too freaking tired.

"You should talk to Ms. Amberly about it. Maybe she can help," Sierra says.

"Maybe." Even though I know I won't. Again, it won't help for anyone on the outside to get involved. They don't know who they're dealing with.

We eat our lunches, listening to the band fumble their way through the songs. Sierra mentions that they seem lost without me. I appreciate her sentiment, but I'm not self-centered enough to think that's the case. Sounds to me like it's just the middle-of-the-week blahs we all have.

The rear auditorium door slams open and Lily flies through in a cumulus cloud of perfume and cold air, like she's been outside and is bringing it in with her. She freezes and scans the seating before Sierra's hiss—"Lily! Back here!"—catches her attention. She bounces on her feet and bolts toward us, clambering over the row ahead to plop into the empty seat next to me.

"Don't tell me you're this excited about writing an extra credit report," Sierra says.

"What? No!" She unzips the pocket of her jacket and pulls out her phone.

"Oh, no—there isn't more video for my dad to freak out about, is there?"

Lily tilts her head at me for a second before going back to what she was looking for. "So, Marina—don't kill me ..."

"Oh man, you know that is never a smart way to start a conversation, right, Lil?" Sierra says. My heart speeds up a bit. What trouble has she gotten me into now?

"My cousin—well, second-cousin, once removed, on my mom's side, but we just make everything easier by saying 'cousin'—I've told you guys about him before. He goes to a performing arts' high school in the city, so we hardly ever see him. BUT—" Lily pauses for dramatic effect. "Have you guys heard of the band Scuttlebutt?"

I nod. I have heard of them. Local band, making some

waves in the indie rock scene. The radio stations aren't playing them yet, but they have a solid following on Instagram and SoundCloud.

"It's HIS BAND!" She thrusts her phone at us. Sure enough, Scuttlebutt is playing on the screen. "Except I didn't *know* it was his band because, due to some family drama, people weren't really talking to each other for a while and he's a year older so it's not like we ever really ran in the same circles, except, like, at family reunions when we were little, but now my mom has made up with whoever she was fighting with and the news has finally reached my ears that Adrian Brooks, my *cousin*, is the lead guitarist and vocalist with Scuttlebutt."

I take her phone from her. "But there's a girl singing here." And she's pretty good. She sounds a bit like a rough Demi Lovato.

"That's their former lead singer. Or she's still their singer —or something—she's had to take a break? I don't know what's going on yet. My mom didn't get all the details because she's clueless, and I'm still waiting for Adrian to explain." Lily leans over and points to the screen to a very good-looking guy shredding on his guitar. "That's Adrian."

Sierra and I look at one another. "He's beautiful," Sierra says. "How could you have a cousin this gorgeous and not tell us?"

"Like I said—family drama—but *anyway*, the point is that I found him on Instagram last night and I messaged him and …," She pauses and locks eyes with me. "I sent him the video of Marina singing."

Adrenaline splatters in my chest. "You did *what*?"

"I wanted him to hear you. Maybe he could help us figure out how to make you famous," Lily says, shrinking back into her seat ever so slightly.

"Did you not hear what I told you this morning in the bathroom? My dad will *kill* me, Lily," I say. I don't want to be angry with my friend—she's only trying to help—but I also can't take any unnecessary risks. Being homeschooled just so I can spend six hours a day at the pool, so Trent Andersen can keep an eye on me? I'll never survive that. My friends are my lifeline.

Lily navigates to Instagram and pulls up Adrian's profile. She shows Sierra and me; Sierra scrolls through each picture slowly, reading the captions out loud.

Adrian Brooks is easily the most beautiful creature I have ever seen. Thick black curls, a stunning white smile accented by dangerously cute dimples, green-brown eyes under heavy lashes. In the photos when he's singing, his big hands are wrapped around the mic like he's telling it all of his secrets, his piercing eyes staring into the camera like he's singing to me and me alone. I can practically hear his voice in my head.

Which is ridiculous because you can't *hear* a photograph— I have no idea what he sounds like. Their videos only show the female vocalist.

Lily flattens her hand between us; Sierra returns her phone. "This is the part where I hope you don't consider murder a viable option," she says, her thumbs dancing across her phone's screen. She clears her voice and straightens in her seat before reading: "'Hey, little Lily, glad to hear from you. I'm so glad we connected! Let our parents be stupid—you always were my fave coz. So that video you sent—WOW— this is a friend of yours? Unreal! Those pipes!'"

Lily pauses to check our faces. Mine is burning with a combination of embarrassment, anger—and excitement.

She moves her eyes back to the screen. "'Are you guys busy this weekend? Any chance you could come out? We're doing a show at the Beanery—got in after another band canceled—and I'd be glad to leave comp tickets for you at the door. Bring your friend—I'd love to meet her and hear her sing in real life, if she's into it. Talk to you soon, coz. xo Adrian.'"

Lily closes out the screen and places her hands in her lap. "Sooo … any chance you could get out this weekend to go listen to Scuttlebutt? Maybe meet Adrian and the gang?" Lily's eyebrows are hiked so high, I'm afraid they will crawl off her face.

I'm already shaking my head. There's no way. "If my dad found out …"

"What, now you're not even allowed to leave the house for leisure?"

"He said last night that I'm grounded."

Lily leans forward, elbows perched on her knees. "And that, my friend, is where Joan of Arc comes in."

Sierra laughs under her breath. "Why do I feel like another Lily plan is about to hatch before our eyes?"

Lily's conspiratorial grin is classic foreshadowing. "Our history teacher just assigned this *huge* project on Joan of Arc. You know, the French peasant girl who saved France in the Hundred Years' War with England?"

Again, I'm shaking my head.

"This project involves a written and oral report with video presentation, to be done via PowerPoint or other preapproved presentation app. It's due in one week. Lily, Sierra, and Marina are to do a co-presentation next Friday."

"We're not even in the same history class," I remind her.

"Don't tell me your dad has memorized the class rosters of every course you're signed up for," Lily says.

She's got a point.

"In order to hit our deadline for this project, we have to meet in real life to work on it. Might as well just sleep over Saturday night so we can work on it all night, especially since you have to be at the pool pretty much all weekend," Lily says. "It's not great that your swimming is getting in the way of schoolwork." She giggles.

"You've rehearsed this."

"A good actress always knows her lines." Lily bats her eyelashes at me.

I lean back in my seat, head against the rear wall, eyes closed. Could I get away with this? What if my dad emails my history teacher to ask about the assignment? What if he wants to see the work I've done for my part of the project? I could always just go to the library and check out some books on Joan of Arc …

I right my head, my eyes still feeling puffy from the recent drama. My friends' faces are expectant, waiting for my answer.

"This is a big story. You guys are going to tell your parents that we're doing this project too, even if we're not."

"Oh, actually we are—well, I am—that's what Ms. Derricks said I could write my extra credit report on. So, you two beauties are gonna help me. We can work on the project for an hour or two late Saturday afternoon to make it look legit, get ready in forty-five minutes, and then we're out the door to the concert!"

"What if my dad calls looking for me?"

"Are you kidding? My mom is asleep by eight on Saturday nights. He'd have to firebomb the front door to get her attention," Lily says. She flashes me the cheesiest smile, all teeth, her nose and eyes crinkled up.

Sierra clasps her hands in front of her and bounces in her seat, making the old wood squeak.

A deep breath leaves my lungs in a long, resigned sigh. "FINE. Loop me into your scheming and let's just hope for the best."

My friends erupt with applause and wrap their arms around me, Lily promising that we will have the best time and "You'll love Adrian" and Sierra already wondering if we have time for a quick run to the mall before Saturday.

If I'm going to take my life into my own hands, at least I'll get to listen to some great music on my way out.

CHAPTER 12

WHAT'S THE SCUTTLEBUTT?

"It's a miracle I'm even here, you know," I say, following Sierra up Lily's front steps. She rings the doorbell and before she can respond, Lily throws open the front door, her blond ponytail bouncing like it's battery powered. Her Maltipoo, Snow White (named after Lily's favorite fairy tale), is at our feet barking and hopping around, also excited to have company as she knows that means extra kisses and hugs and bits of food slipped under the table.

"You're here! You're here! Come in!"

She closes the door behind us, and the house warms my chilled cheeks and nose. I shiver as I bend down to give Snow White the required attention. "Do I smell … cookies?" I ask. My stomach growls its mutual interest in baked goods.

"Of course. We have to have snacks for our epic study session," Lily says, a little louder than necessary. As we follow her and her dog into the kitchen, I understand why. Her mom is in the family room just off the kitchen, watching TV, what looks like a program about a dog trainer trying to wrestle an angry poodle. Lily is obviously playing the part of the studious, diligent child who is welcoming her friends so we can "study."

Sierra and I say hello to Mrs. Bennet; she looks away from the TV long enough to offer a tired smile and wave. "Save me some of those cookies, Lily. And keep them away from the dog if they have raisins in them. You know how raisins make her poop." Mrs. Bennet kinda scares me; I'm glad to get upstairs as quickly as possible.

We flop onto Lily's double bed—she still has the pink-and-white bedspread and matching curtains she's had since kindergarten, but her walls are covered in posters of her favorite fairy-tale movies. I love how my friends' rooms are such a reflection of their personalities. My room used to be that when Mom was alive, but now, other than the guitar and Neptune's big tank, there isn't really anything that if you spent five minutes in there, you'd know something about me.

My dad likes conformity and order these days. No posters, only framed artwork or black-and-white photographs. Books on shelves. Desk tidy. Clothes in dresser, hamper, or closet. Bathroom scrubbed twice a week; fish tank cleaned every other Sunday so it doesn't grow algae. Air purifier filter changed monthly to manage the smell of chlorine and mitigate mildew spores that could infiltrate my sinuses and slow me down in the pool. (Or something.)

I do have a corkboard on the wall next to my bed with printed photos of me and Lily and Sierra and my swimming sisters. Even my trophies and ribbons are downstairs in a proper glass, well-lit showcase. It's so embarrassing.

But Lily's room is like childhood and adolescence have sort of crashed into each other. It smells like a mixture of hair products, body spray, and Snow White, who has obediently crawled into her dog bed tucked next the dresser, concentrating hard on demolishing some greenish bone thing. And right now, Lily's cotton candy-pink bedspread is covered with library books. Her laptop is open with a painting of Joan of Arc on the screen, and poster board sits on the floor with markers and colored pencils and glue and scissors, just waiting for its transformation.

"No detail left to chance," she says, her hands spread to showcase her handiwork. "The stage is set."

It's actually perfect. Now I can take photos of us working and send them to my dad, a requirement to prove that I'm really doing homework and not having fun. Because heaven help us if Marina Andersen has any fun when she's *grounded*. It was my own Oscar-worthy performance to convince him to let me come over at all.

The plan is to work on Lily's project for an hour or so—I've already done some preliminary notes to keep us focused and to help Lily get through this as painlessly as possible. Plus, I had to memorize some quick facts to sound legit with my dad or else I'd be sitting in my room right now with tired muscles and wet hair, just me and Neptune, watching YouTube on my phone.

We'll get as much done as we can in two hours, splitting up the tasks into Joan's 1412 birth and childhood in Domrémy, her time fighting for France in the Hundred Years' War, and then what happened that led to her being burned at the stake at age nineteen in 1431. Even though it's not technically my project, I think I'm going to save whatever research we find for later use—I never knew Joan was so amazing.

About an hour in, Sierra passes me the plate of cookies. "I can't. I've eaten three already."

"But they don't have raisins in them, so they won't make you poop," Sierra teases. Snow White looks up from her dog bed, as if she knows we're teasing her. I take the second-to-last cookie. No raisins, *lots* of chocolate chips.

"Ah!" Lily's shriek makes us all jump. "Adrian just messaged. Tickets are waiting for us and he said to get there early so we can hang out backstage!" She slams closed her textbook. "Come on! We need to get ready!"

"Lil, we've not even left Domrémy yet. Did you guys

know that she started hearing her voices when she was thir-teen, and she didn't tell anyone because she was afraid her parents wouldn't believe her or the townsfolk would make fun of her?"

"What voices did she hear?" Sierra says, looking up from her tracing of Joan on horseback from another book.

I scan through the text. "Archangel Michael, Saint Cather-ine, and Saint Margaret. It says here that she also confessed at one of the trials to seeing Archangel Gabriel and Charlemagne."

"I feel like I should know who those people are, buuuut …," Sierra says, hitching her shoulders.

Lily's head is bent over her phone, thumbs flying. I don't think she's heard a word we've said. "Okay, enough visions and voices and dead people. Seriously, we have to get ready."

"A little respect, Lily," I say, closing the book. "Joan of Arc is a saint."

"Cool. And tomorrow you will think *I* am also a saint because you're going to have such an awesome time tonight. Pencils down, sisters! Prepare for battle!" Lily hops off her bed, her old mattress whining under the loss of her weight, textbooks spilling over the side onto Sierra's feet.

"Ow," she says, tucking her black pencil back into its yellow-and-green cardboard box.

"We'd better do what she says before she pins us down and paints pink cosmetics all over our faces."

"I heard that!" Lily yells from the bathroom across the hall. "And I wouldn't waste it—pink isn't your color. Now, up! *Allons-y!*"

"Uh-oh, she's breaking out the three French words she knows. We should move before she disrespects Joan's native tongue too," I say, helping Sierra up.

~

LILY WASN'T KIDDING about her mom zonking out by eight. We tiptoe through the kitchen to the foyer at eight fifteen, Mrs. Bennet's snores loud enough to mask the squeaky front door.

"I keep meaning to oil that," Lily says as she turns her key in the dead bolt. "Let us be swift of foot! The bus waits for no woman!"

We jog down the block, more challenging than it sounds since we're all wearing shoes that aren't appropriate for any sport other than standing still looking cute. The bus screeches up beside the curb just as we're reaching the corner, and thankfully, it's a driver who waits the extra six seconds for us to throw ourselves through the open door.

"Thank you!" we each say as we tap our fare cards. Well, Lily and Sierra tap their cards—I use cash. No electronic trail that way. And I know my dad checks my tapped fares when he reloads my transit pass.

We slide into the rear of the mostly empty bus, jamming Bluetooth earbuds in so we can share Lily's phone and listen to Scuttlebutt before we get to the Beanery. Their lead singer is strong—though she looks a little intimidating, all dark makeup and black hair and tattoos—she's got to be way older than high school. The band itself sounds amazing together. Some of the videos show closeups of Adrian playing, and he is *really* good. Like, if my dad wasn't being such a turd about all this, I'd love to show him Adrian play. I'll bet Dad knows some people who could hook this kid up.

It would be so cool if some of my rock school friends were able to get this good. We all need something to strive for— and how amazing would it be if one of these days, a real rock band came out of Mr. Malcolm's program and we could all say, "We knew you when!"

The Beanery is only about twenty minutes on the bus from Lil's house. We decide to jump off at the corner before so we can size up the line and who's here and if we know anyone.

Plus, Lily had the genius idea of giving me sunglasses and a ball cap to hide my face a bit better, just in case. Even so, my stomach is not feeling great—I shouldn't have eaten that fourth cookie—because I'm terrified I'm going to run into someone who knows my dad, and then maybe they'll recognize me even with the shades and hat, and then, like the rock school performance, word will reach him that I'm not at Lily's house tonight but here instead, where I most definitely am not supposed to be.

I don't realize I've slowed down until Sierra and Lily stop on the sidewalk ahead of me.

"You okay, Mar?"

"This is a bad idea. I shouldn't be here. You guys go ahead —just give me your key and I'll go back to your house and keep Snow White company."

My two friends flank me, looping one arm each through mine. "You are not going back to hang out with my dog, songbird," Lily says.

Sierra laughs. "Where did *that* nickname come from?"

"Long story," I say. "And it's not a nickname we're using." I give Lily a pointed glare, but it's wasted due to the sunglasses hiding my eyes.

"No one is going to recognize you. We're going to go in and hang out backstage, and then the lights will be out and everyone will be dancing so no one will care who is around them, and then when the show's over, maybe we can go hang out with Adrian again but if it's too late, we'll just head home and your dad is *not* going to find out," Lily says.

"Maybe we should've put a wig on her," Sierra says.

"Yeah, and have it bounce off while she's dancing?" Lily shakes her head, her blond hair like a wave down her back. "No way. Marina's too gorgeous for such dressing. Everything is going to be okay."

"How do you know?" I ask, just as we pull up to the last person in the long line.

"Because we're VIPs," she says, tugging us forward, bypassing all the other concertgoers waiting along the building's front. A few give us dirty looks so I face forward to avoid feeling guilty for cutting in line.

When we get to the big bald dudes in all black at the front, Lily pauses just long enough to open her phone and show them something—a ticket? An invitation?—and they wave us through.

"How …" Sierra starts, looking over our shoulders as we walk into the barely full venue. "All those people are still waiting to get in!"

Lily flips her hair and flashes her most radiant smile. "I told you, baby. We're VIPs now."

We repeat the same drill at the door that leads into the backstage area. My heart is in my throat, just waiting for the two security guards to tell us to get lost.

They don't.

The heavy black door opens into a narrow, industrial-tiled hallway decorated with colorful graffiti and wallpapered with band posters stretching all the way to the ceiling. Up ahead, the familiar sound of musicians tuning instruments leaks into the hall. If I were to close my eyes for even a second, I'd feel like I was six years old again, hanging out in the jam hut with my parents and their friends.

"You ready?" Lily turns herself halfway and asks us, not pausing for our answer. "Mar, sunglasses."

I pull them off and fumble with tucking them into my bag just as Lily pops her head around the doorframe.

"Knock, knock," she says, confidence in motion. One day I'll have to ask Lily if anything truly scares her.

"Cousin!" a deep male voice says. Sierra and I freeze in the door as Lily embraces the tall, dark-haired god standing before us. "Come on in! Oh man, it's so good to see you! You guys look amazing! Introduce me to your friends!"

Adrian Brooks offers his hand first to Sierra and then to me.

"Oh, hey, you're Marina. The singer! Man, you are incredible. Honestly. I was so blown away listening to your performance. It's awesome to meet you." He's smiling at me and I'm imagining that I look like one of those cartoons where the girl melts into a puddle and slithers out of the room because she forgot how to form words.

Sierra elbows me.

"Yeah. That was me. It was just a rock school rehearsal. The girl I was singing with—she's super talented too."

"Talented *and* humble," Adrian says, again flashing his dimples at us. "Come on in and meet the band. We're on in about twenty—I had them reserve you the best table just off the dance pit."

Adrian and Lily walk toward the bandmates at the opposite end of this huge room, the two of them talking as fast as the other about family and how great it is to connect and how they totally have to hang out and catch up. We then stop in front of a trio of raggedy couches and Adrian introduces everyone.

"This is Tyler, our drummer. Damon is the bassist, and Leroy is on keyboards and backup vocals."

Pleasant hellos and nice-to-meet-yous are exchanged.

"Where's Darcie?" Adrian looks behind us to the far end of the room. The vocalist I saw in their videos—the one who looked like she had to be an adult—is on the phone, a clipboard in hand as she paces near a long, fold-out, tablecloth-draped spread of food, coffee urns, cases of water and soda and energy drinks, a big tub of Red Vines (Sierra will be in heaven!), and a clear round bowl of assorted fruits.

In person, it's more apparent their singer is probably closer to our age. She's again outfitted head to toe in black: black hair shaved along one side of her head, huge gauges and multiple piercings on the ear not pressed to the phone, heavy eye makeup, downturned mouth with a blood-red lipstick, black miniskirt over ripped black fishnet tights and scuffed dark purple Doc Marten's boots. She coughs loudly, and then turns to pace in the other direction, revealing that the hand holding the clipboard is tattooed.

I laugh in my head. What would Trent Andersen do if his perfect daughter showed up with a hand tattoo?

"That's Darce. Darcie Drayer—she's our lead singer," Adrian says, waving at her. She points to her phone and turns away.

"Was," Tyler the drummer says under his breath.

Adrian turns to face us, I'm assuming to speak quieter so Darcie can't hear us. "Yeah, she ripped up her voice. Can't sing for at least six months, which is why I'm pulling double duty." He then looks at me. "Maybe we can twist your arm and get *you* onstage with us sometime, Marina."

Lily twists her arm around mine. "Now *that* is an awesome idea."

I whip my head and widen my eyes at her, teeth gritted, before again facing our new friends. "Please ignore Lily. She was dropped one too many times as a baby."

"Weren't we all," Leroy says. Damon chuckles and stretches for a fist bump.

Someone's phone alarm goes off, and the band moves from their perches on the couches. It's all of a sudden awkward to be standing there while these musicians clearly need a few minutes to get focused before they go on.

I grab Sierra's arm, my silent plea for her to get us out of here. "Okay, cool, you guys have a great set. So nice to meet you!" I say.

Lily gives her cousin a quick hug and then leads us out and back into the hallway. Flames burn under the skin of my cheeks—I cannot believe she said that to him about me singing. I love Lily, but sometimes she just needs to keep her mouth shut.

"When she's asleep tonight, we'll use a Sharpie on her eyebrows," Sierra whispers against my ear. I'm so grateful for her perfectly timed humor, even when Lily turns around and asks what's so funny.

We grin and keep walking.

CHAPTER 13

DIRTY FEET: WORTH IT!

When we emerge from the green room, all those
people who were outside are now inside, and
the noise from their excited conversations is
almost like a separate entity in the open space. You can *feel*
their voices, the buzz from the anticipation of what's coming.

And just as Adrian promised, there's a table left of center
stage marked RESERVED FOR LILY & CO.

It's pretty awesome.

When I was little, I'd occasionally hang out backstage at
my dad's shows, thick headphones on to protect my young
ears. I'd wait with Mom until it was her turn to go on for a
song or two, and then one of my many "aunties" would take
me to the green room and we'd hang out and watch TV or
color or play Mario Kart until it was time to go home. I only
traveled with them once—we stayed in a series of really nice
hotels, with huge pools—which was when my parents discovered their little kid had a knack for aqua sports.

Sometimes I wish I'd never jumped in that pool the first
time.

Like Coach Tosto says, "Looking back only slows you

down from going forward." If only going forward didn't mean I'll be spending the next six years in a swimming pool.

Sierra and Lily and I don't even bother with coffees this time, instead deciding we'll grab something on our way out. We'll be dancing in just a few minutes anyway. No need to waste the money, or the coffee.

"Seriously, Lil, I cannot believe you have a cousin who looks like Adrian and you never told us," Sierra says.

Lily laughs. "Well, the last time I saw him, he didn't look like that—plus it's a little gross for me to be into my cousin." Lily's lips twist in distaste.

"I don't know," Sierra says. "How many times removed is he?"

Lily smacks her arm playfully.

"Even Marina is star-struck," Sierra says. "She's stunned silent."

"I am not," I say. "I'm trying to figure out a way I can kill Lily for embarrassing me and hide the body without anyone finding it until I've fled the country."

"I'll help you," Sierra says, offering her hand for a high five.

Lily leans on the wobbly table. "Hey, it was Adrian's idea, not mine." She holds her hands in front of me, like she's showcasing me for a game show. "And why not? You're a singer. They're a band in need of a singer. Match made in heaven."

She leans closer so we have to follow suit to hear her. "Their former lead singer, Darcie? She's, like, their manager now until her voice heals. If it ever does. Adrian told me that they were a thing for a while, but then ..."

She looks around us, as if anyone could hear anything she's saying over the din.

"She cheated on him with Damon, so now she and Adrian are Splitsville."

"But they're all still playing together?" Sierra says. "Awkwaaaaard."

I could explain that my parents met when my dad was dating someone else, when my mom auditioned to do background vocals because she needed tuition money. My parents hit it off, he broke up with the other woman, and voilà!

Except the next thought hits me like a ton of bricks: Was there was someone else for one of them? Is that another reason they were talking about divorce?

Oh man, I cannot think about this right now.

Sierra snaps her fingers in front of me. "Mar, you okay?"

"Yeah. Yeah, fine. I was just thinking about how my dad always says the people in the music business are fickle when it comes to love. Just another reason for him to keep me out of it."

Before my friends can respond, the surrounding crowd erupts in applause and whoops and cheers as Darcie Drayer takes the stage. "Hello, Beaneryyyyyy! You ready to rock?" she yells, her voice little more than a screech in the microphone, as if she's got a terrible case of laryngitis. How in the world will she ever be able to sing again?

"Shut up for a sec. Got a few announcements ..." The crowd settles to a level we can hear her. "Video tonight is cool. Share it widely. Just don't be a jerk and forget to tag us." Applause, until Darcie raises a hand like a kindergarten teacher and the crowd quiets.

"Obviously I'm not singing yet"—she moves the mic aside to cough into her bent elbow—"so instead, you get second best, Mr. Adrian Brooks on lead vocals." The crowd goes nuts.

"Now, give a rousing welcome to the Scuttlebutt knuckleheads, Adrian, Leroy, Damon, and Tyler!" The band members run out onto the stage, waving at the adoring audience as they assume their spots. "Don't screw it up," Darcie says, though I'm not sure we were meant to hear that part.

It's so loud in here, my teeth vibrate.

Everyone's on their feet, tables and chairs pushed aside; the dance area in front of the stage is crammed with bodies, people bouncing and yelling and screaming marriage proposals and "I love you, [insert band member's name here!]" all around us.

We can't help but get caught up in it, laughing our heads off, riding on this wave of pure energy.

And when Adrian dives into the first song, it's like an out-of-body experience. He knows how to get the crowd involved right off the top, making eye contact with people in the crowd, smiling as he finishes a line of a song, getting lost in his smokin' guitar solos, stepping aside to give the other musicians their moment in the spotlight.

I am electricity, my hair and hands and heart on fire with the music, with the force of the combined energy around us. Even when Adrian's vocals falter, he doesn't lose the crowd because his fingers move so fast on the guitar, the vocals hardly matter.

I wish my dad could see this. I wish my dad could *remember* what this feels like.

Because nothing in the world comes close.

If only I could channel my inner Joan of Arc and be brave enough to stand up to him and fight for what I want.

We dance and dance, eventually abandoning our lethal shoes to prevent accidental sprained ankles, ignoring the sticky, stained floor underneath—a worry for another time.

When finally the last song spills from the speakers—a slow ballad that is actually kind of beautiful, even with Adrian not quite hitting all the notes—the three of us are drenched and parched and exhausted. With our shoes dangling from our fingertips (I don't dare look at how filthy the bottoms of my feet are), we wait in the coffee bar lineup, but for juice and water. Who needs caffeine after that raw energy the band just poured into our skulls?

Lily's phone buzzes in her pocket. "The band is asking us if we wanna hang out!" she squeals.

I check my own phone. It's after midnight. And I have to be at the pool by 7:30 a.m.

Sierra sees that look on my face. "Tell 'em thanks, but Marina's got training in the morning, and we don't want to screw up tonight and risk losing her to the homeschool abyss."

Lily nods in agreement and quickly texts her cousin back. I watch her face—I hope we didn't just blow an opportunity to hang out with them in the future. "He says that's cool." Then she grins widely. "He wants to know if I'm allowed to give him your number, Marina."

Sierra howls like a lovesick wolf, startling the people standing near us. "Yes. Of course she gives her permission—"

"Wait—what if he calls me? What if my dad finds out?"

"Then you tell him he's my cousin and you met him hanging out with me," Lily says. "It's not a lie."

She's right. It's not a lie. I *did* meet Adrian hanging out with Lily, and they *are* cousins.

"But … what do you think he wants?"

"Oh, uh, I dunno. You're beautiful, you can sing like a rock angel, and you're single. He probably wants to know if you have a good pancake recipe," Lily says.

"I do."

"You do what?"

"Have a good pancake recipe."

Sierra snort-laughs. "She's right. Marina's pancakes are even better than my mom's."

"You guys are total dorks. I'm giving him your number." Lily's thumbs fly across her screen again; she grins like a bird-stuffed cat and then tucks her phone away. "All I'm saying is that when you guys inevitably end up making beautiful music together, don't forget the little people."

"Well, considering I'll probably be chained to the leg of

our dining room table with some homeschool teacher who looks and smells a lot like Miss Trunchbull ..."

"Come on, Matilda," Sierra says. "Let's get you home before you're thrown into the Chokey." She drapes her arm over my shoulders and the three of us head through the thinned-out crowd toward the front doors, detouring only to drop our empty bottles into the recycling bins.

I pause and take another long look at the now-empty stage and dance pit so I can cement this night into my memory forever, hoping it's not the last time I ever see this place.

CHAPTER 14

WHATEVER, MERMAID

By the time I reach Wednesday of the next week, my shoulders finally relax and my stomach stops aching every time I see my dad, every time I see him with a scowl as he looks down at his phone. If no one has sent a video by now of me dancing at the Beanery last weekend, I'm probably in the clear.

And no one noticed the desperate state of the soles of my feet on Sunday morning when I got to the pool—despite Sierra and Lily and I sitting on the edge of Lily's tub with loofas trying to scrub off the grime from the Beanery's dance floor, I still showed up to swim practice with frighteningly discolored feet. Thank goodness for chlorine—by the time I left Sunday afternoon, they were nice and pink again!

But knowing that Adrian Brooks has my number? Yeah, I basically jump every time my phone dings. So far, he's sent only one text: **Hey, Marina! Nice to meet you—now you have my number!** Followed by a smiley face and microphone emojis. Nothing else. I replied with a lame thumbs-up, not sure what else to say.

For once, I'm glad to have way too much to do, between swimming and homework, so that I don't sit and obsess over a guy, like so many of my friends do. Last year one of my swim sisters, a girl named Lexi who's a year older—she was head over heels in love with a guy she met here at the pool (a water polo player!) and it got so bad with them missing practices and making out in the family locker rooms that at one of the executive board meetings, Coach Tosto tried to get the board parents to agree to a no-romantic-involvement rule for her swimmers. My dad, a board member, was all for it naturally, but the other parents were like, "Nahhhh."

Lexi's still with this guy, and even though they don't constantly kiss all the time now, they've been recruited by the swim departments of the same university. I'd say it worked out okay for them.

I wonder if Dad would let me have a boyfriend if he had gills like I do.

"Songbird, more kicking, less smiling." Oops.

I wrap my arms tighter around my kickboard and slap as hard as I can, grateful that this cool-down will be over in eight more minutes.

I rest my head against the hard, blue foam and groan. After sitting through seven hours of classes and this being the second practice of day, the next eight minutes are going to feel like approximately one million years.

Upon reaching the pool's far end, I spin and turn, head flat against the board, feet and legs on autopilot churning the water just under the surface, muscles burning from fatigue. I tore my bathing cap earlier when putting it on, so a clump of hair has snuck out and plastered itself across my goggles. Head up, I push it out of the way—and my heart stutters.

Ahead, through the glass wall that separates the pool area from the concession and lobby—what is Darcie Drayer doing here?

As soon as the timer goes off, I'm out of the pool, kickboard thrown onto the rack. I scoop up my towel and swim parka and slide into my deck sandals. Coach Tosto hollers at me about dryland cool-down but I respond with an over-the-shoulder "Gotta go, Dad's waiting!" because Darcie Drayer being *here* when my father is also due here imminently—danger! Run!

I jog past one of the lifeguards minding the kiddie pool, slowing when he gives me the "no running" look, but then just past him, I'm off like a shot down the hall. I have to get to Darcie before my dad walks in and sees her talking to me, if she even is here to talk to me. Maybe she's here to see Lily? Maybe she likes swimming?

Except I have never seen her here before today.

This is weird.

And it's not like my dad knows her or anything, but she *clearly* isn't a swim kid, and her outfit alone will lead to a hundred different questions I can't answer without lying. And since I'm a remarkably terrible liar, especially when it comes to my dad, I'd like to avoid this as much as possible.

I toss my stuff onto the bench near my locker, throw on my swim parka, and pull open the main door. Darcie (and everyone else) looks over as it screeches. She squints at me—I yank off my torn swim cap and shake out my wet hair, waving as I approach.

"Hey," I say. "Darcie, right?"

"You look a lot different without all the makeup and stuff," she says, eyeing me from head to toe. Her voice still sounds like she ran it through a cheese grater.

"Are you here to swim?"

She snorts. "Uh, no."

"If you're here to see Lily, she's off today but she'll be back tomorrow, I think. She's always here on Thursdays."

Darcie lifts an eyebrow. "I need to talk to you."

Yup, definitely need to get her out of here before my dad comes in. "This is going to sound nuts, but I need you to come with me."

"Can we go outside? I hate the smell of chlorine."

Over Darcie's shoulder, I see my dad's car drive past the wide glass double front doors.

"NO." I take a deep breath. "Sorry. Um, if you could just come with me, like, right now." I back up, gesturing for her to follow.

"You're super weird." Darcie picks up one heavily booted foot and walks toward me. Thank all the gods.

I shove the locker room door open and lead her down the adjacent hall into one of the family changing rooms. She follows me in, reluctantly, watching as I close the door. The bench is soaked from whoever used the small room last, so I guess we're standing for whatever conversation is coming next.

"What, do I embarrass you or something?"

"No! It's just my dad … it's a long story, but the general idea is I wasn't supposed to be out at the concert last weekend and my father is *very* strict, and if he saw you here, he'd ask questions that I don't want to answer—"

"Your dad—like, the dude from Hidden Villains?" Darcie twists one of her many rings on her fingers, a hefty silver skull. The look on her face makes me feel like she'd rather be anywhere but here.

"Yeah, that's him. And he doesn't want me following in his footsteps," I say, opening my swim parka just a bit, "which is why I am swimming my life away."

"You're a freaking mermaid."

"I guess. Except for the part where I lure fishermen to their deaths with my songs."

"Must've missed that in the Disney version," she says. "Anyway, weirdo, I'm here because I have a problem—I think you're my solution."

How in the world could I be a solution for anything to do with Darcie Drayer?

"You heard Adrian the other night."

I nod.

"He's great on guitar, but he's no singer. No one's ever gonna take us seriously with him fronting the band. Half the time he sounds like he's dying."

A little extreme … "Uh, have you talked to Adrian about this?" This feels wrong—I don't even know these people, and here's Darcie basically airing the band's dirty laundry.

"Of course. He knows where his strengths lie." A dry, rasping cough strains the veins in her neck for a beat. She digs a throat lozenge from her jacket pocket, unwraps it, pops it in her mouth, and flicks the balled-up wrapper into the corner.

I watch it land. "How long are you going to be out, do you think?"

She gives me a hard look and curls her lip in what I think is disgust. "Who knows. Maybe forever. I didn't take care of my throat like the vocal coach taught me—"

"You have a vocal coach?"

"What, because I don't look posh and pretty like you, I wouldn't have a vocal coach?"

"No! That's not what I meant. I'm just envious."

The cough drop clicks against her teeth. "Right. Anyway, Adrian showed me the video his hyper cousin sent him—"

"Lily."

"What?"

"His hyper cousin's name is Lily." I smile; she does not.

"Honestly? Don't care. The video? The one of you singing?"

"Mm-hmm." I flush from head to foot. No doubt I look like one of those agitated squids right now, shuffling through colors as Darcie stares at me.

"I have an idea." She hikes her right foot onto the soaking wet bench and leans on her bent knee. "You can sing. We need a singer." Adrian's voice from the other night echoes in my head—when he was making a *joke*.

I'm shaking my head before Darcie's sentence is even

finished. "My dad would never agree. He'd lose his mind if I even whispered anything about singing, especially in public."

"You wouldn't be singing in public. You and I would go into the studio. My uncle Andy is a sound engineer so we get recording time for cheap or free. He'd record your vocals—then I would lip-sync to your tracks at the gigs we have coming up."

"Won't people know you're lip-syncing? Like, haven't you been out for months now?"

"People will believe what we tell 'em. And you've seen that Scuttlebutt knows how to put on a good show, right?"

I flush again, thinking about watching Adrian up there on stage.

"But isn't that lying? Because it's not really your voice?" I ask.

"So, what, are you the mermaid morality police too?"

"No … it just feels dishonest."

"Seriously, stop overthinking it." Darcie drops her foot heavily onto the coated concrete floor, splashing in a small puddle next to the bench. "*You* sing into a microphone at the recording studio, *I* lip-sync the tracks at our shows, and the rest is nobody else's business. Fans still have a good time, and Scuttlebutt continues on its trajectory toward fame and fortune."

Fame and fortune. If my dad heard Darcie talking, he'd laugh.

Which is what I'm on the verge of doing. And, pardon me, but overthinking is my default setting. I can't *not* overthink this—nor can I ignore the alarms blaring through my head like a finish-line horn.

"Okay, so this sounds good for Scuttlebutt—what's in it for me?" I ask.

Darcie snorts. "Are you kidding? You can swoon all over Adrian."

Now it's my turn to snort. "Yeah, thanks, but I'm not the

swoony type."

She lifts a pierced eyebrow at me. "You'd get to sing with a hot, up-and-coming band. Sounds like singing is not something you're allowed to do much."

"If my dad found out—"

"Your dad, a former rocker himself, would be mad if you were performing?" She coughs again; it echoes off the tiled walls and ceiling of the small space.

"You have no idea," I say, dropping my head. "He's changed since those days."

"Clearly."

I pull my parka tighter around me. "Thank you for thinking I could pull this off, Darcie, but I'm gonna have to pass. With swimming and school, I'm crazy busy."

Darcie bites her throat lozenge in half; it sounds like her teeth are cracking. She glares at me for a second and then digs into the front pocket of her frayed denim cut-offs, from which she pulls a folded gray-and-white business card. "That's my uncle's info—my cell is on the back. Text me if you change your mind, mermaid."

And then Darcie Drayer spins on her booted foot and yanks open the door. "One more thing—you can't say a word about this. To anyone." She then stomps down the hall and out of sight. Only the screech of the main locker room door tells me she's gone.

I examine the card—"Andy Drayer, Sound Engineer, Ambrosia Recording Studios"—before tucking it into the pocket of my swim parka. If my dad were to find this, oh, the questions …

Stick to the plan, Marina.

I pick up Darcie's lozenge wrapper and drop it in the huge gray garbage can on my way past, pausing for a second to pull out the Ambrosia business card. I stare at it for a second —and then crumple it into a ball, dropping it exactly where it belongs.

CHAPTER 15

QUADRATIC PROBLEMS

Dad must not have seen Darcie leave, and if he did, he didn't pay any mind to her.

He's in a decent-enough mood that he picks up a pizza for dinner, a rarity because of my closely watched diet, but this is an artisanal pie from some overpriced restaurant, so while it might look like a chain-store pizza at first, this one is made with kale and goat cheese and organic chicken.

Don't care. I'm starving. I eat half of it by myself and only save him the other half because it's rude to eat all the food when you're meant to be sharing.

Dad makes the usual conversation over dinner—recapping his emails with Coach Tosto, rambling on about some executive board gossip I couldn't care less about, and finally rounds the bend on asking about my schoolwork, i.e. upcoming tests, homework, and the history project I'm meant to be doing with Sierra and Lily.

"I didn't know you were in the same history class with them," he says. The pizza I just inhaled sits heavily in my stomach.

"Yeah, it's a joint class thing. The teachers got together and are team-teaching for this project," I say, surprised how quickly the lie slides off my tongue. I don't make eye contact but rather stand and grab our plates before he can get too far gone with this line of questioning. "I have a bio quiz tomorrow and one in math Friday so I'm heading upstairs."

His phone lights up with a call; I can see the caller ID. My uncle Tim, Dad's brother.

Saved! I offer a telepathic thanks to my darling uncle.

As Dad takes the call, I slide into the kitchen and load our plates into the dishwasher. I give the counters and sink a quick tidy, anxious to disappear before he launches into yet another uncomfortable conversation.

When my bedroom door closes behind me, it's like loosening the strings of my corset. (The only corset I've ever worn was for a school play last year—I do not know how women survived in those things!) I quickly change into pajamas, eager to climb into bed with my math text and get the homework problems done.

But first …

You guys, the weirdest thing happened at the pool today, I text. I wait for the dancing bubbles to start. It only takes a few seconds.

Lily: **You went underwater and saw all the boogers floating around?**

Lily! GROSS! What is wrong with you? I respond. But she's not wrong. Which is why I stay out of the kiddie pool. All boogers, all the time. *Where's S?*

Lily: **Her phone's probably off. Babysitting tonight. She can catch up. TELL ME what weird, booger-free thing happened today.**

So I do. I type as fast as I can, explaining how Darcie Drayer showed up at the pool and basically gave me a heart attack because I couldn't possibly explain to my dad how she and I are friends. Lily offers only emoji reactions as I explain the details of Darcie's proposition.

Lily: **You HAVE to do this. That would be AMAZEBALLS.**

No one older than 8 says amazeballs, Lil.

I know. But it still works here. Why did you say no?

Because my dad would probably forgo homeschooling and ship me off to boarding school.

I've always thought boarding school would be fun. Like sleepover camp, every single day!

LIL, FOCUS.

Right. Sorry. OK, welp, it's a cool idea but I don't know how it could work. Not with your situation with your dad and stuff.

Thank you. I just needed a voice of reason to reassure me I'm not making a huge mistake.

Oh, I didn't say that. I think it's a mistake to say no, but I understand why you're doing it.

Me: Sad face emoji.

I gotta go make my mom something to eat. She has another one of her headaches so we haven't had dinner yet.

K. Sorry. Give Snow White a kiss for me. Hit me later if you're online.

You'll be asleep. I honestly don't even know how you're still awake right now.

She's right. I'm utterly exhausted.

Oh, and Lil—don't TELL anyone this. Darcie said no one could know about this arrangement, and even though I said no, I don't want any rumors to get out that could hurt the band. Know what I mean?

Lily sends a GIF that looks like someone locking her lips with an invisible key. **Love ya, Mar.**

I open my smath book, willing my brain to focus on finding vortices and not on how insanely cool it would be to sing Scuttlebutt's songs in a recording studio. I'm not star-struck by the idea of a studio—been in lots of those given my family history—but knowing I'd be there recording my *own* voice, really singing my heart out? Yeah. Darcie sort of hit the nail on the head there. It would be very, *very* cool.

And even the idea of Darcie lip-syncing doesn't weird me out maybe as much as it should. Sure, fundamentally, it's deceptive, but it would still be my voice. How surreal would it be to be in the crowd at the Beanery while Darcie belted out the music onstage, except Lily and Sierra and I would know that it was actually ME singing those songs?

A smile floats across my face but then disappears just as quickly when I look over at my mom's guitar resting quietly in its stand, at the stupid woodcarving my dad had made that hangs on the wall over my dresser: *Swim. Study. Succeed.*

There's no way I could say yes to Darcie.

Total nonsense.

Head down over math book. "Solve using the quadratic formula. Then graph."

Swim. Study. Succeed.

Ugh.

CHAPTER 16

MIGHTY FORCES IN PLAY

"Are you sure you can't figure out a way to make this work?" Sierra asks. We're in the library for lunch rather than the auditorium as Lily and I have assignments that need attention. Sierra's supposed to be quizzing me with my Advanced Bio flashcards, not harping at me about why Darcie Drayer's harebrained plan is a no-go. She got all caught up with our conversation last night after finishing at her babysitting job, but as Lily predicted, I was long asleep before the two of them spent an hour in our group chat debating the finer points of why I *should* take Darcie up on her offer.

I'm choosing to ignore them.

"Next card, please."

Sierra sets the stack on the table. "LILY." Her tone startles Lily, bent over her own spiral-bound notebook. She sits up straight. "Mighty forces are at work here."

"What are you talking about?" I say, but Sierra keeps her eyes fixed on our other friend.

"Fairy tales," they say in unison.

I scoop up the cards. My friends are looney.

"Okay, so you know in the *Little Mermaid*, the Disney

version, when Ursula comes to Ariel and offers her a deal that if she gives up her beautiful voice, she can walk on land and meet Prince Eric?"

I sigh. "Yes. I've seen the movie."

Lily's eyes widen and she bounces in her seat. "Yes! This is the same!"

"You guys, come on—I have a quiz in, like, thirty-eight minutes."

"Her voice for the boy!" Lily says, ignoring me. She and Sierra lock hands excitedly.

"It's happening again—this fairy-tale thing—we always say it isn't real but then a weird situation comes up, like this one, and it's *totally* like the fairy tale—"

I interrupt Sierra. "Except this is nothing like the fairy tale because Ursula didn't offer me a boy for my voice. Ursula is a sea witch. I am a human female."

"But are you?" Lily says, freeing her hands from Sierra's to flatten them on the smooth, dark blue tabletop. "Because this is sort of what it looks like: Darcie Drayer is Ursula. She certainly sounds like her. And she wants what you have, a beautiful singing voice."

"And what, Adrian is supposed to be Prince Eric? Yeah, she made some random comment about how I could get all 'swoony' over Adrian—that that's what I'd get out of the deal—which is ridiculous. Totally not my style. Plus, you can't promise one human to another human—it's creepy. This deal is good for Darcie and the band only. I'm not getting the equivalent of walking on land or marrying a handsome prince, even if I ever *wanted* to get married, which I do not."

"No, it's not the way the bargain is right *now*, but ..." Sierra says, her eyes dreamy. She and Lily exchange a knowing glance. I swear sometimes they can speak inside one another's heads.

"But what?" I say, ready for this conversation to be over.

"*Buuuut*, Adrian already knows you can sing AND he

asked for your number, which means he thinks you're cool," Lily explains. "If you help out the band by taking Darcie's offer, what's to say he wouldn't fall for you in the process?"

"Yeah! And it could be the best of both worlds! You get to sing, your magnificent voice adored by audiences, and you'd be helping out Adrian and the band at the same time, which would endear him to you." Sierra sits back and crosses her arms, her face reflecting her self-satisfaction. She taps the side of her temple as if to remind me how clever and cunning she is.

"See, darling Marina, we two are your personal Sebastian and Scuttle." Lily gestures between herself and Sierra. "We are here to make sure you—as Ariel—make the right decision."

"Wait—am I Sebastian or Scuttle?" Sierra asks.

Lily picks up her pen. "What is this called?"

"A pen," Sierra says.

"Nope. It's a dinglehopper. I'm definitely Scuttle."

"Wrong—a dinglehopper is a *fork*, Lily. Duh," Sierra says. "Also, that means if I'm Sebastian, I have to sing about Ariel —Marina—kissing Eric, er, Adrian. And it's super gross and wrong to pressure someone to kiss someone else."

"I think the song is actually more pressuring Eric to kiss Ariel, isn't it?" Lily's brows crease in concentration.

"Even worse," I say under my breath. Lily pulls her phone out of her backpack.

"You don't need to YouTube it, Lil," Sierra says. "We've all seen the movie a million times."

"Clearly she needs to see it again if she thought the pen was a dinglehopper," I say, picking up the flashcards. I now have twenty-seven minutes until the bio quiz and I still need to stop by my locker to inhale a protein bar so my stomach doesn't growl in class. "Besides, Scuttle and Sebastian aren't even in the real fairy tale." My words go unheard—they're now leaning into one another's shoulders watching the video for "Kiss the Girl" on Lily's phone, their ongoing argument about which one of them is Scuttle and which one is Sebastian earning an aggressive *ssshhhh* from a nearby table.

Fine. I'll quiz myself.

But as I read the front of each card, concentrating on the correct answer before flipping it over, my brain has other ideas. Musical ideas.

Would singing for Darcie really help the band? Would that be one way to get my voice out there for people to hear, even if they didn't know it was *actually* me? Could that somehow benefit the band *and* me at the same time? I mean, it's always good practice, singing in a proper recording studio with a sound engineer who knows his stuff, right? How weird would it be to go to one of their concerts and listen to myself, knowing it's not Darcie singing up there? Would I feel guilty about betraying the audience like that?

But—and this is the biggest but ever—what if my dad found out? Would he really homeschool me?

I shiver.

The bell rings and I startle. Sierra and Lily have completely tuned out, lost in a YouTube vortex of their favorite Disney songs.

"I'll see you guys later," I say, shoving my stuff into my bag. Now I'm not going to have time to eat something before class. I shouldn't have let myself daydream about ridiculous possibilities. If I don't do well on this quiz, my grade will drop below a 95, and dear old Dad will have something to say about that.

I keep my flashcards out, reading and flipping as I walk down the crowded halls, looking up only often enough so I don't crash into another student.

And yet, it's still useless. All I can think about is Sebastian singing to dumb Ariel in the boat and how creepy that song is for urging Eric to kiss Ariel, even if maybe she doesn't want to be kissed.

A kid bumps into me, hard, sending my flashcards flying. "Oh man, I'm so sorry!" he says, dropping his own textbook. He's younger than me, his voice cracking with his apology. "Let me help you."

"Nah, I got it. Thanks," I say. He nods once, scoops up his book, and skips off.

As I pick up my flashcards, one remains on the floor—from the evolution unit, a question about the differences between *Homo sapiens* and the next comparable genetic species, say, chimpanzees. I flip it over. "Spindle neurons/von Economo neurons (VENs) = advanced motor control, less body hair, more advanced brain (which leads to free will, empathy, embarrassment)."

It's the words "free will" that stick in my head.

Free will, meaning the freedom of humans to make choices or decisions voluntarily.

I am a human, capable of free will. And yet, as the bell rings signaling that I am now officially late for Biology, I know that until I learn to stand on my own two legs—much like Ariel—free will is something only other people can sing about.

CHAPTER 17

SHARP EDGES

"This chicken is good. New marinade?" Uncle Tim helps himself to a second serving from the pottery dish in the table center.

"Greek," Dad says. "One of the swim parents shared the recipe in our Facebook group so I thought I'd try it." He nods at me. "You don't like it?"

"What? No. Yeah. It's great. I'm just tired," I say.

"I don't know how you keep up with your schedule, kiddo," Uncle Tim says, his eyes soft. Sometimes I wish he were my dad instead.

"Speaking of," Dad says, resting his fork on his plate edge. "Coach Tosto would like to see you in the pool five days a week before school up until districts. Your butterfly times aren't where they should be, even after that workshop. She's concerned."

I feel like crying. I am already *so tired*, how can I possibly add two more before-school swim days? "Monday, Wednesday, Friday before school and every day after school isn't enough? Dad, come on, I am wiped out."

"Marina, you're young, healthy, and strong. There's no reason why you can't manage this."

I am so sick of this conversation. I could argue loudly here, spew all my current grades in my classes, including the AP courses, how I'm in the top ten students in the eleventh grade. I could list all my other responsibilities at school, from leadership to writing for the school paper to leading civic-minded activities, such as food drives and community cleanups.

But what's the point? Why should I expend another hundred calories to argue with my dad when he doesn't listen?

I poke at my cold asparagus spears. I hate asparagus.

"Trent, maybe Marina just needs a little break," Uncle Tim offers, raising his eyebrows in the way he does when he comes to my defense, when he's worried about his brother's explosive temper.

"And maybe you should eat your chicken and mind your own business."

"What, Uncle Tim can't have an opinion? He's part of this family too." Maybe I am willing to spend that hundred calories fighting with my dad.

"Marina, I am your father, and I make the decisions for what's best for you."

"But maybe it isn't what's best for her," Tim says, his voice a little stronger. Oh, wow, so he's really going to do this for me. Another point in the Uncle Tim column.

"And what would you know about that, given all of your parenting expertise?"

I inhale sharply and drop my fork. "Dad …"

The room gets deathly quiet. Uncle Tim and Auntie Shelly had a child. A baby girl. She died when she was just a few days old from a terrible genetic condition the doctors couldn't fix. They weren't able to have any more kids.

My father's face shows no sign of regret for what he's just said. "It's none of your business, Tim. I am solely responsible for Marina's future, not you."

Uncle Tim flashes me a sympathetic glance, his eyes pained, wet with emotion.

Now I'm angry. Dad can come after me all he wants, but his little brother has suffered enough crap from being a part of the Trent Andersen Show.

"I'm not going to the pool five mornings a week. Three mornings and five afternoons is enough. I have friends, I have schoolwork, I have responsibilities that need my attention."

My father's laugh is bitter as he picks up his fork and stabs his chicken breast. "Responsibilities. Right."

"Excuse me?"

He looks up, all sharp angles. He's primed for a show-down. "You don't know what real life responsibilities are. You get to live in this huge house, paid for by *me*. You have heat, electricity, running water that won't make you sick, food in your belly, expensive shoes on your feet, a closet full of clothes. You swim at an elite facility with one of the best coaches in the country, again paid for by *me*. What do you know about responsibility?"

"Trent—"

"Tim, shut up or leave," my dad growls. Tim laughs at him, but it's not because he's funny. He retrieves his cloth napkin from his lap, dumps it on the tabletop, and stands. He leans on splayed fingertips, close to his brother's face.

"Keep this up, and you will lose her too." Uncle Tim pushes back and as he passes me, he stops, resting a hand on my shoulder. "I'll text you later, make sure you're okay."

My eyes sting. What I would give to go with him right now instead of staying behind and enduring Hurricane Trent all by myself. The first tear slides down my cheek as the front door clicks closed.

How these two are brothers is a mystery. Uncle Tim is soft and kind and happy to do his guidance-counselor job. His house is an eclectic collection of his favorite things, from comic books to action figures to movie posters to shelves and shelves of DVDs and vinyl albums. I used to love visiting Uncle Tim and Auntie Shelly. Their house always smelled of fresh-baked cookies and flowers cut from Shelly's huge backyard garden. Theirs was a street where kids played outside on bikes and roller blades and where we climbed trees and built blanket forts. When my mom and dad and I would go over for barbecues, my parents would relax and forget they were rock stars. No one bugged us there. They didn't have to be "on."

But then once Mom died, my father's true personality reemerged. Rough, hard, organized, calculating. Uncle Tim said my dad was like that when they were growing up too, that it was music—and my mother—that had sanded down Trent Andersen's sharp edges. But then once she was gone, those edges reformed, sharper and harder than ever.

I sit up straighter in my chair and sniff back my emotion. I cannot look weak in front of him.

"You have to stop trying to control my every move. I hardly ever see my friends the way it is. All I do is swim and study."

My dad exhales and pushes his plate away. He finishes the rest of the lemon-infused water in his glass and leans back in his chair. "We have talked about this more times than I can count, Marina. My house, my rules. You know the end goal here. Scholarships. Scholarships mean you swim, you study, you *succeed*."

"Really, Dad? Aren't you the one who harps all the time about the 'journey'? You, spouting whatever your self-help gurus tell you on your podcasts and audiobooks, going on about how life is a journey and we're meant to enjoy that rather than focus too much on the GOAL, on the destination? What about all that, Dad?"

"I *am* focused on your journey. That's why I do everything I can to give you everything you need to succeed during that journey." He raises his arms to showcase our house, the food sitting on the table in front of me.

"Did you know that if you give me just a bit of slack on my leash, if you give me just a SECOND to breathe, I've been raised well enough to not run out and screw it up? It's not like I'm out looking for trouble every second. For *once*, I just want to sleep in on the weekend, or spend the night at Lily's or Sierra's and not have to sneak out at six in the morning to go to the pool. I want to sing karaoke with my swim-team friends and not have to be back home by ten on a Friday night, just so I can get to practice on time the next morning. I want to maybe go on a date, like normal people my age—"

"A date? Is there a guy? Do you have a boyfriend? Is that what this is about?" His face is dangerously red.

"*No*, Dad, I do not have a boyfriend. How on earth would I possibly have time for that?"

The storm clouds stay in his eyes. "You are too young for a relationship. Trust me, Marina, that is the *last* thing you need right now."

Even though there are exactly zero boys on my radar, it makes me seethe that he is again placing restrictions on what I can and can't do. There is literally nothing under my control right now. At all. I'm helpless to live my own life.

I have to find a way to turn this situation around. "If I agree to the five-days-a-week swim practice before school, will you at least let me do rock school at lunch? It's just singing. The kids are super nice. There's no chance for trouble there. Mr. Malcolm is a cool guy—"

"No."

"Dad, please—"

"NO. This conversation is over." And just like that, my father stands, grabs his plate, and tosses it into the sink hard enough that it breaks. He doesn't stop to clean up the pieces, instead disappearing down the hall and into his study.

I sit there for a few minutes, until my pounding heart

settles and my napkin is soaked with as many of my tears as it can hold. My father doesn't emerge from his study during that time; the silence in the house is punctured by a podcast blaring through his Bluetooth speakers, the thud of his feet as he works out his anger on the treadmill.

The dinner table is still littered with the remnants of dinner. Crockery, dirty glasses, spilled food. I clean it quietly, putting away leftovers, wiping down counters, loading the dishwasher.

Thinking.

As I press the regular-cycle button on the dishwasher's digital face, a sense of peace washes over me.

I unzip the pocket of my tracksuit jacket and pull out my phone.

Since I tossed Darcie's card in the garbage earlier at the pool, I open a text chat to the one number I *do* have.

Hey, Adrian. Tell Darcie I'm in.

I tuck my phone back into my pocket and turn off the kitchen lights, pausing briefly at the fridge to grab some of the specialty fish food for Neptune.

My father's broken dinner plate, still dirty with his unfinished meal, sits in the sink, right where he left it.

CHAPTER 18

GOOD OL' CAP TO THE RESCUE

I wait inside a bus stand to stay out of view of passing cars. With my luck, someone who knows my dad will be out and about buying dog food or going to the chiropractor and will see me, and a *Hey I think I saw your daughter outside Ambrosia Studios today* text will appear in his inbox before the bell even rings on the school day I am currently skipping.

I've never skipped school before. The racing heartbeat and sweaty palms is enough evidence of that. Good thing I'm only here to sing, not take a lie-detector test.

And other than not being in class, everything else about today should be business as usual. I went to the pool this morning like a good little Marina; I will go again after school. I even made it to first period, during which I said I was feeling unwell and might throw up—this always freaks out teachers and they hand over that nurse's office pass faster than lightning splits a tree. I checked into the nurse's office, pretended to call my dad, and waited the appropriate amount of time to exit the school building for my ride home.

Difference is, it wasn't my dad picking me up. It was a

guy named Georgie who drives for Lyft to supplement his "pathetic" night-school work-study income.

And Georgie doesn't care where a sixteen-year-old girl might be going at nine on a school morning, as long as he gets paid and earns a good trip rating. Only when he drops me off in front of Ambrosia Studios does he stop talking about himself and ask me what I'm doing.

"You a musician?"

"Me? No way. Not a musical bone in my body," I lie.

"You be careful around here, okay, kid? This neighborhood can be a little dodgy."

"Thanks for the great ride, Georgie. Five stars!" The door to his Nissan rattles as it closes, and the driver offers a wave as he pulls away, off to pick up the next lucky passenger who will learn the colorful story of how Georgie is going to revolutionize the marketing industry. Or something. He talked a lot about apps and search engines in the twenty-minute journey, but I'm so freaked out about the day ahead of me, I really only heard about 40 percent of what he said, and that 40 percent was filled with acronyms that may have been in Swedish.

"Boo."

I practically jump out of my skin. In my defense, Darcie does, as usual, look a bit like a ghoul. Does she wear her foundation a shade too light on purpose?

"Hey, Darcie."

"Mermaid ... you ready?"

"Umm ..."

"You're not backing out—"

"What? No. I'm here, aren't I?" I try to sound brave.

The smile that follows is the opposite of what I expect, but it looks nice on her. Makes the blue of her eyes pop out against the very heavy black eyeliner.

"Don't be a chicken. This is going to be *incendiary*." Darcie grabs my upper arm and tugs me out of the bus stand and halfway down the block to the bright red door with the word *AMBROSIA* painted on its front in stylish, white block letters. "My uncle is cool," she says, yanking open the heavy door. "He's gonna crap himself when he hears you."

The inside of Ambrosia looks exactly as I expected—silver track lighting overhead painting orbs of light on the polished concrete floors, walls painted in rich primary hues, modern furniture interrupted by an old black-leather couch against the wall, paintings representing an artist's interpretation of who I think are Jimi Hendrix, Eric Clapton, Madonna, Freddie Mercury, Stevie Nicks, and the guy from Led Zeppelin (I always forget his name). Music-focused magazines aimed at guitarists, drummers, bassists, and vocalists sit stacked haphazardly on a long, heavy wooden-and-glass coffee table. Somewhere in here, someone has one of those essential oil diffusers going—this is the first recording studio I've ever been in that smells like lavender and vanilla and not cigarette smoke and body odor.

Then again, I haven't been in a proper recording studio for nearly a decade. Not since before my mom left us.

Darcie hugs a pretty receptionist behind a huge counter that is part wood, part resin—it looks like a river is running through the middle of its front—and again, it's weird to see this side of Darcie. In the few occasions we've spent in each other's company, she's been the exact opposite of the girl I'm watching.

But her voice still sounds awful.

"Marina, meet Tamsin. She basically runs the place," Darcie says. I shake Tamsin's hand. Her tight black pencil skirt and white, short-sleeved blouse say business; the tattoos running up her arms say rock 'n' roll.

"Nice to meet you." Tamsin's accent—she sounds like the Queen of England. "I hear you've got quite the voice. You ready to tear it up today?"

I try not to let my smile quiver.

"Oh, don't be nervous. Everyone here is lovely," Tamsin says.

"Especially me." A man saunters toward us dressed in torn Levi's and a band T-shirt under an open striped button-down with a coffee stain on the left breast pocket. He offers his hand. "I'm Andy, Darcie's uncle." A breath mint just covers the smell of nicotine.

"Nice to meet you, sir." Sir? When did I start saying *sir*?

"You're Trent and Calla Andersen's daughter, yeah? Oh man, I was so bummed when Hidden Villains broke up. I think they were just on the edge of real greatness, you know? So great."

"Thank you." I never know what to say when people compliment my father. It's not like I had anything to do with it. "Um, actually, speaking of my father—"

"Oh, yeah, don't worry. Little Deedee filled me in," he says. Darcie punches her uncle in the shoulder. "Sorry. Darcie. Not Little Deedee. Old habits die hard." He winks at his niece and leans closer to me. "Except she will always be Little Deedee to me. Did you know she couldn't say her own name for the first three years of her life and called herself Deedee? That's where the nickname comes from."

"ANDREW."

Uncle Andy's laugh echoes off the exposed, painted industrial ceilings. "Come on. Let's get busy before I think of more awesome Darcie stories to share."

Darcie throws her gaze skyward for a beat before following after us, unwrapping yet another lozenge. She flicks the tiny, wadded-up wrapper at her uncle this time, pelting him in the neck. He swats it away like he would a mosquito.

The main door behind us opens, throwing a blade of sunlight down the dim hallway. I only turn to look because Tamsin squeals, her stilettos clicking against the concrete floor as she scurries over to greet the newcomer.

Adrian Brooks.

"Hey, you guys weren't going to start the party without me, we you?"

We've stopped in the hall outside the studio door marked with a giant number 2. Uncle Andy throws up a hand in greeting, and we wait for Adrian and Tamsin to finish their quick hug and hello.

Darcie did *not* mention that Adrian would be here today.

Although it makes sense. It *is* his band.

Still …

"Hey, Marina," Adrian says as he saunters toward us. Same outfit as the other night—ripped jeans, worn-out Converse that might have been black at one point—except today he's wearing a thick, off-white wool sweater that looks like it belongs on a guy manning a fishing boat. His curls are gorgeously twisty, which isn't fair given that my hair is still wet from the pool, braided and tucked under a soft, baby-blue knitted hat so I don't catch a chill.

He reaches out for a handshake; I meet it, hoping he can't feel the tremors racing through me. "You ready to make some magic?" he says. I smile because I'm afraid if I speak, my voice will break.

Andy says his own hello (Darcie barely offers a fist bump) and then opens the door, and we follow him in. The studio is super nice. His domain behind the massive sound board is clean and well organized, and the booth where I'll be spending most of the day is softly lit, all the necessary equipment already set up. Large-diaphragm condenser mics with filters, headphones, stand for my sheet music, another tall stool with a bottle of water. Though I'll be singing to prerecorded tracks today, a well-appointed drum set, a baby grand piano, and a collection of guitars sit quietly in the space too.

Goosebumps wash over me. *One of these days, I'll be doing this for real, for people to hear ME.*

One step at a time. First, I have to survive today. I have to survive singing in front of Adrian Brooks.

Uncle Andy points to the coat tree behind the door and then flops into his high-backed mesh office chair. "I'm guessing you've seen the inside of one of these places before?"

I have. Many times.

"So, let's get busy," Andy says. "Fill me in so we can agree on a starting point."

Adrian takes one of the other mesh office chairs, and Darcie plops onto the black couch, a twin to the one out in the lobby. I follow her lead, tucking my hands between my knees so no one will see them shake. From her heavy army-green messenger bag, Darcie pulls out four manila folders and hands one each to me, Adrian, and then Andy. "I figured we'd start at the top of the set list, the stuff we usually perform live. Depends how many takes she needs to get through each track—that'll determine how much time we'll need today."

Andy scans the list, his index finger against his lip tapping out a beat only he can hear, head bobbing as he reads the song titles. "Marina, do you know all these?"

"Most of them," I say. And I do. Over the last ten days, Darcie has overstuffed my inbox with Scuttlebutt tracks, with and without vocals. I've been listening to them every moment I've not got my head underwater, and even then, the tracks play in my head. I also took the very dangerous chance and told Ms. Amberly about it so she could help me work out the songs I wasn't a hundred percent on.

Of course, she's thrilled I'm doing this—and also willing to be sworn to secrecy. She's met my father before, and even though Ms. Amberly is a teacher, she's not even thirty yet, and a former student at our high school. She's the zaniest, kindest teacher on the whole faculty, known for her brightly colored hair and custom-made, crinoline dresses that look straight out of the 1950s.

And I'm so grateful she's been willing to give up her lunch breaks to serve as my interim vocal coach. I definitely owe her one.

"She's only had this stuff, like, a week. I'm not expecting any miracles," Darcie said.

"Deedee, be nice." Andy gives his niece a stern look.

"What? She sings in a school *choir*, not for a rock band." She flops her folder onto the coffee table in front of us and sinks back into the couch. Her earlier smiling face has disappeared. She almost looks … sad.

This can't be easy on her, someone else coming in to sing because she can't.

My stomach sinks a bit. Maybe I shouldn't do this.

But then I hear Lily and Sierra in my head, fighting over which inspirational quote best suits this weird situation. Our group chat is filled with quotes torn off the internet, everyone from the Dalai Lama to Captain America, my goofy, amazing friends trying to outdo one another in their efforts to cheer me on and prop up my confidence.

"Well, by the sounds of it, the only miracles we need have to do with *time*," Andy says. "You need tracks for upcoming shows you can't afford to cancel, Marina isn't supposed to be here, and I have a full month of bookings starting in two weeks with no available space during business hours. So unless Marina can sneak out of her house at midnight to come record, miracles are definitely on the menu today."

Gulp.

"You guys don't need to worry." Adrian says. "I've heard her sing. And I have total faith she's gonna kill it."

Even as I smile tentatively, I swear my insides are going to liquefy and ooze out of my pores and I will die a blob of gelatinous goo right here on Uncle Andy's industrial gray carpet.

Ahem. Stop swooning, Marina.

"Pressure's on if you guys want to get this done," Andy says, flipping through the stapled list and then glancing at the blocky watch on his wrist.

Right as I'm about to grab my coat and run, the voice of Steve Rogers, a.k.a. Captain America, rings in my head: *"I can do this all day."*

He's right. I know how to sing. I know how to make the music bend to my will. I *can* do this all day, even with Darcie Drayer doubting and Adrian Brooks watching.

I stand, pull my own folder of lyrics, sheet music, and notes out of my bag, and nod toward the glassed-in sound booth.

"So, what are we waiting for?"

CHAPTER 19

COMPLICATIONS

I don't even know how I got to the pool. Maybe I sprouted wings during the recording session and flew there?

Coach Tosto nods approvingly as I finish the last 4x100 set and climb out for the dryland cool-down. She doesn't say anything to me—always a good thing when she doesn't bombard you with commentary and criticisms—just points to the section of the whiteboard reserved for the next day's activities, the big box she fills in toward the end of every session so there are no surprises the next time we're in the water. Which, for me, is in, like, twelve hours? Plus, I'm sure anything significant she wants to say will be reported to my father via email before I finish rinsing the shampoo out of my hair in the locker room shower.

Doesn't matter. Nothing could touch how perfectly **perfect** today was.

Adrian and I did a duet just before the session ended—yeah, even though I told myself not to swoon, I did—I swooned! I confess! That duet is going to live on in my Most Romantic Moments Ever memory bank, even if it was just two people singing together and there is zero romantic involvement and I *know* that in my head but my heart was all kinds of squishy and that is probably why I don't remember how I got to the pool this afternoon …

I did need a few takes for some songs—which made Darcie roll her eyes oh so dramatically—but the session was just as she'd predicted it would be: *incendiary*.

And while she was (again) annoyed when I said I absolutely had to leave by three to get to practice on time and not raise suspicions, they all seemed happy with the progress we made, though no one was surprised that we didn't get through the whole twenty-song list. That's an impossible feat for any recording artist. Which means we're definitely going to need another session.

I may have bounced up and down and spilled my honey-lemon tea when Andy said he could squeeze us in Thursday.

Except now that I'm back at the pool, I realize that Thursday is the day before the district meet that runs Friday-Saturday-Sunday. Skipping another school day is going to be tricky, and especially before this huge competition my father is treating like it's the freaking Olympics.

I just have to keep my head down between now and then, not step out of line or give him any reason to get angry. The last bout of grounding sort of faded away, as if he'd forgotten I was grounded, but I don't want to tempt fate. He hasn't mentioned "homeschool" in almost two weeks.

Lily bounds into the locker room, uniform and hair net in place, just as I'm stepping out of my shower stall wrapped in my giant towel. "Sooooo …?"

"Lil," I say, giving her a warning look as I press a finger against my lips.

She lowers her voice. "How WAS it?"

"Amaaaaazing!"

Lily's squeal bounces off the cold tile surroundings. I'm afraid if she bounces any harder, she'll slip on the wet floor.

"Calm down before you break something," I say. We navigate through my swim sisters, the locker room a box of chatter and laughs, the air heavy with the smell of chlorine, hair products, lotions, and the occasional whiff of someone's dinner. Some might think it gross to eat in a locker room, but in a two-hour swim session, we're burning upwards of 1200 calories. I swim three or more hours a day, which means I am constantly hungry. It's not a myth that swimmers eat constantly.

And I think one of my teammates has her mother's famous meatballs in here. It takes everything I have to not go full werewolf and steal them from her water-pruned fingertips.

I open my locker at the row's end, Lily leaning against the slice of wall where it meets the corner. "Soooo, what *can* you tell me?"

I've mastered getting dressed in a room full of people without flashing any important parts, so I hand her my swim parka to hold up between us as a temporary shield and pull on my bra.

"It was *incredible*, Lil," I say, popping my head through my shirt. I take my parka back and toss it onto the bench next to me. "Like, seriously, it was so mind-blowingly cool. Adrian showed up—that threw me off at first but then I got in the swing of things and tried to forget that anyone was even watching."

"Always better than envisioning people in their underwear," Lily says.

"Does that even work?" I'm afraid if I envisioned Adrian in his underwear, it would make things so much worse. I might die of embarrassment. "Anyway, we got through eight songs, I think? Eight. Maybe nine. I can't even remember."

"Is that a lot?"

"My aching throat says yes," I say, keeping my voice low enough that Lily has to lean in to hear me. I cannot risk anyone overhearing this conversation. "It's insane. This isn't how real recording artists do it. But we're short on time, plus Darcie's uncle only has a bit of free space in his schedule."

"Well, it's not like you guys are cutting an album—*yet*." Her grin is blinding.

"Nah, and Andy—Darcie's uncle—he said that the roughness would actually be okay for what we're doing, since live performances are always a little raw, less polished than what you'd get if you were recording an album."

"Did Adrian sing with you?" Lily's eyes sparkle with excitement. I love that about her, that she's so happy for me, even if she knows this situation could explode and end up with me disappearing until graduation.

"He DID. It was … ahhh, it was just so cool," I say. Lily offers her hand for a quiet high five. "And—shocker—Darcie was almost *nice* for, like, five minutes."

"Ursula the Sea Witch was nice to you? Sierra will never believe it." Lily laughs quietly.

"It didn't last. But it was there briefly. I think maybe she might be feeling like I'm stepping on her toes a little."

"That's silly—she asked you to do this."

"I know … but she was definitely back to her snarky self at the end. I think maybe she heard me and realized she can't do that anymore? Like, maybe she's worried about her voice never healing. It happened to Ms. Amberly."

"I've heard their songs with Darcie singing. She's good, but she's not *you*," Lily says.

"Still, I don't want her to think I'm moving in to steal her place."

"It's Adrian's band. That's up to him."

I pull on my second shoe and tie the laces I dropped in the puddle at my feet. "I swear, if Madison doesn't finish those meatballs, I might eat her."

Lily pushes off the wall. "You gonna be online later? I'm here until closing."

"You know I'll probably be long asleep."

"You're like an old lady with your eight-thirty bedtime."

My backpack thrown over my shoulder, I close my locker. "Then I'm an exhausted old lady."

"Follow me to the snack bar. I can slide over a cheddar bagel with cream cheese when the boss goes outside for her break."

"I will love you forever," I say, my mouth already watering. I wave goodbye to my swim family and follow Lily out of the locker room, both of us cringing at the stupid door.

"Why do they not fix that?" Lily says. I follow her to the concession stand, wait for her to clock back in, wash her hands, and take the orders of two little kids from the junior swim program. Man, I miss the days when I could eat a doughnut and chocolate milk for my after-lesson snack.

But soon, Lily hands over a piping-hot, cheddar bagel, the cream cheese oozing down the sides. "I could kiss you," I say, licking my cheese-covered fingertips. "Has Steeeeeve been by yet to say hello to his favorite girl?"

Lily's face lights up like a Christmas bulb. "He did. He's so adorable," she says, eyes dreamy as she leans atop the counter on bent elbows. "But don't change the subject, as gorgeous as that subject might be. What's next with the music stuff? If you guys didn't finish recording?"

I look around us to make sure no one is even remotely close enough to pick up on what we're talking about. "I have to go back. Thursday."

Lily's eyes widen. "How are you going to pull that off with the meet this weekend? I'm scheduled to work all three days because there are going to be, like, a bazillion people here."

"Right? I have heats all three days too. How am I going to skip another day of school without my dad finding out? Two days in the same week?"

"There has to be another way," she says. "Have you heard from him today?"

I shake my head, mouth full of bagel. "I guess I'll know if I'm caught once I climb in the car."

Lily stands up suddenly, straightening her shirt. "Speak of the devil."

My dad has just walked in, the glass sliding doors *whooshing* closed behind him. He sees me and waves.

"He doesn't look mad," Lily says, her lips barely moving with her own smile pasted on.

"I'll see you tomorrow, Lil. Thanks for the bagel." The seconds between the concession counter and when I reach my father is more than just a series of steps. It's me checking the weather in Trentlandia, watching for signs that he's angry, that he's somehow discovered what I did today. With my dad, it's never just *Hey, Dad, how are you*, it's a constant game of analyzing the cues, the body language, the tone of his voice—that's how I know what kind of mood I'm walking into.

Nothing is easy with that man.

"Hey," I say, cupping the napkin-wrapped bagel in my hand.

"You ready for dinner?" He smiles, and it looks genuine. I hope he can't hear my heart knocking against my sternum.

"I'm starving. Lil made me a bagel because Madison has her mom's meatballs in the locker room."

Dad groans. He's had those meatballs too. He knows the deliciousness I speak of.

"You seem in a good mood," I say, following him out of the swim club.

"It was a nice day."

Yes. It was. The nicest day. Please don't mess that up.

He's acting weird. I'm nervous all over again as I throw my swim bag and backpack full of textbooks I didn't use today into the back seat.

"You sure you're okay?"

My dad takes his place behind the wheel. "What, is a guy not allowed to have a nice day after receiving fantastic emails talking about his incredible daughter?"

It feels like that last bite of bagel is lodged in my throat. I can't look at him. I can't tell if he's being genuine. And I don't know what emails he might have received—from Tosto? From another snooping parent? Did someone actually see me outside Ambrosia Studios?

"Coach said you were on fire in the pool today, both before and after school. I love hearing that. It just makes me so proud of you."

"Oh. Cool." I swallow the bite of bagel and chase it with a gulp from my water bottle. "Thanks, Dad."

"Thank *you* for working so hard, Marina." He drops a heavy hand on my shoulder and squeezes before returning to the steering wheel and turning on the car. "In fact, I'm so impressed with what Coach had to say, we've decided that instead of going to school Thursday, we're going to have you at the pool to get ready for the meet. Nothing too strenuous—we want to save your energy for the weekend—but she's giving you some coveted one-on-one time to make sure your head is in the right place, do some visualizations, fine-tune a few things for the individual medley on Saturday. I'm just glad you're doing that in the middle of the weekend …"

His voice fades in my ears, replaced by a panicked roar, as I think about this coming Thursday.

I'm supposed to be meeting Adrian and Darcie and her uncle at the recording studio, not spending the entire day in the pool.

How am I going to get out of this?

"… I know I'm tough on you, Mar, but it's for a good reason. You know that, right?"

"Mm-hmm," I mumble. My chest burns with my duplicity of today, with the worry about Thursday and what Darcie is going to say when I tell her. I'm so grateful my father's eyes are on the road and not watching me.

Because, as he's said a million times before, he can read me like a book.

And right now, the words are written all over my face.

CHAPTER 20

GROUP PROJECT

My dinner disappears so quickly off my plate, I give myself a stomachache. But the reason is twofold: I need to not spend any extra time with my dad tonight, or he will see right through my thin skin and figure me out because I always act weird when I've lied about something; and secondly, I have to text Darcie and Adrian and tell them there's absolutely no way I can make it to the recording studio on Thursday.

At last I'm in my room alone. Neptune has had his dinner, so I grab my phone and open a new group text with Adrian and Darcie. Darcie's response is as I expected—an annoyed emoji face followed with: **Not cool, mermaid. Let me talk to Andy about another session.**

Adrian doesn't respond, even though the text window shows that he's seen the message.

I'm instantly nervous again. Which is ridiculous—I'm the one doing *them* a favor. And I know the tracks sounded good, the ones I did solo and the single we did together. Even Uncle Andy was impressed.

So why do I care if Adrian doesn't respond right away?

Because he's beautiful and he's talented and he's a senior and I loved singing with him today.

The doorbell rings downstairs, the sound so foreign, I wonder if my dad will even know what it is. Uncle Tim never rings the bell, and I know Sierra or Lily would've texted or called before just showing up. I don't think it's cookie season, and Halloween is still a week away …

I listen as my dad's heavy footfalls sound across the hardwood floor. The front door opens. The bass of my dad's voice is barely audible through my own closed door, but when it's met with the low timbre of another male voice, I hop off my bed and crack the door just a smidge.

"Marina!"

The front door clicks closed. "This place is amazing," the other voice says, and the floor drops out from under me.

What in the world is Adrian Brooks doing at my HOUSE?

I don't even have time for a breath mint or to deal with my hair, still a rat's nest from the pool, but I cannot let my dad and Adrian spend more than thirty seconds together.

I fly down the stairs and slide across the floor in slippered feet. "Heyyyy …"

"Hey, Marina," he says. He has a backpack over his shoulder. No tears in his jeans. He's even wearing a pair of black-rimmed glasses. Looks way more science geek than rock star at the moment. "Yeah, I didn't know if you got my text"—he wiggles his phone—"but I know you have that big swim meet this weekend, so I figured we should get a head start on the hydrology project 'cos our time will sort of be limited to get it done."

I stare at Adrian for a beat longer than maybe I should.

"Yeah. Right. Smart—I didn't even think about that," I say, slapping my hand against my forehead. My dad looks between me and Adrian.

"What did you say your name was again?" he asks.

"Adrian, sir."

"I don't remember Marina mentioning you."

"I don't mention a lot of kids in my classes, Dad," I say, trying to hide the quiver in my voice.

"Marina and I were partnered up by the teacher, and we're doing a thing on tidal marsh creation and coastal wetlands," Adrian says, pushing the glasses up his nose. "I reserved us a table at the library for seven, so we should probably go."

"You didn't tell me you needed to study out of the house tonight, Mar," my dad says, turning to face me directly.

I look him right in the eye when answering. "I'm kinda nervous about the meet this weekend, Dad, so if things go unmentioned this week, can you blame me?"

My dad pivots. "The library closes at, what, nine?"

"Nine thirty, Mr. Andersen. I'll make sure Marina is back safe as soon as we're done."

My dad stares at Adrian for a long breath—to his credit, Adrian doesn't wither under my father's scrutiny, instead pushing his glasses up again for nerdy effect (or, maybe they really don't fit).

"No later than ten."

"I'll grab my stuff," I say, taking off like a shot up the stairs. I don't think I've ever moved so fast. Rinse with mouthwash while trading track pants for cute jeans, cozy baby-blue beanie for messy hair, lip gloss in pocket, favorite warm sweater, backpack, phone, slippers discarded for socks and actual shoes. I'm back downstairs in under two minutes, grateful to see my father has again disappeared into his study, leaving Adrian to scroll through his phone without further interrogation.

His smile alone could power an electric car for a week.

I throw a quick look over my shoulder and then press a finger to my lips. I don't want any words exchanged until we're out of the house.

Except once we're out of the house and down the long

walkway that connects the sidewalk to the porch, I realize that we're not walking to the library—Adrian has a car, an old Honda, parked in front of the neighbor's.

"You brought the backpack in for effect?" I ask.

He opens my door for me and tosses said backpack into the rear seat. "Of course. Lily filled me in on Mr. Trent Andersen, former rock god, and his jailhouse tendencies," he says.

I'm not sure if I will have to scold or thank Lily for giving out such details about my dad.

I slide into the car before Mr. Trent Andersen, former rock god, changes his mind and chases us down the block.

Adrian climbs in behind the wheel, his breath exiting in a cold plume. "So—are you mad? Is this too much?"

"It's a bit nuts, yeah, but I'm not mad," I say. "It just caught me off guard."

"I thought maybe it would be cool to hang out a little more before we get back into the recording studio. Because today was amazing, wasn't it?"

I smile like the cat who caught the canary; Adrian grins back.

As he pulls away from the curb, he again pushes the glasses up his nose.

"Are those real?"

"Yeah, I usually wear contacts, but I figured your dad would be more trusting if Nerd Adrian showed up at the house."

"As opposed to Rocker Adrian."

"Dads tend to get a little nervous when that persona shows up out of the blue to take their daughters to the library."

"Do you show up at a lot of girls' houses and ask them to the library?"

He laughs. "Only once last year for a social studies project and it made the dad so nervous, he actually drove us there and sat at a nearby table to make sure we were doing the project on Mesopotamia."

"Was it real, or a ruse, like this?"

"Mesopotamia is the birthplace of writing, the wheel, and beer, I'll have you know." He grins. "And what? You're saying you don't want to learn about tidal marsh creation and coastal wetlands?"

"As a creature who spends most of her waking hours in an aquatic setting, of course I am naturally concerned about coastal wetlands," I say, pointing out the window, "but since we're passing the library *right now*, I'm guessing our destination is otherwise?"

"The Beanery okay? I hear you have a special place in your heart for their vanilla lattes and homemade cookies."

"I really need to get a muzzle for your cousin," I say, pulling my phone from my pocket and tapping out a quick text to Lily: ***I'm deciding whether to kiss you, or kick you.***

It only takes a few seconds for the bubbles to dance back: **I have my shin guards on just in case. xo**

CHAPTER 21

WHIPPED CREAM MAKES EVERYTHING BETTER

The Beanery is super quiet. Adrian explains that they only have live music Wednesdays through Saturdays, and Sundays are reserved for comics and writers who want an open-mic opportunity. He waves at the manager as we walk in.

"Pick us a table," Adrian says. "Regular vanilla latte?" He nods toward the coffee bar.

"With whipped cream. And a peanut butter cookie, if they have any."

"Coming right up."

I slide into a table against the wall that gives me a clear view of the door—one of these days, I won't be so paranoid about my dad following me around—but until then …

With my bag on the floor, I turn toward the wall and use the darkened screen of my phone to apply some lip gloss, hoping I've not slimed it outside the confines of my lips. My hair is a hopeless mess, though I quickly finger-comb and fix my braid before replacing my hat. If I'd *known* I'd be "studying" this evening with Adrian Brooks, I would've taken care to not look like a swim bum.

Oh well. This is who I am. Take it or leave it.

Adrian pauses for me to take the small paper bag pinched between his fingers—his hand covered in a plastic glove—and then slides a delicious-looking, whipped-cream-topped mug onto the tabletop in front of me, followed by his own identical drink. "It looked so good, I had her make me the same."

"I have excellent taste," I say.

"I've heard that about you." He sits and slides the glove off.

"What's with that?"

"Peanut allergy."

"What? Oh! Adrian, I am so sorry! Why didn't you say something?" I grab the cookie bag and shove it into my bag.

"And ruin your chance at the best peanut butter cookies in the city? I wouldn't dream of it." He grins and takes a drink of his coffee, coating his upper lip in whipped cream. "What? Do I have something on my face?" I hand him a napkin. "Mmm, you're right. You do have excellent taste."

"You've never had a vanilla latte before? Doesn't get much more boring than that." I sip from my own drink, cupping the mug and shivering against its warmth.

"I've never had a vanilla latte with whipped cream before. You're definitely onto something." He sets his cup down and tucks his hands under his folded arms. Maybe he's nervous too? "I got your text about Thursday. Don't let Darce freak you out. We'll get the tracks down. Andy's a great guy and I'm sure he can squeeze us in somewhere. And we owe you so much for doing this."

"I'm glad I can help," I say, cheeks warming. "And I was having such an incredible time today, I didn't even think about the swim meet this weekend. It was nice, actually, to forget about it for a few minutes."

"Your dad's pretty tough on you ..."

"*That* is the understatement of the year." I don't want to

talk about my dad. "What about your parents? Do they support your wild rock star dreams?"

Adrian laughs quietly. "They do, weirdly. I'm the baby, so I get away with a lot. I have two older brothers—one's an accountant and one's almost a pediatrician, in his residency right now. My parents have their smart, respectable kids—I guess I get to be whatever I want."

"And being a musician isn't respectable?" I ask.

"You of all people know the answer to that." He lifts an eyebrow.

"You did your homework." I take another drink from my coffee.

"A little. Google is this thing we can use to look stuff up on the internet. Maybe you've heard of it?"

I nudge him under the table with my foot. He fakes like I've broken his leg.

"You googled my dad, which means you know more than maybe what Lily told you."

"I know about his musical career, how awesome he was—and of course, I know Hidden Villains' music. But your talents, those are rare. You could be a huge star. You have that thing that most performers only dream about."

As cool as it is to hear someone say nice things about me, it's making me uncomfortable.

"Okay, so let's talk about something else," he says. I'm guessing my inability to make eye contact was enough to clue him in. "Favorite food."

"Really? Twenty questions?"

"Come on. It'll be fun. I'll start. Favorite food is pretty much anything with cheese."

"And no nuts."

"Just no peanuts."

"Do you think it's weird that we're all allergic to stuff all of a sudden? My dad thinks it's some sort of conspiracy," I say. "Then again, my dad thinks a lot of things are a conspiracy."

"We're not talking about your dad right now, remember?" His smile makes my heart skip a beat. "Okay, soooo, favorite band."

"Like, classic or modern?" I ask.

"Either. Both."

"Heart. Ann and Nancy Wilson," I say. He doesn't need to know why they're my favorite. "And current band …"

"Don't say Coldplay."

"What?" I laugh. "What's wrong with Coldplay?"

Adrian groans and throws his head back.

"I wasn't *going* to say Coldplay but maybe I should," I tease. "I listen to mostly alternative. Some of my favorites—Tegan and Sara, Phoebe Bridgers, Regina Spektor, Aimee Mann, and I love this performer named Aurora—and oh man, Fiona Apple. And I recently discovered a singer/songwriter called VÉRITÉ—I'm into female vocalists who really know how to use their voices."

"You know how," he says.

"I also know I'd be better with a vocal coach."

"You don't have one?"

"Just the choir teacher at school. Swimming is job one," I say. "Your turn."

Adrian lists his favorites, which leads him to talk about how he got into music in the first place. He had some behavioral issues in elementary school but as soon as his folks put him in a music program, he was hooked. No more trouble in class, no more driving teachers crazy. In sixth grade, he transferred to a private performing arts school but hated it because they wanted him to learn classical music and he wanted to be a rock star. That's how he ended up at the prestigious Lange Performing Arts.

I tell him about rock school, how I want so much to be a part of it but my dad freaked, about my duet with Tandy, how

I write my own music and lyrics but I never get to perform them unless my dad's out of the house.

"I'd *love* to see some of your stuff."

"Nooooo, I'm not ready to share it with anyone."

He tilts his head. "You cannot keep it all bottled up, Marina. Share it with me. Please? I promise I won't laugh."

Am I worried about that? About someone laughing? The music I've written lately has been so personal, it would be like letting someone read my diary. If I kept one. The songs are my diary.

"The music isn't quite where it should be. I definitely need work on that—I play my mom's guitar when I'm writing to try to noodle it all out, but I don't have arrangements for, like, a whole band or anything."

"Luckily for you, I happen to know a whole band, and I'd love to help."

"Maybe."

"You think about it, but I'd be honored to hear what you've got." He fidgets with a woven black bracelet around his wrist. "It's really scary showing people your work. I get it. I've been luckier than most because I have to show my stuff at school—and then it gets torn apart in front of everyone, which actually makes it easier. Eventually. Once you get done being annoyed that the instructors are right about how much it sucks." He laughs under his breath.

"I cannot imagine what it would be like to have my parents so behind my musical aspirations," I say, instantly regretting it. I'm trying to keep the conversation off Trent Andersen, but somehow all roads lead back to him.

Adrian leans forward on his bent arms on the tabletop. "Why is your dad so uptight about you singing?"

I stare at him for a beat, trying to get a read on whether I want to talk to him about this. Just because we sang a song together today …

Might as well. Then we can just get past it.

"My mom died. Drunk driver. She left the house in the middle of a big fight—about their separate music careers"—I stop short of talking about the potential divorce, that information still too new and raw to talk about out loud—"and she was killed. My dad blames himself, and the music industry, for everything that went wrong that night. Now he's basically obsessed with keeping me away from anything resembling a music career."

Adrian reaches across the table and places a warm hand on the back of my wrist. "That sucks. I'm so sorry, Marina."

I nod and pick up my mug, sipping the last of the now-cold coffee just to get my eyes anywhere other than on Adrian's face. I don't know him well enough to show him tears.

He releases my hand and again sits back, his chair squeaking under him. "Most embarrassing moment ever. I'll start," he says. "Fifth grade. I wet my pants in front of the whole school."

I laugh loudly, not because it's so funny but because I'm so relieved he's changed the subject. "You did not."

"I swear." He flattens his hand over his heart. "We were doing this dumb Christmas performance, and I was playing the guitar—badly, I might add—and I'd had way too much ginger ale at our class party before the show and I meant to pee before I got up on stage but I didn't so yeah, right in the middle of our rocker version of *Little Drummer Boy*, I got a little excited about my big solo moment and let loose."

And then I really am laughing, envisioning an adorable ten-year-old Adrian with his mop of dark curls, his little nerd glasses, playing the guitar, peeing his pants.

"Good thing I switched schools soon after," he says. "I still run into people sometimes who I went to elementary with, and lucky me, it's the first thing they remember. Little Pee-Pee Boy, *pa-rum-pum-pum-pum*." He gives me a second to dab the corners of my leaking eyes. "You'd better not tell anyone."

"If we ever perform live together, promise me we can sing that song."

He offers his hand for a fist bump. Singing together ... again ... I feel light-headed. Performing the duet with Adrian will definitely be added to the Top Ten Moments of My Life list.

"Hey, can I ask you a question?" I don't even know why I say that. It's a question just to ask if you can ask a question. "Is Darcie upset that I'm singing with you guys? She seemed weird when I left today."

Adrian exhales heavily. "Darcie is a handful," he says. "She's obviously bummed about her messed-up voice, but she loves this band. She wants what's best for Scuttlebutt. Which is why she came up with the idea of asking you to sing for us."

"That was her idea?"

"Yeah, I showed everyone the video that Lily sent me. We need stronger vocals if we're going to get any traction. Darcie knows that."

"But she seemed mad earlier. I just hope she knows I'm not, like, trying to sneak in and take her place or whatever."

He leans forward again, closing the distance between us. His aftershave wafts toward me. "Darcie and I have ... a tiny bit of history. It didn't work out, which is totally cool because we both just love the music. But don't let her get in your head. Don't question what you can do. You have an incredible, powerful voice. And if your future includes a few sets with Scuttlebutt, either behind the scenes or on the stage with a mic in your hand, we'd be honored to have you."

My face hurts from blushing so hard—and because I'm trying really hard to control the Christmas-morning grin tugging at my cheeks.

"Thanks for saying that, Adrian. Whatever happens, I'm really glad your obnoxiously naughty cousin introduced us," I say.

"Me too. Me too." He flattens a hand on the tabletop, almost like he was going to reach over and touch me again but then didn't.

The barista slides up next to the table. "Hey, guys, sorry—gotta kick you out." She taps her wrist, even though there's no watch on it.

And at once, I'm nervous again—I grab my phone. Holy cow, it is really nine thirty? How did two hours go by so quickly?

"Don't worry," Adrian says, unzipping his backpack. He hands over a bunch of stapled pages about coastal wetlands and estuaries and marshlands. Some text is already highlighted, notes scribbled in the margins. "I really did this project, so I got your back."

We say goodbye to the barista, who then locks the door and turns out the lights behind us. We really were the last people in the place. Adrian drives probably a little faster than he should, but he manages to get me home just under the wire. He unlocks his seat belt and makes to get out of the car.

"No—you're cool. I can walk to the door by myself," I say.

"I was trying to be a gentleman," he says. "My dad would kick my butt if I weren't."

"Well, my dad will kick your butt if he realizes we didn't actually go to the library."

"And your dad seems a little scarier than mine, not gonna lie," Adrian says.

"He drinks a lot of kale."

"Oh man, you really are in bad shape." He grins. "Okay, so—I look very forward to seeing you again, and I'm sure Darce will let us know about studio time and *hopefully*, you can sneak out long enough to dazzle us with more vocal stylings. And maybe we can get some food that doesn't involve kale."

"Or peanuts."

He snickers. "I always have an EpiPen with me, just in case you can't control yourself around the cookies."

Everything inside me feels like butterflies instead of flesh and blood and bones. "I can't wait."

Adrian extends his arm for a handshake, and when I meet it, he kisses the top of my hand, quickly. "Until next time, then."

I'm grateful that the outside air nips at my cheeks just enough to redden them before I reach the front door. It helps conceal the blush that starts in my feet and ignites the ends of my hair so that when my dad, sitting in the living room watching another of his self-help documentaries, doesn't notice anything out of the ordinary as I sail past and up the stairs, a "good-night" thrown over his shoulder just as my bedroom door clicks closed.

CHAPTER 22

SWIM FAST, LITTLE FISH

The rest of the week is all about the district meet. I guess it's good that my father is so preoccupied with my upcoming performance in the pool that he doesn't seem to give the sudden "library night" with Adrian a second thought—at least he doesn't bring it up again.

Instead, it's all visualizations and meditations and things I'm supposed to tell myself as I'm preparing to swim, as I'm climbing onto the starting block, as I'm positioned and waiting for the starting beep, with every stroke as I'm racing, how I'm going to outpace the swimmer beside me, as I'm climbing out of the pool, as I'm stepping onto the winner's podium to claim my medals.

All visualizations, all the time.

(Not going to lie. All that time spent with my eyes closed meant to be thinking about swimming and winning does mean I doze off now and again, instead thinking about the back-and-forth text messages with Adrian this week, the videos he sent me of him playing an acoustic guitar, working out some new lyrics. Means I jerk back to the present when either Dad or Coach Tosto startles me with "WAKE UP, MARINA! FOCUS!" Scares me every time.)

And Friday morning en route to the first day of the meet, while Dad is giving me one of his famous, podcast-fueled pep talks in the car, I'm thinking about if I'm brave enough to record myself playing Mom's guitar with my own original compositions, if I'm *crazy* enough to share it with Adrian. And then there's last night's brusque text from Darcie asking if I can manage to sneak out a night or two next week to finish recording the tracks.

As my dad said last night over a huge bowl of chicken and pasta, "Your head is not in the game."

He's not wrong.

But as we're driving to the pool where the district meet is held—one of the local community centers instead of our home club—I realize there really is no magic flu or broken neck coming to save me from the next seventy-two hours, and life will be easier if I just go along with Trent Andersen's Plan for World Domination and actually get my head in the game. The only way through this weekend is through it.

And this process is made easier by the presence of my swim-team siblings. Someone always arrives earlier than the rest of us to claim the best corner so we can camp out with chairs, blankets and pillows, coolers full of healthy, energy-focused snacks, even waterproof camp mats so we can snooze between heats. Swim meet days are very long, and if you're a swimmer who places in the top eight in her event—which I almost always do—the day is even longer as finals are usually held in the evenings.

My first heat is right at eight o'clock. The pool bleachers are already crammed with spectators, mostly parents and grandparents because it's still so early, but it's a day off from school for our district, so it'll be standing room only in here before lunchtime. Sierra and Lily promised to come see me too, threatening big signs with quotes from the *Little Mermaid* to cheer me on. That should be fun trying to explain to my dad later.

I'm able to pull my focus where it needs to be, and I finish first in my 8 a.m. race. As the day progresses, I finish second and first again in the two later races, which, at day's end, puts me in the top four swimmers for the day. But as it's only day one of three, it's not the time to get complacent or cocky.

I do see Lil and Sierra briefly in the afternoon, but it's best for me to stay with my swim team while I'm in competition mode—and it makes my dad and Coach Tosto happier if I'm at least giving the impression that I'm focused on swimming things and not whatever my real-life friends might bring.

The irony? When I'm with my swim team, we don't talk about the pool or our heat times or how much we love trying to squeeze into our ridiculously tight kneeskin suits—we play video games, listen to music, and talk about boys, music, romance, the latest gossip floating around amongst the squads, even a few rounds of truth or dare. Yeah, pretty much the last thing we're talking about is swimming.

But if we at least look like we're dutiful little dolphins? That's worth a gold medal all on its own.

By the finals on Sunday afternoon, my dad is prowling around the pool edge like an anxious tiger, his own stopwatch and clipboard at the ready, despite the fact that meets are drenched with parent volunteers and stopwatches in official timing capacities. It's not like my dad needs to time anything. He could just be one of those chill parents who sits in the bleachers and hoots and hollers for me.

Yeah, I know. Makes me laugh too.

This is the final race of the weekend, and I've swum very hard all three days to get here, much to my father's utter delight. Even my third-place finish in the butterfly yesterday didn't dampen his mood too much. (I hate the butterfly.) Coach Tosto whispers in my ear how this race is mine for the taking, to race the swimmer in the lane next to me and not the entire field, that a first-place finish will put me in the top ten swimmers for both juniors and seniors, and that I might as well sharpen my pencil to start signing early intent offers because there are university scouts here, frothing to sign me to their squads, even though I'm still only a junior.

Coach knows when to stop talking, though, and she leaves me to get my mind on the race. It's the 100M freestyle, my best event. I adjust my cap and hang around near the back tiled wall, facing away from everyone else, stretching my arms, making sure nothing is tight or hurting, splashing with water from the nonstop shower spigot. Every swimmer has their thing they do—I sing quietly to myself, under my breath, my mother's voice in my head, dancing across my lips:

> *Always here, by your side,*
> *I am the sand, you are the tide …*

My own personal good-luck charm.

Finally, the race officiant calls the swimmers poolside. First whistle, we hop onto our blocks. I take a deep breath, focused only on the blue water stretching in front of me. Coach is right—this race is mine.

Second whistle: Move into ready position.

"Take your marks."

Slow breaths. Wait for the beep.

Beep!

I hit the water as hard and fast as I can, streamlining underwater and then hitting the surface in full stroke, my body falling into a rhythm it knows. All I have to do is push as hard as my muscles will let me, watching that I breathe at the right intervals, kick at the right cadence, stay tight but relaxed at the same time so I don't cramp, not let the girl in the silver suit next to me get ahead.

Even when she does.

I can still catch her.

She's a half-body's length ahead as we hit the flip turn. We don't check clocks while we're swimming—we just instinctively *know* when we're lagging behind where we think we should be, based on other swimmers or our own body's feeling. While I know my dad is probably going to be hoarse later from yelling poolside, I can't hear him, and it's definitely best that I not try.

My entire focus is on beating the swimmer next to me.

I throw everything I have, scrape every last ounce from the tank, and yet she *just* beats me to the touchpad on the wall.

We throw off our goggles and watch the scoreboard—it's confirmed. Even though I've beaten my seed time by almost an entire second, she's finished 0.9 seconds ahead of me.

Which means second place.

She throws her arm over the lane rope for a quick handshake and once the other swimmers have finished, my opponent is hoisted out of the water by her cheering coach and teammates. My swim siblings do the same for me, all of them so proud and excited. Second place in the district finals is still a big deal for our swim club, and it secures my spot at the regional meet in two weeks.

Even Coach Tosto wraps an arm around my shoulders, handing me a towel, speaking right into my ear that the swimmer who beat me is a senior and this is her last year before college, that I nearly swam faster than a girl an entire year older and I can beat her at the regional meet, as we move away from the starting blocks so the final results can be announced and certified by the race officials.

At this point during a meet, everyone's tired and wants to go home and either celebrate or lick their wounds, but number one on the swimmers' minds? FOOD.

The medal ceremony is quick and raucous, and I'm so excited to see Lily and Sierra screaming at the top of their lungs from the bleachers when I step onto the second-place podium. Wrapped in my swim parka, I graciously bend forward and accept my medal, scanning the crowd for my dad.

He's standing at the very end of the bleachers, clapping with the crowd, and he's smiling, but the smile doesn't reach his eyes.

It makes my heart pound. Fresh sweat breaks out under my chilled armpits.

My fastest 100M freestyle ever.

And he's not happy.

CHAPTER 23

SIX THIN STRINGS

Uncle Tim scoops me off the ground as I emerge from the locker room. He's so excited, counting the medals hanging off my swim bag from the weekend's events.

I'm so tired, I could fall asleep standing right here.

"You are a force of nature!" he says, my medals splayed across his outstretched hands. "You're going to need another one of those light-up cases your dad loves so much. All this bling."

"Thanks, Uncle Tim." I hug him again. "Where is Dad?"

Tim nods. My father is hunched over in conversation with Coach, a serious look on his face, head bobbing as Coach speaks. "They're already strategizing," my uncle says. My eyes, tired and dry from the pool, meet his. "It won't always be like this, Mari. One of these days, you'll grow up and you'll get to call the shots."

My throat is so tight with emotion, I can only nod in silent agreement. Even if Uncle Tim is right, that day feels like a million years away.

"Marina!" I turn toward the voice. It's Ms. Amberly, wearing another of her crazy dresses—this one, the fabric is printed with mermaids. It's adorable. She's holding hands with a tall, skinny guy with a red goatee who looks like he could be a lumberjack if he'd just put on a hundred pounds.

She gives me a big squeeze. "I cannot believe how *fast* you were out there!"

"You saw?"

"Of course! I always try to come out for big stuff my kids are doing. My kids—listen to me," she says. Her red lipstick looks like it's been painted on by an artist. "This is my boyfriend, Stephan. Stephan, this is Marina."

He offers a freckled hand. "I've heard so much about you. Well done out there. Really incredible."

"Thanks," I say, tucking my hand back into my pocket. "This is my uncle, Tim."

The adults shake hands and talk for a moment about where they work, exchanging pleasantries about the high school teacher/counselor life. Ms. Amberly's Stephan is also a teacher—earth sciences and math—but at a local middle school.

I look over just as Dad finally shakes hands with Coach Tosto and joins us near the vending machines that are basically cleaned out after a long weekend of hungry teenagers and younger siblings.

"Dad, this is Ms. Amberly, my choir teacher, and her boyfriend, Stephan."

My dad shakes their hands, his guarded-but-pleasant face installed. He gets that way when he's not sure if someone is going to bring up his past rocker life. Says that "fans show up in the weirdest places."

"Mr. Andersen, I am not supposed to have favorites, but your daughter," Ms. Amberly says, winking at me, "she's incredible. Quite a talent you have here. I've never heard anyone else like her!"

Trent Andersen's smile tightens a notch. "Thank you."

"And today! That was nuts! I didn't know a human body could move so quickly! You must be very proud of her."

"I am." My dad drops a firm hand on my shoulder. "It was nice to meet you both. I should get Marina some dinner. It's been a long weekend."

"Oh, yes, absolutely." Ms. Amberly gives me another quick hug, and then her boyfriend helps her into her vintage leopard-print coat. "See you tomorrow, Marina!" Her peep-toe, blue-green heels click against the industrial-tile floor as they scurry toward the sliding doors that allow in a blast of cold air every time someone triggers the sensor.

"Dinner? I could eat," Tim says. "We must feed our champion!" He pats my back in victory.

"Marina needs to get home. I'll order in. School tomorrow," my father says.

"Oh. Okay. We could just get a quick bite, talk about how awesome she did today ..."

"I'll call you later this week." My father nods at his younger brother and pivots toward the exit.

"Should I follow as backup?" Tim asks next to my ear.

"It'll just end up in a fight," I say. "Go eat a pizza for me, something layered in cheese."

"If you insist ... but it won't be the same." He leans in and kisses my cheek, wrapping his arms around me. He's squishier than my dad; it's like being hugged by a friendly bear who smells like shaving cream and licorice mints. "I'll check on you later."

We walk out the front together, the cold, damp fall air rushing into my tired lungs, but Uncle Tim is parked in the opposite direction, so we wave goodbye and I hurry toward my dad's car, already idling impatiently at the curb.

I slide my swim bag onto the back seat and climb in, my stomach in knots. I can't take the silence as he pulls out of the community center parking lot. "Soooo ... are you unhappy with how the meet went?"

He shakes his head. "Not at all. You swam your heart out. Sure, I would've liked to have seen you in the first-place spot, but that swimmer from Highlands was good."

"She's also a senior."

He nods.

"I saw you talking to Coach. Does she have some ideas to get ready for regionals?"

"Not much else we can do that we're not already doing," he says. "Regionals will be a tough competition. The same scouts that were here today will be there. We'll have a debrief with Coach this week, see what we can troubleshoot. Definitely the butterfly."

"Right. That makes sense." I don't know what else to say to cut through the tension. Sometimes the simplest conversations with my dad are like trying to walk through a giant pool of Jell-O. Every step, every word, is a major effort.

"Nice of your choir teacher to come out today," he says.

"Yeah … she's amazing. Everyone at school loves her."

The rest of the drive is quiet, even when he stops at our favorite Italian restaurant and pops out of the car to pick up an order he must've placed while waiting for me to emerge from the locker rooms. I hurry and pull out my phone to see what I've missed—tons of notifications from Sierra and Lily— and even a text from Adrian: **Heard you killed it today. Congrats, little fish!** followed by a corresponding emoji.

Flame on, cheeks.

And then I see my sour-faced father approaching the car, so I tuck my phone away again and lose the smile. As soon as he climbs in with the paper bag full of takeout containers, my focus shifts from deciphering his mood to contemplating what I'm going to eat first. We could've just as easily invited Uncle Tim to have dinner with us—Dad has ordered a ton of food here—but clearly something is up.

Now I get to worry if it has something to do with me, and

if it does, what the next four hours, four days, four weeks are going to look like.

Upon arriving home, I follow him into the house, my empty stomach growling its excitement over the bag of deliciousness that leads me into the kitchen like some sort of oregano- and parmesan-infused Pied Piper. I don't risk delaying this meal by running up to change or hang up my swim gear—I need food *now*, and if I wait, he might pick whatever fight is brewing beneath the surface of his sullen face.

I grab plates, glasses, and silverware and quickly set the table as my dad unloads the restaurant bag. Given how quiet he is, I think he's thinking the same thing as I am: eat first, fight later.

I inhale my fill of this massive feast that is definitely not on the clean-eating menu. A steaming plate of fettuccine Alfredo with grilled chicken breast, two tubes of spinach manicotti oozing with fresh ricotta, three pieces of garlic bread, a can of sparkling lemon water, followed by a square of fresh tiramisu and two tall glasses of ice-cold milk to wash it down.

Once I have food in me, I'm even more wiped than before, if that were possible. I know there's homework simmering in my backpack upstairs, but there's no way. I'll just have to take a photo of my medals from this weekend and show my teachers I was a *little* busy, paddling for my future.

But with the food gone and the plates loaded into the dishwasher, the silence gets louder.

"I'm gonna go up and change. Exhausted," I say. My dad leans against the counter, swallowing his evening load of health supplements one horse-sized pill at a time.

"You did great this weekend, Mar," he says, pausing between capsules.

"Thanks, Dad."

I slide out of kitchen before he has a chance to say, "You

did great this weekend *but* ..." Grab my swim bag, slog up the stairs because my legs are so, so tired and my belly is so, so full, close my door quietly.

The shower at the community center was cold and quick —a lot of swimmers wanting to rinse off and get home—so I stand under the pulsating shower head, singing to myself as I slather my hair with a deep-conditioning treatment, the strong smell of coconut filling my steamed-up bathroom. I'm happy with how the weekend turned out—mostly relieved that it's over—so that I can take a breath and *maybe* find a way to get back into the studio with Darcie and Adrian to finish recording those tracks.

Adrian's text from earlier wasn't the first of the weekend. He messaged on Friday afternoon to ask if I wanted more cheerleaders at the meet, but I begged him not to show up. It's one thing to convince my father that we're science-project partners, but if he thinks Adrian is potential boyfriend material, that's a whole different can of worms.

And I'm so relieved Ms. Amberly didn't say anything more about singing. The fewer buttons we push on Trent Andersen, the better for all of us.

Plus, giving my dad the wrong impression about Adrian means I'll never be allowed out of the house without supervision. And Adrian and I hardly know each other! I am *so* not his type. He dated Darcie Drayer, for Pete's sake. She's, like, sophisticated, and tough, and a proper rock star in the making. We couldn't be more different. He probably dates other rock star types, or maybe even actresses or artists from his school. People who run in his same social sphere.

I'm a swim kid. I chronically smell like a chlorine tablet and I have red raccoon rings around my eyes most days from my goggles. I live in tracksuits or yoga pants and Converse; makeup is something reserved for special occasions when Lily and Sierra get a hold of me.

I'm an athlete, he's a performer. Two very different worlds.

But then why am I smiling, thinking about Adrian in his thick black glasses telling me bite-size factoids about estuaries on the drive home from the Beanery, as the shower water pelts my face?

I've never had a boyfriend. Well, not unless you count Daniel McCarthy from second grade, but he wasn't really my boyfriend. He was just this new kid who would bring his favorite stuffed giraffe to school and we'd hide under our desks at lunchtime and make up stories about his giraffe's grand adventures because I felt sorry for him being the new kid.

Anyway, my dad would lose his mind if I had a boyfriend. Adrian is just a *friend*. We can be friends. There doesn't have to be any weird romance involved.

Then, Marina, explain why you find your thoughts drifting to his blue eyes and long lashes and how well he plays the guitar and his dorky laugh and how he holds the door for you and how he asked you about your personal stuff and then when it got too hard, he made you laugh.

I'm too tired to even have this argument with myself.

I rinse, dry off, comb and braid my hair, brush my teeth, moisturize everything as the pool water tends to dry me out. And I can say with confidence that pulling on my flannel pajamas and thick socks is basically the best feeling in the entire world.

Towels hung up and bathroom tidied, I grab my robe and open the door, startled to see my dad sitting in my room, his lanky form draped over the antique wooden desk chair I rarely use because it's so uncomfortable. Across his lap is my mother's guitar, plucked from its stand in the corner.

"Hey ..." I say. The warmth I absorbed from the shower dissolves into a cloud of cold.

He nods at my bed. I sit, hugging my robe to my stomach, as if it can protect me from whatever is coming.

He reaches into his back pocket and pulls out a small white-and-gray business card, leaning across the space to offer it to me.

I recognize that font even before I take the card.

Ambrosia Recording Studios.

"I know Andy Drayer. Had this card forever," my dad says, running a finger along the neck of my mother's Martin. "I didn't know his niece, though."

The air is sucked out of the room.

"Darcie? Is that her name? She sent me an email. Told me you're a terrific singer. Attached a video." My dad chuckles under his breath. "Your generation will never learn. It's kind of sad, actually. You can't get away with anything."

I can't get on top of the racing thoughts—WHY would Darcie *do* this?

"Dad, it's not what you think. They just needed some help —I wasn't going to perform in public or anything—"

"Stop." My dad sniffs, and when he looks up at me, the flame in his eyes is underscored only by the rim of moisture along his lower lid. "Apparently Andy Drayer was absolutely 'blown away' by your talent. That he hasn't seen that kind of raw power come through his doors in a decade." He swallows hard and looks down. "Not since your mother was there. At least that's what the email said."

"Please—"

My father raises his hand to stop me from speaking. I then watch him twist behind him and grab something from my desk.

Wire cutters.

"I told you, Marina"—*sproing!*—"swim"—*sproing!* —"study"—*sproing!*—"succeed."

One at a time, he cuts through all six guitar strings. One snaps back and hits him in the cheek, immediately drawing a thin line of blood. He doesn't flinch as he replaces the wire cutters on my desk and stands, his hand white around the guitar's neck.

"It's not about the music now, Marina. You lied to me. More than once. I thought we were a team."

"We're a team as long as I play by your rules." My voice is barely a whisper.

"My rules are the only rules," he says, crossing my room in slow, defeated steps. "I'll be calling about the tutor tomorrow."

He doesn't even slam the door.

That's how I know I am in deeper than I ever have been before.

CHAPTER 24

SAIL STRAIGHT

I write my father a short apology letter on beach-themed stationery I've had since I was little and slide it under his bedroom door as I'm leaving for the pool the following morning. Which I do extra early so that he can't stop me from actually going to school in favor of me sitting at the kitchen table with the first Miss Trunchbull he finds.

The look on his face as he left my room last night—and now the glaring absence of my mother's guitar in the corner —the sadness living in my father's head that pushes him to make the decisions he does is not something I can fix on my own. He can give the world his best face forward, the doting father committed to raising an elite athlete and student, but I know what's going on behind the scenes.

Trent Andersen is broken.

And even though singing is absolutely the only thing that brings me real happiness, if it's making my dad miserable, I need to stop poking the wounds, at least until I can get my uncle to help me figure out how to help him.

But I'm furious, to the point where thinking about it makes me dig my short fingernails into my palms, about

Darcie going behind my back like this. WHY would she do it? Does she not care about the band? All that stuff that Adrian said the other night about how Darcie is committed to Scuttle-butt—is it total crap? Does she have him fooled too? And they were a couple—why would she do anything that could potentially hurt Adrian? Is she still mad about their breakup? Does she think maybe he's into me and now she's jealous or something?

That can't be it—Lily said Darcie cheated on Adrian with another band member, and that's why they broke up.

I've composed a dozen texts to Adrian over the last ten exhausting hours, and deleted every single one before I could hit Send.

It makes no sense for Darcie to sell me out. This whole thing was HER IDEA.

I can't hide under my covers and wish this would all just go away, especially after last night, after watching my dad's face and hearing the anger and sadness in his words.

After watching him clip the strings of my mother's beloved guitar.

I should never have said yes to Darcie. Lily and Sierra were right. She is Ursula the Sea Witch.

And yet, this is all my fault.

SIERRA AND LILY are outside the school waiting for me as I lock up my bike, both of them chattering nonstop about how awesome I was this weekend and didn't I get their texts and I have "so much to catch up on in our group chat," and as they drag my tired butt down the hall, I can see they arrived even earlier than I did. My locker is decorated with balloons and streamers and fake medals made of craft paper and hair ribbons. And then Lily opens her locker just a few spaces down and pulls out a telltale pink box filled with my favorite maple- and chocolate-glazed doughnuts.

I really do have the most supportive friends ever.

I eat one of the beautiful pastries, my thoughts spinning. When the warning bell sounds, Sierra loops her arm through mine and leads me to English.

"You okay, Mar?" she asks.

I'm not—and I need to tell them about last night, what Darcie did—but I need my friends in the same place at the same time, without a teacher pacing the front of the room to get started. And after this second incident of my father catching wind of what I'm doing because of our easy access to phone technology, I'm actually sort of afraid to have this conversation via text message. "Just tired. Long weekend."

"Your dad should've let you take the day off to sleep," she says, sliding into the seat next to mine.

My dad should've let me do a lot of things.

By the time English is finished, I just feel defeated. I should talk to Lily and Sierra, but my heart ... it feels broken. I don't know how to make words come out of my mouth to explain all this. It feels pointless.

So I manage to hide behind the excuse of being overtired for the bulk of the school day, my two amazing friends carting me around the campus and intercepting questions from people who either saw or heard about the swim meet, as well as from the few rock school kids who ask when I'm going to come jam with them again.

And the text messages on my phone, from Adrian ... they go unanswered. I don't know what to say without screaming DARCIE TOLD MY DAD AND NOW I AM IN SO MUCH TROUBLE. But I know I can't help the band. I can't risk it. I can't sneak out and disappoint my father again. That look on his face last night ...

Adrian is great, and I love spending time with him, but

he's barking up the wrong tree. He needs to get things straight with Darcie before I get involved. This whole thing was just a huge mistake. I know that now.

Swim. Study. Succeed.

There is no fourth S. Singing can wait.

CHAPTER 25

LOOK FOR SOLUTIONS

"**Y**ou've twisted that dial way too many times to get the lock to open," Sierra says. She's leaning against the lockers next to mine, eyes on her phone. The halls are quickly emptying as kids feel that end-of-day freedom. "Need some help?" She stuffs her phone in her pocket.

"I think my brain is waterlogged," I deflect. "Where's Lily?"

"She has to present the Joan of Arc project. Finally," Sierra says. Even though the project has been done for a week, Ms. Derricks, the social studies teacher, managed to catch a flu so she's been out. "I told her we'd wait. Or I would since you have to get to the pool."

"I don't, actually. Rare day off." I'm not even excited about it. Just means more time in the house with my dad.

Sierra flattens a hand on my arm. Her coral-colored finger polish looks nice against the dark blue of my sweatshirt sleeve. "You don't seem okay," she says.

I pause, considering unloading everything on her right here in the hallway. Instead, I give her my most reassuring smile. "Told you, I'm just tired."

"Maybe we can go to karaoke this weekend? Or, hey,

when are you going to finish the THING with Scuttlebutt?" she says, lowering her voice to an excited whisper.

"Yeah, I'm not going to be able to finish that for now," I say, sliding my math text into my backpack. "Hey, tell Lil I'm sorry I missed her. You guys text me later, yeah?" I give Sierra a hug and then turn to jog down the hall toward the rear door to the bike racks before she can see the tears falling down my cheeks.

As I round the corner, I nearly crash into another person, this one wearing a floofy, off-white-and-black skirt, the fabric printed with giant black music notes interspersed with red and pink roses that look like they're from one of those old-fashioned postcards.

"Marina? Heyyyy," Ms. Amberly asks. The second I make eye contact, I know the charade is over. "Oh dear, okay, come on." She drapes an arm around my shoulders and steers me down the hall toward her office connected to the cavernous music room. She closes the door behind us and gestures to one of the comfy chairs that was probably manufactured before either of us were born. With the second door to the music room closed, her office is quiet like a grave, only the whirr of the fan from an old PC on her cluttered desk.

"It always smells so good in here," I say, sniffing as she hands me a wad of tissue.

"I'd ask you if you want to talk about it, but I can see by your current state that talking is going to be mandatory."

I nod. She's right.

"My dad."

"Ah. Yes, the notorious Trent Andersen strikes again." I look up at her. "Sweetie, teachers talk. Plus I've known you now for three years *and* I know who Hidden Villains is." The chair across from me squeaks as she sits. "What has you running down the hall in tears? After such an incredible weekend? It has to be more than fatigue, although frankly, the fact that you can move at all today ..." Her eyes sparkle when she smiles.

"I hate swimming. I mean, I don't *hate* hate it. But I want to sing. A friend invited me to do this ... thing ... where I get to sing with this band, but it had to be, like, a total secret so my dad wouldn't find out."

"And your dad found out."

"Yeah—and the worst part is that the girl who asked me to help out the band—SHE is the one who ratted me out."

"Not cool."

"It just doesn't make any sense. She asked *me* for help, and then she turned around and did this? Now my father is threatening to homeschool me."

The soft smile slides from Ms. Amberly's face, replaced by that look of concern that always freaks me out on adults.

"He wants me to get a scholarship. 'Swim, study, succeed' is his mantra."

"And you just want to sing. Because that is what you were born to do," she says, flattening a hand against her throat. "Marina, can I ask about your mom? Can I ask why your dad is so against you sharing your talents?"

For the next however many minutes—minutes that feel like hours because my sinuses are congested and my head and face hurt from crying—I explain to the kind Ms. Amberly all the reasons my father doesn't want me anywhere near the music scene.

When I'm finally finished, Ms. Amberly smooths her skirt before resting her hands on her bent knees. "As your teacher, I am limited in what I can say. It's important that I not create an alliance here with you that would threaten whatever your relationship is with your parent." She takes a deep breath. "However, I'm only twenty-eight. It wasn't that long ago that I was going head-to-head with my parents over this, that, and the other thing. I *know* how it feels to not be heard. I'm not going to tell you to take a deep breath and wait to turn eighteen so you can move out, because that's not helpful advice."

Ms. Amberly scoots forward in her seat. "What I *am* going to tell you is that you need to be solutions-based here with your father, rather than problem-based. We need to identify what the problems are and see if we can brainstorm solutions to those problems that will satisfy both parties. Do you have any other close family members?"

"My uncle. Tim. You met him yesterday."

"Right. Of course. How is your relationship with him?"

I laugh sadly. "Sometimes I wish he were my dad instead."

Ms. Amberly goes on to suggest that maybe I should get Uncle Tim involved in the conversation, that maybe if we can show my dad that I am working the program he has set up for me—for school, for swimming, for all the other stuff I do—that allowing me to sing, either with rock school or whatever—is not the end of the world, and in fact, will do so much to support my health and happiness.

But even as Ms. Amberly's pep talk flows from her brightly painted lips, I know that much of what she's suggesting will fall on deaf ears. My dad controlling my every move is how he keeps a hold on whatever is chewing him apart inside.

"Would it help if I talked to the counselor or maybe even Mr. Malcolm? Maybe if we invited your dad in for a meeting to explain how you're feeling—"

"No. Please. Don't. Let me handle it," I say. "It'll just make things worse."

She nods and sits back, interlocking her fingers. "I know how tough it is," she says. "My parents divorced when I was young. My mom had some mental health struggles, so I had to go live with my dad and stepmother when I was eight." She swallows hard and looks down at her clasped hands. "It sucks growing up without a mom. I know. And it sounds like your dad is overcompensating to make up for her absence."

"Which is why this is so awful. I *warned* Darcie that my dad is impossible. So WHY did she do this? Why would she tell him when she came to *me* for help in the first place? I'm so confused, I can't even talk to Lily and Sierra about it."

"The boy—what's his name?"

"Adrian Brooks. He's Lily's second cousin. Or something. Scuttlebutt is his band. But he and Darcie used to be a thing for a while. They broke up, and then she hurt her voice. She can't sing for them, and Adrian's an amazing guitarist but he's not a singer."

Ms. Amberly is already nodding her head. "Darcie is jealous. She heard you in that studio—she saw her future flash before her eyes, and it showed you on stage with the band, not her." She sips from her ever-present water bottle. "I know that feeling, the powerlessness and anger and resentment that comes from losing the instrument that meant the most to you."

"So you're saying I should forgive her for this? For telling my dad?"

"Not at all. That was a crap thing to do," Ms. Amberly says. "But understand the reasons why she did it. She let her emotions get the best of her. She heard you sing and realized she will never be that again, if she ever was that good to begin with."

"I'm not that good," I say.

My teacher snorts. "Plus there's the drama of Darcie maybe still having feelings for Adrian. Then you come in and she hears you, and she sees you singing with Adrian. You know how sommotionalsy provocative music can be. Think about how YOU feel when you're up there singing. How you felt when you were singing with Adrian."

Singing with Adrian made me feel like I was made of starlight.

"You need to talk to Adrian about this. You can't just ignore him. He's not going to understand what happened, and if the band is relying on you to help them …"

"They're not. I recorded enough songs, they should be okay. At least until Darcie's voice heals."

"That may never happen."

"But this can't be my problem. My dad is micromanaging every second of my life. It's only going to get worse now, thanks to Darcie." I inhale deeply, exhausted to the last blood cell.

"Remember: solutions-based thinking. But I want you to know, Marina," she says, leaning forward again and wrapping her hands around mine, "you are not alone. And you have a gift. Your voice—it is all yours. And no one, except maybe a haphazard surgeon"—she sniffs back her own emotion—"can take that away from you. I will do whatever you need to help you find your true voice, and preferably in a way that doesn't require you to skip school." She lifts an eyebrow for a beat and then smiles.

I nod, and then we're both crying. She stands and pulls me into a hug. "I always wanted a little sister," she says, laughing as she dabs at the black mascara dancing down her cheeks.

"Thank you for talking to me. It really helps," I say, glancing at the clock. "I should probably go. You have a life outside this building."

"Hardly," she says, laughing once. "You have my email, right? It's on the class syllabus thingie."

"Mm-hmm."

"I want you to use it. Okay? Email me. Whenever you need to talk."

I shake my head yes again because I can't make any more words. "And Marina, if you reach a point where we should get the counselor or principal involved, *please* come talk to me. Promise?"

"I promise."

She clears her throat gently and again smooths her skirt. "So, find a way to talk to Adrian, let's get through the next big swim meet, and then we can revisit talking to your dad about the singing. Yes?"

"'K." But even as I agree with her idea, I hate it. I hate that everything I do is meant to keep Trent Andersen from losing his temper.

As Ms. Amberly walks me from her office to the bike racks out back, I can feel the vibration of my phone going off in my pocket. I wait for her to say goodbye and disappear back into the school, and then I pull out my phone.

Eight new messages. From Adrian.

I delete them all.

CHAPTER 26

DISCONNECTED

Even though I technically have the day off from the pool, I don't want to go home. I don't want to talk to my dad, not about last night or the letter I wrote him or whatever tutor he may have found today that will seal my fate. I don't want to talk to Uncle Tim right now, even though I told Ms. Amberly I would. I don't want to talk to Adrian or even Lily or Sierra. And I don't trust myself to not send Darcie a text that will melt her painted-on eyebrows.

I turn off my phone and stuff it into the bottom of my bag.

I keep spare gear at the swim club—I won't have to stop at home first. And the big pool will be quiet today, since Coach gave the team a free afternoon to recover.

It's almost like my bike knows the way, my tired legs pedaling. In my head, the unfinished lyrics to "Counting the Stars" bounce around …

> *I can't bring her back, neither can you,*
> *Her absence, like a black hole,*
> *It hurts me to remember her too.*

It's an original song I've been trying to nail down for the

last six or so months, since stuff with my dad started to get really intense. A few lines just aren't fitting—maybe too many beats? A mixed metaphor?—so my brain defaults to melodies and notes when I'm on my bike, riding alone and in the quiet.

But today I'm too tired, too sad, to sing anything, especially a song about my mom, about my dad seeing ME instead of wishing she were still here.

I lock up my bike and head in, changing quietly and quickly in the near-empty locker rooms. Poolside, I grab a kickboard and slide into the water, smooth like glass, disturbed only by wrinkles from the slurping filters along the walls. Even the lane ropes are absent today, rolled and quiet on their giant silver spools against the wall.

Because I'm not sharing the lane and there's no one with a stopwatch nearby, I can go as slow or fast as I want. I relax against the kickboard, letting the lyrics play in my head, humming when I can't help myself. My heart aches all over again as I think about my dad snipping through the guitar wires last night.

I swim for an hour, until the fatigue from crying earlier and the exhaustion from the past weekend takes the last ounce of my energy. I climb out and drop the kickboard into the bin, pausing at Coach's whiteboard, already updated with the countdown to the regional meet, a giant number **13** taking up the space usually reserved for the day's in-pool and dryland exercises.

Thirteen days to do nothing but swim and study, to keep my father from doing anything worse than cutting guitar strings.

I PUNCH in the garage code so I can put my bike away, not surprised to find our car parked in its spot. Warmth hits me hard as I push open the interior garage door and enter the kitchen, a shiver rushing through me. Voices float in from the living room.

"Marina?"

No use ignoring him.

I drop my backpack on the top stair and prepare for whatever battle is coming. The living room's French doors are open; I step inside, surprised to see Coach Tosto sitting on one of the plush oversized chairs, a delicate teacup cradled in her large hands.

"Where've you been?" my dad asks. Not even a hello.

"I went to the pool."

"On a day off?" He's testing me to see if I'm lying again, but the raccoon rings around my eyes are proof enough.

"Just felt like it."

"Come in and have a seat," he says. It's not a request. I nod hello to Coach. "We're just going over what the next two weeks are going to look like."

"Thirteen days," I say. "The board at the pool says thirteen days." Now he knows I'm not lying, that I truly was at the pool.

The next half hour is my father and Coach Tosto going over the detailed plan of attack they've worked out to make sure I'm a hundred percent ready for the big competition. And it includes pulling me out of school all next week, with the support of a tutor, so that I'm swimming six hours a day instead of three.

I don't even have the energy to argue.

"Can I go now?" I ask, rising from my seat. "I'm hungry and I have homework."

My father gives me a hard look. "I'm also going to need your phone."

"What? Why?"

"We want to make sure you're focused and not distracted by any of the petty nonsense you and your friends get up to."

"Dad, come *on*, I use my phone for everything. And what

if I'm out and I need a ride or something? You do know pay phones don't exist anymore, right?"

He gives Coach Tosto a tight smile and then looks at me. "I have a pay-as-you-go phone for you to use for now, to keep in touch with me. You can leave your iPhone on the counter. I'll give it back to you when the meet is over."

"This is unbelievable," I say, storming by his perch on the sofa's edge. He reaches out and grabs my wrist before I can get past.

"I only want what's best for you, Marina," he says.

"Keep telling yourself that." I yank my arm free and take the stairs two at a time, slamming my bedroom door behind me.

By habit, I look to the corner where my mother's guitar usually sits on its black stand. Another punch to the stomach to see that it's still missing, that my father's performance last night will endure.

I know I probably only have a few minutes before Coach Tosto leaves and my father comes knocking for my phone, so I quickly text Lily and Sierra, and then Adrian: *In jail until further notice. Please don't make it worse.*

The text flies out, followed in short order by a response from Sierra: **Is he taking your computer?**

No. Not sure if he will cut the house Wi-Fi though.

Seriously? Ugh! Lil and I will find you online tonight, 9 p.m. I hope you're OK.

And just as I expected, as soon as the front door closes downstairs, my dad is knocking and entering my room, hand outstretched for my phone as I did *not* leave it on the counter as instructed. I've changed the lock-screen code so he won't be able to guess it. Last thing I want is him reading through my messages with Lily and Sierra, or worse, Adrian. The way he's acting, I wouldn't put it past him.

My phone firmly in his grip, he repeats his prior senti-ment: "I only want what's best for you."

Ms. Amberly's talk about a solutions-based approach with my father rings in my head, but the look on his face tells me any attempt at such a conversation would be a waste of time.

I turn away and pull my textbooks out of my backpack, making it clear that I'm done talking to him for the night.

CHAPTER 27

HARD TRUTHS

The week creeps by. Other than at-school or swim-club interaction, my connection with my friends has been cut off at the knees since my father took my phone. And as I feared, he's started turning off the Wi-Fi at nine o'clock every night, "until we get through the regional meet."

Sitting in Bio on Friday, I'm just finishing up the in-class exercise when an office monitor slides quietly into our classroom and hands Mrs. Martinez a yellow attendance note. "Marina Andersen," she says, the note pinched between two fingers. "Just grab your stuff. Only ten minutes left anyway."

Everyone looks at me; my heart stutters. Is my father here now to pull me out of school? He said the tutor was starting Monday, and just for the week—he wouldn't have done anything earlier, would he?

Worse, did Ms. Amberly make good on her suggestion of talking to the counselor and principal? Am I being summoned to an ambush?

My cheeks are on fire as I hand in my worksheet, take the note from the teacher, and exit the room. The office monitor is already long gone, so I can't even ask him if he knows anything.

I pause outside the class and unfold the yellow rectangle: "Your cousin is here to pick you up for your doctor's appointment."

My *cousin*?

I don't have a cousin, at least none I've ever met.

I hustle to my locker. There's only one class left for the day, but I will need all of these textbooks, plus the detailed lists from my teachers of what I'll need to cover next week with the tutor who, by the way, looks more like Miss Honey than Miss Trunchbull.

With the yellow notice in hand, I hurry toward the front office, but on the bench just outside, to the left of the bronze tiger statue that represents our school pride, sits Adrian Brooks.

His face lights up when he sees me. My face does not.

He stands, casual, like we've known each other for years and not weeks.

"What are you doing here?" I ask.

"What, can't cousins drive their younger cousins to their doctor's appointments?"

Ohhhhh, man. "Are you even serious right now?"

"Come on," he says, looking around us. "Halls are getting busy. We should skedaddle."

"Adrian, I can't—if my dad found out, he would—"

"He would what? Ground you? Take your phone away? Pull you out of school and make you study with a tutor?" His smile has faded. "Yeah, I talked to Lily. Come on. We need to go before the bell rings."

"My bike. I'll need it."

"Where is it?"

"On the racks out front." I was late this morning, and the racks I usually use in back—closest to my first-period class—were full.

"It should fit in my trunk." He winks and takes my backpack from my shoulder, making a face when he realizes how heavy it is. I pull my hood up to block out anyone seeing my face—but mostly to block out me seeing anyone else's face when they notice I'm leaving school early with a guy who doesn't go to our school, a guy who looks remarkably like the lead singer of that up-and-coming band Scuttlebutt.

I scurry to the racks, unlock my bike, and then jog it over to Adrian's car that sits with its emergency flashers blinking in the traffic roundabout. The two of us muscle the bike into his trunk, but even with his back seats flattened, it doesn't fit all the way in. He scrounges under the front seat and yanks out a bungee cord.

"Voilà!"

"You're ready for the zombie apocalypse now," I say, an edge to my words.

"Sometimes we have to use Hero the Honda to move drum kits. Bungee cords are never a bad idea." With my bike secured, he opens the passenger door. I slide in, knowing that skipping the last class of the day is not going to end well for me. But like Adrian said, what else can Trent Andersen do that he hasn't already done?

He turns off the hazard lights and pulls out of the half circle. "Where can we go that your dad wouldn't have spies?"

I chuckle. "Mars."

"You hungry?"

"Always."

The car is quiet until, at a red light, he risks a huge ticket by scrolling through the playlists on his phone. When my voice filters through the car speakers, I stiffen in my seat.

"You think you're being funny?"

Adrian pushes his black glasses up his nose, but his face looks sad. "I don't think any of this is funny, Marina."

"Ironic. Darcie Drayer sure thought it was funny." I look out the side window, my own hooded image reflected back at me as the rare fall sunshine blasts through. The tracks playing sound amazing—Adrian and I sound so good together in the duet. Warmth that might be a bit of pride eases the chill in my nervous stomach.

"I'm so sorry. Honestly. I can't believe she did that."

"I can." Now that I've had a week to think about it, I agree with what Ms. Amberly said about Darcie still having feelings for Adrian.

He's silent until he pulls into the parking lot of a small diner near the edge of town.

"You like pancakes?" he says, and without waiting for my answer, he unbuckles and climbs out of the car, jogging around the front end to open my door for me.

Inside the restaurant is quiet—only a few older couples huddled over newspapers and crosswords in the worn booths. Adrian waves at a gray-haired waitress in pink and white behind the long, dark red counter and leads me to a booth near the back. He offers me the side facing away from the door. "You're hidden in here. You can take your hood off."

I do. The waitress shuffles over with menus; I order peppermint tea, Adrian orders coffee.

"I'll give you a minute to decide," she says, the aroma of old-lady perfume and bacon grease lingering.

I'm looking at the words and pictures describing their entrees on the sticky, laminated menu but none of it is registering. Too many alarm bells sounding in my ears for me to focus on anything. I shouldn't be here.

I glance over the top of my menu at Adrian, his eyes bouncing around his own as he bites his lip in concentration. Seeming to have decided on something, he sets the long plastic sheet down at the table's edge and folds his hands in a knot.

"So. I was relieved to know that you weren't ghosting me because I offended you with my winning personality."

I set my menu aside. The words might as well be written in Aramaic.

"I shouldn't be here," I say, grabbing the paper napkin off my lap and setting it on the tabletop.

"Wait—"

The waitress chooses that moment to reappear. "What will you kids be having?"

Adrian orders a stack of buttermilk pancakes with a side of hash browns and an orange juice. She looks at me. "That sounds fine. Thank you," I say. Hash browns are definitely not on my curated diet plan, and I might regret that grease later when I'm in the pool, but for now, I just need the waitress to go away.

When she finally does, Adrian leans forward on bent elbows. "Don't go yet. I just want to talk."

I sit back in the booth. In that moment, a wave of tiredness washes over me.

"I am so sorry that Darcie got you in trouble," he says. "Andy is furious. He actually has a pretty strict rule about people not recording videos in his studio."

"Darcie must've missed that memo."

"Anyway, it was total crap that she did it."

"Why did she, though, Adrian? What did she gain by outing me to my father?"

He shakes his head. "I don't know. I've been thinking about it nonstop all week. If you'd seen my messages, you'd know that."

"I think I know why she did it," I say, folding the corners in on my paper napkin. "She's jealous." There. I said it. "She wants to be able to sing, and she can't. She saw us performing together, and it was more than she could handle."

His head bobs. "That sounds like Darcie."

"And after you told me that night over coffee that she was a team player, that she was only worried about Scuttlebutt."

"I know … I thought she was, Marina. Honestly." He leans forward on bent arms. "I like you. A lot. You have to know that."

My skin erupts with heat.

"I told you before … Darcie and I used to be a couple. It wasn't for that long, and then it ended badly," he says. I watch his face, as hard as it is to keep eye contact, but I need to know he's not lying. "She sees what I see in you—the talent, sure, but also that you're a fun, cool, smart person." His quiet laugh sounds nervous; he rubs at the guitar calluses on the fingertips of his left hand. "When I'm around you, I don't have to be Adrian Brooks from Scuttlebutt; I can just be Adrian, the dorky kid in the black glasses who peed himself on stage once."

I smile but then remember I'm still in very real danger. Danger of my father finding out I'm here, danger of losing my last shred of freedom.

In danger of losing my heart to someone I'm not yet sure deserves it.

When I don't say anything, Adrian continues, his own face awash with red. "Anyway, I'll deal with Darcie. What she did was wrong. But I still wish your dad would've heard you on that recording and instead recognized how you come alive when you sing, instead of freaking out."

"My dad hears me sing all the time. We live together, remember?"

Adrian takes a deep breath and folds his hands together. "But the work you're doing in the studio … it's different than singing while doing the dishes. You know that."

"It was one session, Adrian. There won't be another—not after this. And I shouldn't have done it in the first place. I wanted to help you guys—I thought Darcie's proposition was really because she cared about the band. But now I just have to do what my dad says and get through this."

"And I'm not saying you shouldn't. All I'm saying—you have this gift that so few people in the world have, and your dad is being a bully by keeping you locked up in some creepy tower."

I laugh and shake my head. "Wow, you really have been hanging out with Lily." More talk of fairy tales? "I'm not Rapunzel or Ariel or even Cinderella being kept from some ball. My dad is suffering—he's hurting—and me being rebellious so I can sing songs is hurting him more."

"So, what, you're supposed to suffer because *he's* suffering?"

"You don't know anything about it. You don't know what you're talking about."

He snickers once. "Sorry, Marina, but you don't have the market cornered on sad families." He sits forward again and takes off his black glasses. "The feud that kept our weird family apart? It's because my mom was diagnosed with MS, and my dad had a total meltdown. Instead of being the supportive husband, he did everything wrong. The opposite of what he should've done." He pauses, clears his throat, fidgets with his glasses on the table. His shoulders rise and fall with a deep breath.

"My dad ... the family sort of broke apart. People took sides, and some still aren't speaking to one another. But then he got some help—to deal with his grief, the guilt he felt, like it was somehow *his fault* that multiple sclerosis found her ..." Adrian swipes a tear away quickly, as if he doesn't want me to see it. When he looks up, his blue eyes blaze like oceans on fire.

"Everyone's family is damaged. Everyone has problems. But your father keeping you from being who you are here"—he pokes his own chest over his heart—"just because he cannot get over your mom ... Marina, it's not right. And there are people who want to help."

I take a shuddering breath. "You think he's going to listen to you or Ms. Amberly the choir teacher or Andy Drayer or even my school counselor? He won't even listen to his own brother. He won't listen to his own *daughter.* The only way I can get him to loosen the collar around my neck is to not make him mad. I just need to get through this next meet. I need to win. I need to show him I am worthy of—"

"Worthy of what, Marina?" Adrian's raised voice draws the attention of the table across from us. "Worthy of his love? So, what, you go and swim and you win this big meet, and then what? He's going to lock you in your house for the rest of junior year and all of senior year, waiting for the next big meet where you can swim your butt off, just to make him happy? To get a scholarship to some school so you can swim for another four years? Do you even LIKE swimming? Does swimming do for you what I see happen when you sing? Because I'm going to guess it doesn't.

"You're a human being, Marina, not some wind-up toy who can swim fast to make Dad proud."

The waitress looks sheepish as she slides the first two plates in front of us. "You kids okay here?"

"Fine, thanks," Adrian says, not taking his eyes off me. The waitress walks away. "Say to my face that I'm wrong, that you can't wait to get to college and swim for another four years. Tell me I'm wrong that you struggle to fall asleep most nights because your brain is dreaming up new lyrics, new tunes, to express how you feel. Convince me I'm way off base about all this, and I'll never bother you again."

"You're just annoyed that I can't come in and finish singing your stupid songs so you guys can dupe all your fans into thinking Darcie is okay, that Scuttlebutt is who they say they are. This is all about a record deal for you—this isn't about what's best for me. It isn't now, and it never was."

Adrian opens his mouth to speak, but then closes his lips

again. His cheeks are bright red, his lashes still wet from the tears that snuck past.

I push my steaming, untouched plate aside and hold out my hand. "Keys."

"What?"

"Give me your keys. I need to go."

"Marina, come on—let's just eat."

"KEYS!" I yell. The restaurant freezes. Adrian drops his fork and reaches into his pocket, pulling out his car keys. But when he hands them to me, he also hands over a folded piece of paper.

"Read this. Later. When you're done feeling sorry for yourself."

I crumple the paper and shove it in my pocket, sliding out of the booth and running through the diner to the exit. At the car, I grab my backpack and then wrestle to unload my bike from the back end of Adrian's car. He's followed me out but I refuse to let him help me.

"Marina, please, wait—"

"You don't know me. You don't know anything about me."

"I know that the only time your eyes look alive is when you have a song pouring from you."

"Oh, please. Save it for your cheesy lyrics."

He laughs bitterly. "Cheesy or not, I know that the music is the only thing that makes you feel alive—because I feel the *same way*. What else is there to know about you?"

I'm shaking too hard with unspent rage, with the effort to keep from crying in front of him. I am *so tired* of crying all the time.

He closes the distance between us. "Don't be a coward, Marina. Stand up to him. *Fight* for this."

His words sting like a slap to the face.

I toss his keys at his feet and climb on my bike. If I leave now, before I say something terrible, I should be able to make it to the swim club on time without anyone noticing anything out of the ordinary.

"Read the letter!" Adrian calls after me, but I pedal hard enough, my hood down, to let the rain and wind against my ears deafen the sounds of life rushing past me.

CHAPTER 28

SEE YOU MONDAY

I fall into a hypnotic routine of sleep, eat, swim, and study. The tutor my dad hired, Alysha, is a graduate student at the local university, and she's actually really cool. She's focused, for sure, but she softens a bit when my father leaves the house for whatever errands or meetings he has. Yesterday, after we finished the day's academic tasks and my dad had stepped out, Alysha opened her laptop and we watched the latest episode of a show we both happen to love.

Without the Wi-Fi on at the house at night, and no phone, I've been strangely disconnected from the outside world. And two weeks is a long time in the land of my favorite Netflix shows.

Although I desperately miss Sierra and Lily—their efforts to pop in unannounced were met with my father's stern reminder on the front porch that I will be available next week, after the regional meet has concluded—I have managed to sneak in time to say hello and to finally fill them in on all the drama, for the *real* reason I'm on house arrest. The pay-as-you-go phone is useless; my dad monitors every minute spent based on how much time is left on the prepaid balance.

Alysha has been cool about letting me login and chat with

Lil and Sierra when my dad leaves. Lily even faked a stomachache the other day to excuse herself to the bathroom in the middle of history class so we could talk on FaceTime. Plus they've promised they're going to be at the meet this weekend.

I just have to remind myself that this is almost over.

Except ... it's not. I'm still angry at Adrian for thinking he can tell me what's best for my life—for calling me a *coward*—my chest burns thinking about him saying that. The nerve! Like, seriously? Who calls someone they hardly know a *coward* to their face?

And yet, I know that so much of what he said is true. Even if this thing hadn't blown up in my face thanks to Darcie's big mouth, none of this will be over on Sunday night when the meet is done. I have the rest of the school year to get through, plus prep for spring competitions starts the day after Thanksgiving, like our very own aquatic Black Friday. Then senior year.

Man, if the pressure is on now, I can't even imagine how terrible my father is going to be next year, my last year in high school, my last chance at securing those coveted, prestigious scholarships.

And then what? I get a scholarship to a great school and I swim for them for four years? Four more years of trying to balance the rigors of swim life with university-level classes? I don't even know what I want to major in yet.

Which, of course, is silly. I know exactly what I want to major in.

But my dad has already made it clear that a music degree is not an option.

Maybe I truly am a coward.

Like Adrian knows anything about me or my dad. Jerk.

So far, any attempt to stand up to Trent Andersen has not gone well. The tutor camped out next to me right now is proof enough of that. The rest of my friends and classmates are sitting in regular classrooms, listening to Mr. Brody drone on about droids and the Death Star, or listening to Ms. Derricks get super excited about some bloody world war. I can't believe I'm envious of them.

We hear the garage door activate and Alysha quickly clicks off the music app and closes her laptop. A check of the clock reveals we're done for the day anyway. The only benefit to this homeschool thing is we're done with classes by noon. Everything goes so much faster when there aren't twenty-nine other students to deal with.

But then being done by noon means I'm at the pool at one fifteen until long after most families have finished their dinner dishes.

Alysha tucks her laptop into its pouch and gathers her materials as I slide today's work into my designated folder for my father to inspect later. She's just zipping her backpack as my father comes through the door attached to the garage, two cloth grocery bags in hand.

"Ladies," he says. "Alysha, join us for lunch?"

"Ah, no thanks, Mr. Andersen. I have a lab at one thirty." She throws her bag over her shoulder and waves goodbye to my dad. I walk her to the front door.

"Break a leg this weekend," she says. "Or are we supposed to say that to swimmers?"

"Every bit of luck helps."

Alysha leans in for an unexpected hug. "You're gonna do great. I can't wait to hear all the news."

"Maybe I'll finally get my phone back next week and I can text you."

"Or you can tell me Monday. I'll go easy on you—you'll be exhausted from the weekend."

I freeze. "Monday? I thought we were done today. I mean, at least until the next meet when he bribes you to come back."

She looks confused. "No, your dad hired me for at least a

month." My chest seizes with panic. "Did he not tell you, Marina?"

I don't know what to say. My thoughts race, everything coming at me all at once. At least a month? That puts us into December—I can't be away from my friends, from choir and Ms. Amberly, for a whole month. Choir is already starting on the holiday program. If I'm gone all that time, I won't be able to participate in one of the few opportunities I get to sing at school without my dad freaking out.

"I'm sorry ... I should probably go," Alysha says, her hand gentle on my upper arm. "Good luck at the meet."

With the door closed behind her, I watch through the leaded-glass panels as she hurries to her car parked at the curb. She waves again just before climbing in behind the wheel; a little voice in my head screams to run after her and hop in her car, just to get away from what's coming as soon as I walk into the kitchen.

Don't be a coward, Marina.

My slippers pad across the hardwood floor, muted briefly by the long Persian rug that runs down the main hallway. I stop behind my chair at the rectangular dining table, watching as my father prepares lunch at the island.

"You've hired her for a month?"

He doesn't look up as he answers. "You did so well without all the extra distractions, I don't see the harm in extending this little experiment for a while."

"The harm is that I have a life at school. I have friends there and things I've committed to."

"And we've talked about this before, Marina. True friends aren't going to abandon you, plus you have a swim team full of friends. The choir can survive for a little while without you."

"This is crazy."

He stops slicing tomatoes and looks up at me. "What's

crazy is blowing an opportunity like this. You should be thanking me instead of nagging me."

"*Thanking* you? For controlling every facet of my life? What's next, Dad? Are you going to install an app in my head so you can control how many times a minute I take a breath?"

He snickers as he layers the tomato on the open sandwiches. He finishes with a leaf of fresh lettuce each. "You're being melodramatic." He slides a plate toward me. I don't move to take it. "If you don't eat, you'll pass out in the pool. Stop being a brat. Take the sandwich, eat, and get changed. Coach is expecting you. Shorter practice today and then dinner and rest tonight. We have to be at the swim club by six tomorrow morning."

"It's like you're not even hearing the words coming out of my mouth." I flop into my chair. "It's like nothing I say matters to you."

He picks up both plates and walks to the table, sliding my lunch in front of me. "I am hearing the words coming out of your mouth, and what you say does matter. However, you are sixteen years old with very little real-world experience. You make decisions fueled by impulse and hormones and whatever is popular at the moment. It's only natural—I remember —I was sixteen once," he says. "One of these days, you're going to look back on this perceived hardship, and you'll thank me."

I look up at him, my eyes saying the words in my head my lips don't dare utter.

His jaw clenches. "I have a few calls to make. Eat and get ready."

CHAPTER 29

BREAKING DOWN WALLS

The sandwich from this afternoon sits like dead weight in my gut through the entire afternoon practice, slowing me down. Coach doesn't ride me too hard, chalking it up to precompetition jitters. While she works with everyone on the squad, I get the lion's share of her attention because I'm poised to win big this weekend, if I follow the plan like a good little Marina.

My father sits in the stands, alternating between checking his phone and clenching his beloved stopwatch. He shakes hands and puts on a good show for the other parents. When the conversation is clearly on me—based on the fact that my father's plus four other parents' heads turn to look at me motoring along with my kickboard—I stare back hard without a pleasant, friendly smile, and then face forward.

I'm not giving him an inch.

An hour later, Coach pulls everyone out of the pool for cool-down dryland training and then a pep talk. It goes in one ear and out the other. I know what I need to do this weekend to keep everyone happy. Just plug that key into my back and wind it up.

When Coach Tosto and my father continue talking poolside long after everyone else has left and the surface of the water is resting after the calamity of thrashing teenagers, I sit out in the concession area humming to myself, wishing I had my stupid phone so I could at least listen to music. A quick glance behind the counter reveals that Lily isn't working today—it's some new kid named Devin whose ineptitude with the microwave means the whole lobby stinks through his entire shift.

Finally, Coach and my father are done plotting. Dad opens the heavy glass door and waits for her to pass through before sighting me and bobbing his head. Guess it's time to go.

The drive home is more of Dad talking at me, recapping his chat with Coach about the plan for the weekend, how scouts will be everywhere so "be on your best behavior, be prepared to answer questions about your intentions for after high school, give them my email address so I can handle inquiries," and on and on through dinner until we're loading our spaghetti-stained plates into the dishwasher.

"Shower and early bed," he says. Like I'm four years old again.

I go upstairs without a word. I don't think he even notices that I've not uttered a single sound over the last seven hours, not since Alysha left.

I do what he says, shower and prepare for bed, pausing only to feed Neptune and give the side of his tank a quick swipe with the algae brush. The tank needs to be cleaned, but this week has been so nuts … "I shouldn't complain about swimming to you, should I, buddy? At least we have that in common. Two fish just trying to make their way in the world." I watch as his big goldfish lips slurp up the food floating at the top, the flakes sinking just until he swoops past and swallows them whole.

I slide between cold cotton sheets, stretching to pull an extra blanket over my shoulders, but my eyes aren't ready for sleep. I can't concentrate on the novel I'm halfway through; I don't have a phone to browse photos or watch videos or talk to my friends; and even though I still have my laptop, the Wi-Fi is off so I can't chat with Lily and Sierra or even click on a movie to lull me to Dreamland. And I'm sure as heck not going to study.

The regional meet is a big deal—I feel like I should be more nervous about the next three days speeding at me like a boat with no driver. Swimmers from all over, held in the Olympic-sized facility at the university. It's the only venue big enough to accommodate all the swimmers and accompanying family and friends.

So why am I not more excited? These events are always fun, I'll admit. Sure, they're competitive and nerve-racking, but it's awesome to hang out with my swim siblings and make new friends from different clubs and schools. I barely qualified last year as a sophomore, which is why my father has been so intense about my training over the last twelve months, but it was the highlight of my swim year.

Yet instead of thinking about friends, old and new, instead of hearing Coach's earlier pep talk playing in my head, I hear Adrian. Again. I think about how playful he was in his text messages, how it felt to sing with him at Ambrosia, and how funny he was that night at the Beanery when we were meant to be at the library.

About how nervous and awkward he was at the diner, apologizing for what Darcie did, telling me about his family.

How he told me to my face that he likes me.

And then I was rude. Told him his lyrics are cheesy when he was just trying to say something nice.

Oh, Marina …

I'm too young for a heart attack, but my chest aches all the same.

I think about how unbearable life is going to be with just swimming and studying, my only reprieve the online chats with my friends at night, *if* my dad relents and gives me my phone and internet back. Will he let me out on weekends to sing karaoke with my girls? Will I be allowed to attend school dances and choir competitions? How will I ever get to see Ms. Amberly and Mr. Malcolm and all my rock school friends if I'm nothing more than a waterlogged receptacle for facts I can regurgitate on college entrance exams?

Knuckles rap against my door, followed by it opening and my father's head poking around the edge. "Set your alarm for five, yeah?" I don't acknowledge him. And then the door closes. I listen as he walks down the hall to his room. When I hear his own door close, I throw the covers back and grab the coat I was wearing at the diner last week.

Adrian gave me a letter.

I'd forgotten about it.

The letter is stuffed right where I left it, the paper textured and stiff from having gotten damp from the raindrops absorbed as he handed it to me.

Nerves hop around behind my sternum; my fingertips tingle.

It's actually two pieces of paper: the first is an email, to Andy Drayer from another guy named Red Jones. I scan it, not sure what it has to do with me—until I get to the line about how he listened to the demo Andy sent over and "Is that seriously Trent Andersen's kid? Where the hell has he been hiding her? When can I hear more?"

Oh my god. Oh, no, no, no. I definitely have to keep this away from my father. I can't even imagine the depths he would go to if he knew a music producer had heard the tracks from the recording session. So now it's not just Darcie screwing things up—her uncle has his own agenda too?

I drop my eyes to the signature line on the email. Red Jones is a music producer with Big Town Records.

Big Town is huge. My dad recorded with them years ago.

And Red Jones wants to hear *more*? From *me*?

The second page—it's a song, handwritten in pencil with

some of the words scribbled out and recast with better choices. At the top, in pen, is a note from Adrian: "Marina, I wrote this … would love to work on it with you, if you're ever interested. Be who you were born to be. xo, A."

I set the email aside and read the lyrics:

Breaking Down Walls

I wish I could take back what I said,
All my words they came out wrong,
And my mind keeps circling back,
To those words, and all that they lack.

You know I can't really explain,
I'm stuck on the sound of your name.

And I've seen you wandering these halls
With your heart hanging low, putting up walls,

Please don't be just a face in the crowd,
When you should be singing out loud,
Not hiding the strength of your light,
'Cos when I look, girl, it shines so bright.

And you're not the only one,
It's easy to fall into step,
I've been wandering these halls
And I've been putting up walls,
With my heart hanging low,
'Cos I had nowhere to go.

But then you came along,
With your face in the crowd,
And you were shining so bright,
That I felt the strength of your light.

You know I can't really explain,
But I'm stuck on the sound of your name.

I've seen the way that you smile,
Even if it's only once in a while,
And I've got so much to say,
But words only get in the way.

You know I can't really explain,
I'm stuck on the sound of your name ...
You know I can't really explain,
I'm stuck on the sound of your name.

Oh man ... I should be angry that this virtual stranger is getting into my head, but the tears that soak the page are evidence enough that anger at Adrian is not part of this equation.

I'm stuck on the sound of your name.

I am in so much trouble.

CHAPTER 30

MOCHI ICE CREAM FOR
THE WIN

My bedside alarm clock screeches at me to get up. My eyes pop open as I remember what today is. Upon throwing my legs over the side of the bed, I'm grateful to feel like I may have actually gotten some sleep. The pages from Adrian are tucked under my pillow, but I know they need to be somewhere way more secure before I leave the house.

I look at the lyrics one more time.

I'm stuck on the sound of your name.

Is this meant for me? Or is it just a song he's been noodling with and I happen to have the right voice to make it work? Did he write this a long time ago for Darcie and then they broke up and *this* is why she's so mad, because he isn't singing this song to her anymore?

Don't overthink it, Marina.

I laugh to myself. It bounces around the quiet of my bedroom.

I have a treasure box hidden in my closet where I keep personal, private things. My dad has never gone looking in there—and I know he won't because it's filled with mementoes from my mother. It would be too painful for him.

I slide Adrian's pages inside it, the box hidden under some of my mother's sweaters that I took from their closet years ago, before my father purged everything to save his own heart. They used to smell like her, leftovers of perfume and her personal scent … not so much anymore. "Keep those safe for me, Mom."

And then with my dad's three knocks against my bedroom door announcing the day has officially begun, it's like someone pushes fast-forward. To the university pool, sign in, set up, team meeting, first heat, lunch, second and third heats, afternoon snack, first-round semifinals to see who goes on to tomorrow's biggest races and at what times. I manage to sneak off to the locker room for a few minutes with Lily and Sierra, where they deliver an oversized GOOD LUCK card signed by Ms. Amberly, Mr. Malcolm, and everyone in the choir department and rock school. It's pretty awesome.

As far as my races go, I finish third, second, and third, and then only fourth in the semifinals, but it's still good enough to earn me a spot for Saturday's heats. Coach is surprisingly enthusiastic about my performance, even if it's not the first-place finishes my dad would've preferred. When she sees that look on his face as we're preparing to leave the pool, she stops and reassures him that it's only the first day and that preserving my energy for the higher-stakes races over the next forty-eight hours is a solid strategy. She also reminds him that she's had detailed conversations with several scouts today about me, so things are looking bright and shiny.

I'm grateful she did this. It means my dad is pleasant—and calm—enough to agree to dinner out with Uncle Tim and Auntie Shelly, and when I ask if Lily and Sierra can come along, he nods agreement.

Victory!

We end up at a sushi restaurant, which is perfect—my dad

and uncle and aunt can sit at one table, and Lil and Sierra and I can sit at another, away from the adults. Finally, a break!

I am practically delirious with happiness as my friends take turns recapping everything I've missed in the last week. Stories of romantic drama, including a fight that broke out on the football field over some cheerleader; one of the biology teachers left the lid unlocked on the in-class terrarium where his ball python, Furiosa, lives and she escaped the other night, giving one of the night cleaners an actual heart attack and the fire department had to come save the guy. (He's apparently fine. So is beautiful Furiosa.)

"All the insane stuff happens when I leave!" I say, shoving a piece of California roll into my mouth. "Tell me more." They do, filling me in on the happenings in their own lives, Lily and I pausing now and again to howl and make fun of Sierra because she is the literal worst with chopsticks and half of her food ends up back on her plate. When she finally gives up and goes to ask for a fork, we laugh her all the way back to the table.

The three of us talk so fast and so much, and I know it's because we're all dreading that moment when my father is going to slide up next to the table and yank me back to jail.

We order *taiyaki* (traditional pancake batter cooked in a fish mold that this restaurant then stuffs with delicious mochi ice cream), even though we're so full already—but if my dad sees we're still eating, maybe we won't have to leave quite yet. And Sierra's grateful the *taiyaki* comes with tiny pink spoons and not more chopsticks.

Lily leans in and lowers her voice so only Sierra and I can hear her. "We debated telling you this," she says, licking melting ice cream off the side of her pancake "cone."

"Seriously, how much worse could things get?" I gesture subtly toward my father at the table across the small restaurant.

My two friends lock eyes with one another, and then Lily

takes a deep breath. "Scuttlebutt is playing tomorrow night. At the Beanery. Adrian has been bugging me all week to get a message to you somehow, to let you know."

I shrug, acting like it's no big deal. But my friends know me way better than that.

"He said they're going to be using your songs, to give Darcie a chance to try stuff out."

My cheeks catch fire. "But we didn't finish the recordings." A pause. "It would be weird for me to see her in person, you know, after what she did."

"Right. Yeah. That would be weird," Sierra says. Lily nods her agreement.

I contemplate telling them about my dad cutting the strings and taking my mom's guitar, about the incredible lyrics from Adrian and the email from the music producer. But what good would it do to give them more fuel? It's not like I can do anything about it.

Sierra drapes her hand on my arm. "Is there any way you can go? We could be there as backup, so Darcie can't cause any trouble. Maybe if you do really well tomorrow, would your dad let you come out for just a little while—"

My sharp laugh pierces the low din of the restaurant. It's all the answer Sierra requires.

"Are you guys gonna go?"

They look at each other. "We were thinking about it," Lily says, "but it's just not the same without you."

"Yeah, no fun getting dirty feet without our Marina." Sierra rests her head against my shoulder. It makes my throat ache, trying to hold back the burn of tears—I'd give anything to be able to hang out with my friends.

"Make sure to take a few pieces of rotten fruit to throw at Darcie for me, would ya?" I want it to be funny, but it just hurts.

"Adrian told me you guys talked last week, at the diner?"

Lily watches my father, currently paying the bill, as she speaks. "Said it didn't go so well."

"Yeah, well, he said some stuff that stung a little."

Lily finishes the last of her dessert in one bite and then leans as close as she can with the square black table in the way. "He likes you, Marina. Like, *likes* you. So he's worried about you."

"We all are," Sierra says. She's put her dessert aside unfinished, patting her stomach to indicate she can't take another bite.

Lily's words bring about a not-unpleasant warmth in my chest. *He likes you, Marina.*

Thing is, I like him too. But it's ridiculous. I hardly *know* him. I try to tell myself that I only took Darcie's offer because I wanted to help the band, but that's not a hundred percent true. There were selfish reasons for me wanting to sing with Scuttlebutt—beyond the fact that I *love* the actual singing part.

In Adrian, I saw a handsome musician who wasn't a total egomaniac, who has real talent, who was able to tell me stuff about himself—private stuff—without turning it into a weapon just to get girls. I don't know ... maybe he does do that. Lily hardly knows this older version of Adrian, even though they're cousins, given their family's weirdness since the two of them were kids. But I'd like to think if Adrian were a jerk who chases every girl who throws her Snap at him, we'd know. We'd see that.

Wouldn't we?

Lily *did* say that it was Darcie who cheated on him, not the other way around.

My brain hurts from too much thinking.

"Thanks, you guys. For coming today. For being my people," I say.

"We will always have your back, even when King Triton over there does his best to keep us apart," Lily says. Sierra snort-laughs, which always sends us into fits. It feels so good to laugh with my girls again. I've missed them so much.

"Hey, when he falls asleep tonight, sneak in and steal his trident," Sierra says. "Then he would be weakened against your mighty powers!" She cackles, sounding much like the famous sea witch.

"You've been practicing that laugh," I say. "Should we be worried?"

Lily rolls her eyes. "You have no idea. It's been a long week."

CHAPTER 31

IT'S NOT STEALING IF IT BELONGS TO YOU

My dad plays chauffeur, dropping off my friends at their respective houses. They each promise to try to come out to the final races on Sunday since tomorrow Lily has to work at the swim club and Sierra has her babysitting job. I'll definitely miss seeing their faces in stands, but maybe it will help too—*not* seeing them will keep my mind on the races, and not on the Scuttlebutt concert they're going to at the Beanery tomorrow night.

Ha. Yeah, right.

As soon as Sierra has flashed the porch light indicating that she's safe inside her house, my dad pulls from the curb and starts in on everything Coach said earlier. It's like he was holding his breath, waiting for it to be just us again, before unloading everything he needed to say. I let him talk, I nod at appropriate times, say "mm-hmm" and "okay" just so he doesn't get angry and question if I'm listening.

But Sierra's mention of me stealing King Triton's trident …

Interesting idea.

My father waits for the garage to open, muttering something about how the motor must be going out because it's so slow to raise the wide, impossibly heavy door. He finally parks, reminds me for the millionth time to grab my swim bag out of the back, and hops up the three stairs that lead into the kitchen.

"Gonna grab a shower. See you in the morning. Set your alarm for five again," he says as he finishes punching in the code on the alarm keypad. "Good job out there today. Tomorrow will be better."

I move to the fridge and linger with the door open, grabbing the ever-present pitcher of lemon water, as I watch him climb the stairs.

Pour a glass of water.

Listen for his bedroom door to close, followed by his footsteps on the hardwood floor over my head.

Wait for the sound of his bathroom's pocket door to bang shut.

The shower turns on.

Still, I stand in the kitchen, frozen and listening, though I know my window is tight.

Put the pitcher back into the fridge.

Slide off my shoes.

Tiptoe down the hall to his office, grateful the door is open. It isn't always, and sometimes it's even locked with a key only he has.

His desk is an antique, carved-wood behemoth—it took four guys to move it in here. I know which drawers make noise when you open them, so I'll avoid those until absolutely necessary. The desktop is surprisingly cluttered, considering my father's tendency toward near-obsessive organization and cleanliness. Gently, I lift pages and piles, search in the desktop file organizers, open the top middle drawer, holding my breath when it squeaks with the movement.

Rummage through the drawer's contents. Pause, hands splayed on the messy surface.

If I were my dad, where would I hide my daughter's phone?

I scan the room, looking for potential spots. He wouldn't have put it in his wall safe, or worse, in his room where I would never venture, would he?

I flop into his fancy leather desk chair.

The grin spreads across my face when I see it, its corner peeking out from under a pile of dry-cleaning and grocery and drug store receipts. Even knowing that taking it is going to get me in the biggest trouble, I gently pull it out by its edge, careful not to disrupt the mountain of receipts, hoping he won't notice anything amiss.

The shower overhead turns off, and with my heart pounding like I've just done a 200M medley, I bound up the stairs and into my room, careful to not slam my door from the adrenaline.

I bide my time, plugging in my dead phone under the bed so if Dad walks in to say good night, he won't see it.

And then when I'm positive we're done interacting for the night, I quietly lock my bedroom door, slide under the covers, and turn my phone back on.

The home screen blazes with dozens of unanswered messages across all my apps.

But opening them might show that I'm online, and I don't know if my dad follows me on any of the social media platforms. A week ago—before he took my phone—I'd say you were full of it if you told me he was monitoring me that way.

Today, after a week of basically house arrest, I'd say anything's possible.

Text messages should be safe enough. There's no indicator that I'm online in the text app, is there?

Worth the risk.

I scroll through the group chats where Sierra and Lily have carried on conversations, including me even though they knew I wasn't there, promising we'd talk about this or that when we finally see each other.

A few texts from rock school and choir friends, wondering if I'm ever coming back to school.

Even one from Ms. Amberly who says she hopes she isn't overstepping but she got my number from Sierra and just wanted to check in after our talk last week, and she hopes I'm doing better.

The last name I tap on … Adrian Brooks. Text after text.

I'm sorry. I didn't mean to hurt your feelings at the diner. I should just shut up more often. I couldn't even finish my pancakes. Which is a crime. Pancakes are my favorite food.

Did you read the lyrics? Oh man, if you think they suck, tell me. No. Wait. Don't.

Hope you aren't still mad.

You really thought the lyrics sucked. I knew it.

Hello? Hello? Anyone?

I talked to Darcie. Told her what she did was the worst. She hardly seemed remorseful, but I warned her that if she did anything like that again, she was out of the band. We had a fight. It was ugly. But she's still wrong. Please text me back, Marina.

Come on, seriously? Ghosting is so beyond you. You're not that girl.

Did you even READ the email from Red Jones?

Fine. Whatever. I get it. Bye.

A break in the texts, followed by:

Ahhhhh, oh my god, Lil says you don't have your phone. So basically you're not seeing any of these messages and I have been giving you crap and being a jerk for no reason? Maybe I should just tell you all my deepest, darkest secrets since you'll probably never see them.

OK, I already told you about peeing my pants on stage.

Next secret: I still sleep with a night light because I'm convinced a monster lives under my bed. Actually a monster does live under my bed and her name is Pickles

and she's a 20-pound street cat who eats socks and sometimes flesh if you're not careful WHICH IS WHY I HAVE A NIGHT LIGHT. #stoplaughing #cannibalcat

Second secret: I actually *love* that series of books about the sparkly vampires. DO NOT REPEAT THIS INFORMATION OR I SHALL DENY DENY DENY.

Last secret for the day, more like a confession: I met this totally cool girl and now I never get to see her because her dad is meaner than Shrek (before he meets Fiona) and it really sucks, so if you happen to run into her, tell her I said hi ... and I miss her.

I've been muffling my laughs into my threadbare stuffed goldfish, but I'm not laughing now. Just smiling, so hard my cheeks actually hurt. "I miss you too, Adrian," I whisper.

I reread his last secret a dozen times before scrolling on.

After another break between messages, based on the time stamps, there's one from yesterday: **Not sure if you'll even see this or if you'll talk to Lil in time, but we're at the Beanery Sat. night—gonna run your tracks with Darcie up front. Her last chance to make up for being a raging jerk. Ticket for you at the door, just in case ... xo, A.**

A plan slowly blossoms in my mind.

Heck, I already stole his trident tonight by taking my phone back.

Now I have a few text messages of my own to send.

CHAPTER 32

COVERT OPERATIONS

y only other race of the day, after finishing second in this morning's heat. I'm shaking out my hands, arms, and legs, waiting for the first signal, the swimmer who won first earlier again next to me. My suit digs into my shoulders—the tighter the suits, the more aerodynamic. Anything to make us just that tiny bit faster once we hit the water.

The crowd in the stands buzzes with conversation and nervous anticipation, but the swimmers all have eyes on the pool, waiting for the whistle to climb up onto the starting blocks.

My stomach is in knots.

But it has less to do with swimming the 400M freestyle faster than the other athletes in the pool and more to do with what comes after.

The first whistle goes; we climb up. Second whistle, we take our marks. When the beep sounds, I am in the water with all the energy of a shooting star. I need to be top three in this heat, if not first, to keep my father happy, and to make sure I get a good spot for tomorrow's finals.

Like every race before, my body knows what to do—at

this point, it's a mental game. I just have to outmaneuver the other swimmers, believe I can win this race, want it more than they do.

Faster, harder, leaner.

By the third flip turn, everything is on fire—lungs, legs, arms—but based on the position of the swimmer in the adjacent lane and on the cheering of Coach and my teammates, I'm very close.

Faster, Marina. FASTER.

My hand hits the touch plate and I grab the wall, throwing my goggles back to check the scoreboard.

Second. Again.

It's not terrible.

But it's not first.

As soon as the rest of the field finishes, the swimmers are out of the pool so the next heat can go. My teammates and Coach Tosto congratulate me, though it's immediately followed with Coach leading me away from the other swimmers with a few tips about what I can improve on for tomorrow's heats. The thing about swimming—there is no rest. We are never quite as good as we could be, our form is never a hundred percent right, and there will always be someone faster. It's what keeps us competitive, knowing that milliseconds stand between us and a medal.

Or in my case, a scholarship.

As Coach talks, voice low and serious, her head bowed between us, I'm grateful that at this meet, parents aren't allowed in the team areas. Last thing I need right now is my dad lecturing me about what *he* thought I did wrong.

As soon as Coach is done with her notes, she pats me on the back and tells me to cool down. There are still races to come, including the second-tier heats for those swimmers who didn't place in the top five. When Coach asks if I'm sticking around for those, I nod.

Even with my fingers crossed behind my back.

I see my dad climbing down the bleachers, so I move toward the metal-and-fabric barricades that keep swimmers safe from meddling parents and guardians.

"Looked good," he says. "A little slow in the last 50M but the swimmer next to you was so quick. Something to strive for, yeah?"

"Yup."

"You talked to Coach?" He knows I did. I always do after a race. Plus, he saw us. "Are you cleared to leave, then?"

"No, I should stay and support the team. Not everyone had as good a day as I did," I say, hoping he'll buy it.

He's nodding. "Right. Makes sense. So, I was talking to the scout from USC—and he's interested, Marina. Excellent school of business there, plus their swim program is among the best in the country—"

"Dad, can we talk about this later? I need some water and a snack." The last thing I want to study in university is business, but this is definitely not the right time to have this conversation, which will inevitably lead to an argument.

"Right. Sorry. Just got excited about the possibilities."

Yeah. Me too. Studying subjects I don't care about and swimming nonstop for four years for a team that treats me like a robot. Sign me up.

"I can get a ride home with one of the girls when we're done," I say, praying in my head that he will agree.

His eyes are on the pool. It's gotten really loud in here again as another race is underway.

"Dad, you look tired. Just go home and I'll get a ride with Madison or Olivia or something. No big deal."

He's thinking.

The race behind us finishes; the crowd goes crazy, as they do with every race. I'd probably be smart to wear ear protection when not in the water.

"Okay, that might work. What time does it wrap up today?" He pulls the heat sheet from his back pocket. "Last heat is at seven, followed by results and probably a team meeting … so I should expect you at, what, eight? Nine?"

"Yeah. That sounds about right."

"Do you have the burner phone?"

I nod. I also have my regular phone, but he doesn't need to know that.

He reaches into his other pocket for his wallet, opening it to hand me a few bills. "Get something to eat," he says. "You can't live on energy bars alone."

"Thanks."

"Good job again, Marina," he says, and then walks away. A wave of nerve-induced nausea washes over me as I watch him go, again recalling the look on his face after he got the email from Darcie, after he realized I'd lied to him.

But as soon as I see he's out of the building, I swallow the discomfort, steel my heart, and move to our club's area. My swim siblings are all very congratulatory about my last race, and I have my own hugs to pass around to the swimmers who have worked so hard today. We really do have an awesome team. These people are like sisters.

I sit with my team for about a half hour more, watching the clock like I'm waiting to meet a CIA operative who will deliver secrets from a rogue nation.

Flurries of anxiety swirl in my stomach every time the second hand passes twelve and I grow that much closer.

Just a few more minutes.

I wait until the clamor calms and more races are on so I can quietly excuse myself to the locker room to shower and change before the flood of athletes drains the hot water tanks or crowds the mirrors. When I'm sure Coach Tosto is preoccupied with our swimmers in the water, I take the route I mapped out earlier, one that goes under the bleachers and away from the prying, nosy eyes of other swimmers, coaches, and well-meaning adults.

I shower as quickly as I can, relieved that when I check my

dry bag, my clothes are, in fact, dry. You never know with gear left on the pool deck.

Instead of changing into the usual team sweat suit, I pull on Lily's soft lavender T-shirt with the white rose, a cute cardigan, black jeans with holes in all the right spots, three inches of bracelets for my left arm, rings on both hands, and my favorite low-heeled, weathered-leather boots. A few swimmers are starting to filter in, so I need to hurry. Makeup would be great—although I should probably do my hair now while I have access to electricity and then do makeup in the car.

I check my phone to make sure everything's on schedule.

A text awaits: **Hey, Mari, we still on for 7?**

I text back: *I'll go out the side door, northeastern side, near the first row of parked cars. Thank you so much.*

I finish drying and adding some curl to my hair, but my hand shakes as I try to draw on the cat eyes Sierra is so good at. By the time I'm done, I've used every last cotton swab in my bag, and some twisted-up tissue, and I look like I've been punched.

Whatever. I try to compensate by smearing more eye shadow over it. I really should take a page out of Lily's handbook and spend some time on YouTube watching makeup tutorials.

I check my phone again. Rendezvous in five minutes. I will have to fix this disaster later.

I pack my things, keeping out only the purse I've now stuffed with my phones, lipstick, and my ID. The money my dad gave me, I put into my swim bag. Later, after all this comes crashing down—as it inevitably will—I can give him back his twenty bucks.

The noise level in the locker room is picking up as more swimmers file in. I need to get out of here before Coach or one of my swim siblings sees me.

Out the main door, I detour down a side hallway and to a

door marked EMERGENCY EXIT. However, I saw a janitor go through it earlier, so I know it's not alarmed. Still, my heart pounds as I put my hands on the bar to push it open. *Please don't be alarmed. Please don't be alarmed.*

It's not.

And sitting at the curb, just like the text promised, is my ride.

The driver waves, and I wave back, running to the car like a dragon is chasing me. The locks click open as I approach; throwing the door open bathes me in the scent of familiarity, of peppermint licorice and homecoming.

"Hey, Uncle Tim."

CHAPTER 33

YOU ARE NOT ALONE

"You do know there will be murderous rage to deal with once we're found out," I say.

"And you remember that I grew up with that hothead. Let me deal with him," Uncle Tim says. When he pulls away of the swim club and onto the street, my entire body exhales with relief.

"How'd you do today?" he asks. I recap my races, explaining there were only two today but that potentially means four tomorrow.

"And you'll be able to handle it after a crazy night out on the town?"

I laugh. "Adrenaline has gotten me this far. I guess we'll see if I sink to the bottom tomorrow."

"Oh, dear, not in front of the college scouts, please." We laugh. It's not that I want to make fun of my dad for being so serious about the scouts, about my future—but it has gotten to the point where everything is almost a farce, that no matter what I do, nothing will ever be good enough.

If he's going to accuse me of robbing a bank, I might as well rob a bank. Well, metaphorically. I'm not actually turning to a life of crime.

Although the fact that I've snuck out of regionals before being properly excused by Coach, riding in my uncle's car after a premeditated plot to willfully disobey my father so that I am now on my way to the Coffee Beanery to meet my friends and listen to Scuttlebutt, *very* much against my father's wishes?

Yeah, that definitely sounds like a life of crime.

"Are you going to come in and listen?"

"I don't know … am I?"

"I asked Adrian for two tickets." As much as I want to just hang out with Sierra and Lily—who will be waiting for us at the door by seven forty-five—I also know that if my Uncle Tim is in on my misdeeds, I may have a buffer against my father's wrath. I am afraid of my dad; Uncle Tim is not.

"As long as you won't think it's too uncool to hang out with your dorky uncle."

"Are you kidding? You're awesome. My friends love you."

"It's easy to love me because your dad is so scary," he says, chuckling. "I win by default."

"Nah. You'd win anyway. My friends have been my friends for a long time. They are very familiar with the Trent and Marina Show."

"Speaking of," he says, his face more serious. "I didn't want to text this to you, just in case. Your choir teacher emailed me."

"Ms. Amberly?"

He nods. "Looked me up via the school district staff directory. We had an interesting talk."

My mouth feels like I've just chewed a piece of chalk. But why am I worried? This is Uncle Tim, not my dad. "What did she have to say?"

"That she's concerned about you. That you've been really upset at school and she thinks we should get the counselor and maybe the principal involved."

"I begged her not to."

"Which is why she emailed me instead," he says, looking over at me briefly at a red light. "It's also why I agreed to this nefarious scheme tonight." He smiles. "We are both considering an intervention on your behalf."

"Oh my god, no. That would make everything so much worse."

"But would it? Your father's iron rule is bordering on child abuse at this point. There is such a thing as being *too* involved, too controlling over your child's life, you know."

"What would that mean, though? He wouldn't get in trouble or anything, right? Because you know—we both know—he is this way because he's broken. He's hurting, so much. And me being a spoiled brat doesn't make things easier for him."

My uncle's chuckle sounds sad. "Little Mari ... you are so far from a spoiled brat, you're not even in the brat ballpark." He pats my shoulder across the space. "My brother has always had some stuff going on in his head. It doesn't take a degree in clinical psychology to see that—and I have one. After your mom died, your dad did fall apart. And the only way he knew how to keep going was to duct-tape everything together again. You got caught up in all that."

I put my head back. All this poorly applied eyeliner and mascara is going to end up on my cheeks.

"Your dad needs some help. Yes, he is a devoted, attentive parent, but he's gone to an extreme. You're just a kid. You are carrying more than a full load of AP courses; your grades are outstanding; you're involved in civic and volunteer activities at your school; you are an elite athlete; you are a talented singer; and you are a really, really nice human. Marina Padrina, you are every parent's dream for their child."

He hasn't used that nickname in a million years. I snort-laugh as I open the glove box and pull out a fast-food napkin to soak up disobedient tears. Thank heavens for my frugal

Auntie Shelly. If I were in the mood for ketchup or soy sauce, I'd have that covered too.

"We need to sit down with your dad and let him know that he needs to talk to someone. He's grappling with some issues that are too big for him to manage on his own, and because of that, he's adding all this extra weight onto your shoulders, shoulders that are often squished up next to your ears because you're so tense when you two are together." I look over at him. "Yeah, I see it. You're a walking ball of anxiety when Trent Andersen is in the room. It's a wonder you can still use your hands at all with how high up your shoulders ride."

As he says it, I realize my shoulders *are* tight and tense. I focus on relaxing them, letting the muscles loosen and drop to a normal position.

"So—tonight, you are going to go out with your friends and listen to this band you're so enamored with, and when my brother freaks out, I'm going to be there with you. If necessary, we will pack you a bag and you'll come stay with me and Shel for a bit."

I whip my head toward him. "Really?"

"Really. This is a crossroads for your father. He has to see what he's doing is not healthy, not for him and certainly not for you. You only get to be a kid for such a short time, and life in the big, grown-up world is really damn hard, kiddo."

I sniff and dab. "Wait—what about Neptune?"

He laughs loudly. "Neptune comes with. We never leave a man behind."

"Or fish," I say. I reach across and grab my uncle's hand. "Thank you. I feel like a weight has been lifted off my chest."

He nods. The lights of oncoming traffic reflect on the tears poised in his own eyes. "I knew things were bad. The email sealed it for me," he says, taking a deep breath and clearing his throat. "Please, next time—talk to me. Talk to Auntie

Shelly. We are *here* for you. You're like our daughter too, you know?" He squeezes my hand.

We drive the rest of the way to the Coffee Beanery in quiet, pleasant silence.

And it's so nice, for once, to not be afraid of the quiet in the car.

CHAPTER 34

LA PETITE SIRÈNE

Uncle Tim finds parking in a sort-of scary garage a few blocks from the Beanery. "Twelve bucks?" he asks the pimply-faced kid taking his money.

"Busy downtown on Saturdays, mister. Complain to the boss."

Tim takes his lot ticket and tucks it into his pocket. It's closing in on eight o'clock, so we hurry.

I loop my arm through my uncle's, huddling against his overstuffed, dad-style jacket for warmth in the light mist. My own father would never be caught dead in something so lumpy or practical. Another blaring difference between my uncle and father: Dad cares (too much) about what other people think; Uncle Tim cares about *how* people think.

"Adrian said he'd leave tickets for us at the door."

"Ah, just like old times. VIP is the only way to fly, kid," Uncle Tim teases.

We hustle to the Beanery, bypassing annoyed concertgoers lined up outside, just like last time. And just like last time, I keep my head down so I don't feel bad about getting special treatment.

The guy at the door gives my uncle a once-over, and then

asks him to unzip the big coat to check that he's not smuggling anything in. "What? It's cozy. Just wait until your forties," he says to the guard who scans Tim with the metal-detector wand. "I'd rather be warm than fashionable."

"Obviously," the guard says, satisfied my uncle isn't sneaking contraband into the venue. He pulls out two tickets from an envelope marked "Adrian/Guests" attached to a clipboard and waves us through. "Have a good night."

We stop briefly so Uncle Tim can hand over his legendary coat to the girls manning the coat check. I pull my phone from my small purse to check messages. A text awaits, from Adrian: **Let me know when you're here. I'd love to say hello.**

The butterfly flock in my stomach wakes again, all rested from their brief nap.

And then Lily's and Sierra's shrieks echo down the narrow hallway that attaches the front door to the concert space and coffee bar.

"You're here! You're here! I can't believe it's really you!" A bouncing group hug ensues. My uncle chuckles, but then Sierra throws herself at him.

"Thank you, Uncle Tim! Thank you for saving our mermaid from the Kraken!"

It's a good thing my uncle is so comfortable around kids. I'm not sure Sierra ever wants to let him go.

"Did you guys get a table yet?" I ask.

Lily spins, her blond hair a shelf of platinum shininess, and points. "See the one with the VIP card on it? Yeah, that's us. It's good having friends in high places." She blows on her fingernails and pretends to polish them against her fuzzy pink, short-sleeved sweater. Pink is definitely her color.

Uncle Tim offers to buy our coffees, even though we try to tell him we won't be sitting for long. He reminds us that his bad knees mean he *will* be sitting, and he'd love to have some caffeine to keep him company.

As he breaks off to line up at the counter, my friends and I move to our table before it gets too crowded to squeeze through. "Your dad gave you your phone back?"

I laugh once—it comes out sounding a bit more wicked than I intend.

"You stole it?" Sierra's eyes widen.

"I *liberated* it," I say.

"You are such a rebel."

"Speaking of phones … Adrian texted and told me to let him know when we're here," I add.

Lily and Sierra share a conspiratorial smile. "Text him now. Go backstage and say hello. We'll wait here for you." Lily bumps into Sierra's shoulder and arches an eyebrow.

"What? You guys are acting weird."

"Nope. Not weird," Sierra says, pulling out her chair. "Just excited that you are out in the world again. Excited that when you say Adrian's name, your face lights up like an LED bulb."

"No! Her face lights up like one of those bioluminescent squid—all sparkly and fluttering—she is a mermaid, after all," Lily says.

"No more fairy tales. You guys are nuts."

Sierra leans forward on the small round table. "We may be nuts, but we also know when the fairy-tale goddesses are busy weaving their tangled webs." She and Lily exchange a high five. "Now: text Adrian. This second."

I look over at the coffee bar; my uncle catches my eye and waves. He mimes to ask if we want anything to eat. I shake my head no, but he will inevitably come back with a variety of snack options. I don't need a grandmother constantly trying to feed me—I have Uncle Tim and Auntie Shelly. Thank heavens. I am actually starving.

I slide my phone from my pocket, my cheeks already ablaze with anticipation.

Open Adrian's latest text and type my response: ***I'm here. Made it!***

Darken the screen, phone clutched in my hand. Waiting.

It only takes a few seconds for it to buzz against my palm.

Meet me at the stage door in 30 seconds.

My insides feel like a bottle of sparkling water, all bubbly and fuzzy.

"I'm gonna meet Adrian for a sec," I say, standing to push my chair back.

Lily stands too, fluffing my hair over my shoulders and inspecting my face. "Radiant. Go get him, songbird."

"Will someone please tell me where that nickname came from?" Sierra whines. I laugh and weave through the tables that are slowly filling with excited fans. I squeeze past the barricade that separates the seating from the performance/backstage area, nodding once at the bald, black-clad security guard waiting there.

"Can I help you?"

"Um, yeah—" But before I can finish, the backstage door swings open, and Adrian is there. My heart skips a beat.

"It's okay, Jacques. This is Marina. She's with me."

Jacques the bald security guard smiles tightly and nods, taking the handle to hold the door for Adrian and me to walk back through.

The hallway looks the same as it did the last time I was here.

And Adrian looks as beautiful as ever in his torn jeans and curly hair and knee-weakening smile. "Hey," he says, stopping against the wall covered in band and concert posters. The door to the green room down the way is open, allowing the telltale sounds of musicians warming up to escape.

"Hey yourself," I say. It's then I notice his T-shirt. "Oh my god, is that a mermaid?"

He laughs. "Inside joke. For you. Because Lily told me she thinks you're living a fairy tale right now. Because Darcie is actually kind of Ursula the Sea Witch."

"You are such a dork! So, what, I'm Ariel?"

"That would probably be logical?"

"Oh, and I suppose that makes you Eric the dashing prince Ariel is just dying to marry."

He grins like the Cheshire Cat. "I was thinking I'm more like the crazed little French chef who's trying to capture the crab—"

"Louis! The chef is Louis!"

"Yeah. That guy." Adrian chuckles, but then he reaches for my hand, interlacing his fingers with mine. "I'm glad you're here. I know it's a huge risk."

"It is … but my uncle is in on it, so at least I have an added layer of protection."

"Your dad *is* an awful lot like King Triton," Adrian says. His smile warms me down to my stress-chilled toes.

"And *you* have been spending way too much time talking to your crazy cousin."

"Only because she has excellent taste in friends."

"She does," I say. "I cannot disagree with that."

The air between us is tense, but not in that bad way, not in the way you feel when you're about to have a fight with your dad or when your coach is about to scold you because you didn't swim fast or hard enough.

This tension, it's the good kind. The kind that makes me feel like I could leap tall buildings in a single bound.

A raspy, barely there voice yells from down the hall. "Ten-minute warning." It's Darcie. She disappears as fast as she appeared.

Oh man, I forgot she was even here. Good feeling gone.

"Hey, don't worry about her," Adrian says, grabbing my other hand.

I shake my head, trying to act like it wasn't a big deal, even though we both know it was a *huge* deal.

"Is she nervous? About singing with my tracks tonight?" I ask. "That's still the plan, right?"

"Yeah. And I don't know if she's nervous. She's been mostly avoiding me."

"Good." I don't mean to sound possessive, but I'm not done being mad at Darcie Drayer yet. "I hope for you guys, everything goes okay."

"It should. Andy's gonna be in the booth for us—he's a little nervous about the Beanery's sound tech, and their equipment isn't great. But we're playing everything else live —it'll just be Darcie lip-syncing."

"Do you think people will know?"

He shrugs. "I guess we'll find out soon enough."

A silence unfolds between us.

And then Adrian lets go of my left hand, moving his fingers to my chin to tip my head back so I can only look at him. In that moment, his cheek twitches, and he looks like nervous Adrian, the nerdy kid standing in the foyer at my house, waiting to see if my dad would strike him dead, rather than rock star Adrian who has legions of adoring fans waiting just on the other side of that Jacques-protected door.

"Would it be weird if I kissed you?"

"It would only be weird if you didn't."

He smiles and leans down, his lips feathering a light kiss against mine, and then another, and then he gently cups the back of my head, kissing me a bit harder, and I unlock my fingers from his to wrap my own hands around his neck. He tastes like a little like honey.

I never want this moment to end.

But then voices from down the hall interrupt us, and Adrian releases me from his spell, his forehead against mine, our eyes soft. He then presses his lips just below my hairline and wraps his arms around me, whispering in my ear. "I am so glad to see you again."

I squeeze him back, just as Tyler the drummer lets out a loud whistle. He then hollers, "Adriaaaaaaaaaan!" like he's in some sort of physical pain.

Adrian laughs and moves back just enough to allow a breath between us. "He thinks he's funny. It's from a movie. *Rocky*? The boxing movie? When he's yelling for the woman he loves?"

"Yeah … I've seen it."

"The curse of my parents choosing that stupid name."

I grab his cheeks and pull his lips to mine again for a quick kiss. "It's a great name."

"Thanks," he says against my mouth, finally releasing me when it's clear his bandmates are not waiting for us to wrap it up. "You found your table okay?"

I let him go and take a step back. "We'll be cheering the loudest."

"See you after the show?"

I grin so hard, I'm afraid my face will shatter. "Counting the minutes." I spin on the ball of my foot, all the fatigue of two days of hard swimming and months of practices and competitions and the stress of my father's militancy melting away like a snowball dropped in a frying pan. I push open the door and give Jacques a pleasant smile, buoyant as I float back to rejoin my friends and wait for the show to start.

Maybe Lily's on to something. Maybe this is a fairy tale after all.

CHAPTER 35

PLEASE STAND BY

I slide back into my seat, trying—and failing—to keep my smile under control.

"Ohhhh, now *that* is a face we haven't seen in a while—or ever," Lily says, her chin resting smugly against her palm. "Tell us, Ariel, did you find your prince?"

I flash a look over my shoulder at my uncle, sitting just far enough back that he doesn't seem to have heard Lily.

I lean in close to my friends. "A mermaid never kisses and tells."

And then, of course, they dissolve in a fit of giggles and shrieks, Sierra bouncing so hard on her chair, I'm afraid she'll tip over backwards and break something.

"I knew it. I knew the minute we met the band that he would fall head over heels for her," she says.

"You guys"—I press a finger against my lips to quiet them—"and he's not head over heels. We're just … friends."

"Mm-hmm. Also, he's head over heels," Lily says. She flattens her palm between her and Sierra. I watch as Sierra sighs dramatically, digs into her pocket, and pulls out a crunched-up five-dollar bill.

"I'm sorry—what just happened?" I ask.

"We had a bet. I knew he'd kiss you; Sierra didn't think he would. Not yet."

I open my mouth to protest, but Lily cuts me off. "Don't even try to deny it. You had more lipstick on when you went through that magical door."

I crumple a napkin and throw it at her, grinning like an idiot. I can't help it.

As Lily stuffs her newly won cash into her small beaded purse, I quickly check my phone. It's eight thirty. My dad will be figuring things out soon.

Again, I sneak a look over my shoulder at my uncle, his eyes on his own phone, probably playing one of the word games he's so fond of. I'm just glad he's here—he's keeping me calm. Reminding me I'm not alone. And when Trent Andersen figures out that his daughter is not where she should be, this time I'll have reinforcements.

A shift happens in the noise and energy all of a sudden as someone bounds onto the stage, a guy with long, brown bangs that flop over his right eye, a huge ring in his nose, and tattoos covering arms exposed by his short-sleeve black Coffee Beanery T-shirt. He grabs the mic and waits for the raucous whoops and applause to calm.

"Gooooooood evening, ladies and gentlemen! Welcome to Saturday Night at the Bean!" More applause. He again waits a beat to be heard over the racket. "I'm Sean, the manager in charge of booking killer acts like the one we have for you tonight." More noise. "I don't want to take up any more of your precious time, so if you could please help me welcome to the stage, our very own local, homegrown talent, SCUT-TLEBUUUUUUTT!"

And then everyone is on their feet, including us, screaming and shouting, bouncing with excitement as Leroy, Tyler, and Damon take their spots. The decibels nearly blow off the roof as Adrian jogs out, followed quickly by Darcie Drayer, arms flailing in welcome to the roaring crowd.

"Heyyyy, everybody!" Adrian shouts into the mic.

Darcie stops before reaching her mic stand and tears off the worn leather jacket she came out in, tossing it theatrically across the stage. Lily, Sierra, and I howl when we see what's on her shirt.

"Oh my GOD, is that the Ursula the Sea Witch?" Sierra yells against my head. She and Lily are laughing so hard, I'm afraid they won't be able to stand up much longer. And I'm never going to hear the end of it, about how this is an actual fairy tale.

The guys fiddle with their instruments, a quick jumble of sounds as they get situated. Adrian, guitar draped over his upper body, strums the strings once, and I think the girls at the table next to us are going to pass out. One of them might even be crying, her hands stretched toward the stage like she wants to grab Adrian and stuff him in her purse.

Adrian catches my eye and smiles; I smile back. He then steps up to his mic and waits for it to quiet down a bit.

"Thanks for that warm welcome. We're Scuttlebutt."

Crowd goes wild.

And then Adrian throws himself into the first song, the band hot on his heels, as Darcie grabs her mic from its stand and bobs her head to the beat, waiting for the vocals to start.

Angry as I am, I'm super nervous for her, for all of them.

I look back at Uncle Tim who is, as promised, still seated but his phone is put away and he's clearly enjoying the energy coursing around him, his feet and hands tapping out the rhythm. I hop close and lean in so only he can hear me. "Watch the guitarist. He's incredible."

Tim nods and smiles. He knows. The guitarist is incredible not just because he's a talented musician with hands that play his instrument like it's part of his body but because he's so much more.

Just as I'm about to pull away, Uncle Tim grasps my wrist and whispers against my ear. "That's you singing, isn't it …"

"Maybe," I say, winking.

"Sounds fantastic." And for a second, his eyes widen and he looks almost sad, despite his smile. "Your mom, Mari … God, you sound so much like her."

I squeeze his hand wrapped around my wrist and then throw my arms around my uncle's neck, for fear we will both lose it.

He pushes me back. "Dance! You must DANCE!"

I kiss his cheek and then turn back to my friends. Lily and Sierra and I clasp hands and push toward the front of the stage, bouncing and dancing and singing and yelling with everyone else. The vocals DO sound good, and with the live music alongside it, the difference between our voices isn't so obvious, especially not to people who don't know any better.

We dance and dance and dance, singing along with the rest of the crowd—which feels really weird for me since I'm actually singing along with myself. But it's so loud and wild and free … I want tonight to last for a million nights.

We have enough space between songs to take a couple of breaths, and then Leroy, the keyboardist, eases into the next piece with nimble fingers across his piano, sending the crowd into a renewed frenzy. This song has a nice long intro, which lets Leroy really show off his crazy talent. Adrian on guitar and Damon on bass join in next, followed by Tyler on drums who picks up the pace, taking this number from slow ballad to rock anthem in no time.

Darcie grabs the mic and opens her mouth to sing—

And there are no vocals.

The guys are jamming, Darcie's mouth is moving, but no vocal track comes through the speakers.

The band keeps playing, but then Darcie realizes something is definitely wrong. She spins to face her bandmates, tapping her ear with a tattooed finger, one hand upturned in question. The band stops abruptly; Adrian grabs the nearest mic.

"Hey, guys—sorry—technical difficulties here. Give us a sec."

Then the crowd quiets to a dull roar, everyone sort of looking around at each other, trying to figure out what's going on. A few people holler at the stage. When the break drags on into more than just a sec, the commentary around us gets a little tense as people start asking if she was lip-syncing and not actually singing. One girl says if that's the case, she's demanding her money back.

Slowly, fans shiny with sweat from dancing give up their spots in the pit to wander back to their seats, the conversation growing louder in fits and starts. A handful even gather coats and bags off their chairs, moving toward the main exit, grumbling about this turn of events.

Sierra and Lily and I just watch, though my gut is twisty and nervous as the crowd thins, as I watch the band huddled and talking into an earpiece.

And then Andy Drayer is there, looking flustered, joining the huddle, his back to us so I can't read his face.

Scuttlebutt is losing the audience. More fans are getting annoyed. People are on their phones again and plans are being made to leave and find something better to do.

I look back at my uncle, who shrugs his shoulders, seemingly as confused as the rest of us, and then I look to my two friends standing next to me, both scrolling through their phones and showing each other dumb memes and dorky pictures of their respective boyfriends to pass the time.

I lean against the metal barrier between the crowd and the stage. "Andy!" I yell.

He turns at the sound of my voice.

"Let me," I say, miming as if I'm holding a microphone.

His eyes widen. He then swivels to the band, points, and just that quick, Adrian is taking off his guitar and gesturing toward the stage door.

It's then that Sierra notices I'm not standing right next to her. "Um, what is happening?"

"Guys, wish me luck."

And before they can say another word, I'm pushing through people, moving as fast as I can without running, to the stage door. I squeeze Uncle Tim's shoulder as I swoop past—he looks perplexed for a beat, but then his sneaky grin tells me he's figured out what's about to go down.

The stage door is open.

Adrian stands waiting for me, a smile as wide as the ocean on his face.

"You sure about this?" he asks.

I'm not, but I am. "My contract stipulates that I require pancakes," I say.

"Hmm," he says, tapping his index finger against his lips. "I might know a place ..."

Adrian then offers his hand, and I take it.

CHAPTER 36

HIDDEN DEPTHS

As soon as I'm backstage, Andy buzzes like a fly on old meat, fussing around to fit me with an earpiece so I can hear myself sing.

"Okay, so here's the set list—you know all this, right?" He hands me a piece of paper with a list of songs, not waiting for my answer as he weaves the earpiece cord under my hair. "You're saving their butts, kid."

Adrian, standing next to me, wraps his warm hand around my clammy one. "You're shaking."

"This is terrifying," I admit.

Andy squares my shoulders with both hands. "You ready?"

I nod aggressively, almost displacing the earpiece. Out of the corner of my eye, I see Darcie lean over and pick up her leather jacket from where she tossed it earlier. The look on her face—yeah, this definitely sucks.

"Let's finish the show and worry about politics later, shall we?" Andy says, whipping me around. He exchanges a quick word with Sean from the Beanery who then sails past to the lead mic as the band members hurry back to their positions.

"OKAY, we have a fix! Ladies and gentlemen, so sorry

about that." Applause, though not as enthusiastic as before. "Come on back in so we can get things moving again." A few people put their phones down long enough to look up at Sean, and then me, standing awkwardly next to him, like I don't know what I'm doing.

Because I sort of don't.

Of course you know what you're doing. This is in your blood. This is your heritage.

This is who you were meant to be.

"We have a late-game substitution, flying in to save the day!" More people file back toward the performance area. Sean continues: "Folks, how many of you've heard of the band Hidden Villains?" THAT gets their attention. Whoops and hollers from the re-gathering crowd. "Well, let's just say that this gorgeous creature standing next to me *might* be our very own rock royalty, that rock 'n' roll blood coursing through her veins. Ladies and gents, performing for the first time at the Beanery, let's give a warm welcome to rock princess, Marinaaaaa Andersen!"

It's amazing how just a few words can change the entire vibe of a room. The eyes of the concertgoers are heavy on my skin as they lean next to one another and whisper, a few scrolling through their phones and then looking from the screen to me. This happens sometimes when people learn who my father is. *Is she really Trent Andersen's daughter? What happened to Hidden Villains? I heard he went out in a blaze of glory. Is she really his kid or someone just trying to get famous?*

I've heard it all before.

I am Trent Andersen's daughter, but I am not Trent Andersen.

I am Marina. And I'm ready to show these people exactly what that means.

Adrian gives his bandmates a nod and starts in on a riff they all know, something to get people riled and engaged again. I grab the mic and wait, watching, feeling the beat like

I feel my own pulse. As the crowd refills the dance pit and the people seem ready to listen, Adrian winds everyone back to a tune I recognize. With a deep breath in, and a look down at my cheering friends, I open my mouth …

And sing.

I sing and sing and sing, throwing everything I have into this microphone, letting myself get carried away on the smoking guitar behind me, riding the glorious wave these insanely talented musicians are creating, their hands flying over strings and keys and across the tightly stretched drumheads.

Three songs in, everyone is back to full throttle. The questions on their faces of whether I am worthy of this stage have evaporated. I am electric, every part of me a live wire as I bounce and lean in close to Leroy on backup vocals, to Adrian where he shares my mic, his fingers flying across the neck of his instrument. The way the music pours out of me like a broken dam, the way we sound together. To borrow from Darcie's earlier estimation, before she threw me under the bus to my father: we sound *incendiary*.

After the next song, once the audience stops screaming so we can hear ourselves think for a beat, Adrian steps up and grabs hold of my mic. "Hey, who's interested in hearing something a little quieter?"

Uproarious applause.

He turns and nods to Andy, now offstage rather than in the magical hidden sound booth. Andy trades out Adrian's electric with an acoustic guitar and then hurries out with two wooden stools. I'm watching like I know what's happening. Yeah, I don't.

And then Adrian is walking across the stage, another acoustic guitar in his hand, stretching it to me. He nods and points to the stool. He then leans close and whispers against my ear. "Can we do a Hidden Villains song?"

My eyes widen. He wants to sing one of my dad's songs?

And instantly I know which one he's talking about—the stools and the acoustic guitars—there were only a few Villains songs that were quiet enough to use acoustic guitars.

This one, my dad wrote for my mom. They performed it together at every show in the year before she died.

My throat aches.

"'Hidden Depths' ... Can you do it?" he asks. "If not, we can do 'Yesteryear.' You know that one—it's a Scuttlebutt tune."

I shake my head, fully aware that the audience is watching this entire exchange, even if they can't hear us. "I can do it." Adrian leans in and kisses me, slow and gentle, and I swear I hear the hearts of three hundred girls breaking along with their chorus of "Awwwww!"

I climb onto the stool, closing my eyes for a second to refocus, to remember the song my father wrote for my mother, the one he refuses to listen to anymore.

My favorite song of theirs.

Andy positions a second mic so there's one each in front of us, and I watch Adrian as he counts our start, talking over the first few bars. "Some of you might recognize this one ..." The crowd erupts with applause and laughter, hoots and hollers almost drowning out Adrian's guitar. As soon as he finishes the first line, someone shouts out "Hidden Depths."

I laugh, happy but sad, that someone out there remembers a song that was so special to my family.

As the crowd quiets, I join Adrian, letting muscle memory take over. I've played this song a thousand times in my room on my mother's Martin, and even though this isn't her instrument, it molds to me, like it understands that what is about to happen is really beautiful, really important.

> *I've been playing this role,*
> *But I'm done with it now*
> *I've forgotten my lines*

'Cos they never made sense.

Standing backstage with my heart inside out
I need you, I need you to see me
'Cos you're the one all my songs are about.

I see you pretending, just like me
They think all I do is strum strings,
Break dreams,
But baby, I've got hidden depths.

Maybe if I write loud enough
You'll finally, finally hear me?
I'm giving you all these words
But will you ever just see me?

You're on stage with your heart inside out
I need you, I need you to see me
'Cos I'm not the kind to call out.

I've been playing this role,
But I'm done with it now
I've forgotten my lines
'Cos they never made sense

Standing backstage with my heart inside out
I need you, I need you to see me
'Cos you're the one all my songs are about.

Adrian quiets and lets me finish it on my own, that final line falling off my lips as the tears creep down my face.

The audience eats up every second of it, everyone on their feet, shouting their affection, whooping and hooting and making a terrific tempest of noise.

I love it, I love it, *I love it.*

Adrian hops off his stool, sets his guitar on it, and gives me a tight hug around my own guitar, right there in front of everyone. He then hands me a folded handkerchief from his back pocket. The crowd *awwwws* again.

His lips tickle my ear. "I planned for tears. That was beautiful."

And then just as quickly as he appeared with the stools, Andy is back out to remove them and we're rejoined by the rest of the band to finish the few songs left on the set list. The energy in this place is like a real, tangible thing you can reach out and touch—I've never experienced anything like it.

I know now what my father was talking about, the addiction of it all.

I could get used to this very quickly. Nothing else in my life—and certainly not the swimming—ever makes me feel this alive.

As I approach the mic to launch into the next song, I glance down at Sierra and Lily, both of them clapping and cheering and making the heart symbol with their hands. A quick look over to Uncle Tim—I know that song must've been hard for him to hear too—but he's not at his table.

I close my eyes and fall into the song, bouncing and plucking the mic from the stand as the tempo increases, singing to Adrian and then with Leroy, whose backup vocals are so freaking good, I don't know why they didn't have him fronting the band in Darcie's absence.

The last line roars out of me like a freight train—I surrender to the music, to the beat around me, to the perfect synchronicity with my fellow musicians. The audience rides and soars right along with us, their bodies moving like one of those sound wave illustrations in a science textbook. It's not until Tyler finishes that last clash on the cymbal that I tuck the mic back into its stand, the tsunami of adoration washing over the stage.

Adrian slides next to me and kisses the side of my head,

holding his hands out to me, clapping and encouraging everyone else to follow along. They do.

I'm eating it up, like the most delicious sundae I've ever sunk a spoon into, when my eyes land on the reason Uncle Tim is no longer holding court at his table stage right.

He's got his hands full dealing with my father, who stands at the back of the Beanery, his eyes lit like nuclear reactors.

CHAPTER 37

COUNTING THE STARS

This could go very bad, very quickly, in front of a lot of people with cameras.

When our eyes lock across the space, it's like being kicked in the stomach. I've hurt him again.

Adrian's voice is next to my ear. "You okay? We usually do one more song as an encore."

I spin and look up at him, the crowd now chanting for us to keep going. Frantic, I look around the stage, the other musicians still at their instruments, waiting for Adrian to lead what happens next. The stools from earlier are just behind the side curtain.

I pull Adrian down so I can talk just to him. "My father is here. I have to do something."

Adrian straightens and brushes a thumb against my cheek. "Anything you need."

I nod, and he moves, signaling to his bandmates that they're vacating the stage. He then gestures to Andy to bring a stool and acoustic guitar. Darcie is offstage right, arms crossed, watching. She looks defeated—how can I be mad at her when she looks so sad?

I clamp my hand around the mic and raise an arm, met

with spirited cheers and bouncing bodies. My father and Tim are still at each other over by the far wall, at the edge of the seating area. I paste on a smile, trying not to worry as Sean and another Beanery employee approach my dad and his brother. My dad puts his hands up before him, like he's not trying to make trouble, but the look on his very angry face says otherwise.

"Thank you for being so understanding tonight, folks," I say into the mic, trying to bring down the noise a little. "Can we all just give a huge round of applause for the amazing Darcie Drayer? We can't wait for her to be back in action." I throw an arm out, summoning Darcie to emerge. She steps out of the shadows, and the crowd eats it up.

The rush of fan love seems to melt something in her glacial exterior. Darcie grins, waves, and bows a few times, then stretches her arms and claps in my direction. More deafening applause.

One more enthusiastic wave to her fans, and Darcie disappears behind the side curtain again, though when she spins on a heavy boot to face the stage, she no longer looks like she wants to feed me to her eels.

By now a tall wooden stool has been positioned behind me, and Adrian stands patiently waiting to hand over the acoustic guitar. My palms are sweaty; I'm afraid I might drop the mic and chicken out if I don't get going.

"This one's for my dad … and my mom." Applause and whoops. Adrian rubs my back; I relax into his touch, not aware he was even there but grateful to not be up here alone. I swipe at a rogue tear and clear my throat. "It's called 'Counting the Stars.'"

I nod at Adrian. He slides the mic back into its stand and leaves me to it. The audience offers a soft applause as I settle myself and the guitar onto the stool.

My fingers find their place. Eyes closed. Deep breath in.

"I love you, Mom," I whisper to myself.

The introductory notes float just over the tops of the hushed spectators, and when the first line is poised on my tongue, I turn my eyes to my father, standing with arms crossed defiantly against the wall; my uncle, right next to him, nods once in support.

I can't bring her back, neither can you,
I know, I know, I know that it hurts
It hurts for me to remember her too.

But don't you get that I'm her daughter,
So sometimes when you're not looking,
I do all the things that remind me of her

Like writing down words,
Like strumming a song,
Like singing out loud,
Like counting the stars.

But I can't bring her back, neither can you,
It hurts for me to remember her too.

The way that she sang,
The shape of her laugh,
The smile in her eyes,
The sound of her words

And yeah, I know, I know that it hurts,
But I can't bring her back, neither can you
I know, I know, I know that it hurts
It hurts for me to remember her too.

I hope that somehow, you'll see through the pain,
See the light again, dance in the rain,
Know that the stars have welcomed her home

And among their fair hearts, her love she will share.

Don't you get that I'm her daughter,
So sometimes when you're not looking,
I do all the things that remind me of her

Like writing down words,
Like strumming a song,
Like singing out loud,
Like counting the stars.

And yeah, I know, I know it hurts you,
It hurts for me to remember her too
It hurts for me to remember her too.

The last line almost chokes me, but as the final notes vibrate their end through the guitar's strings, there's not a dry eye in the place. After a beat, the crowd jumps to their feet. I look down to Lily and Sierra, my view of them occluded by my own tears, but I can see mascara smeared down their cheeks even as they cheer and shout my name.

And then Adrian swoops back on stage, wrapping me in a hug, followed by the band who climb behind their instruments. Tyler slams the cymbal once and then after a quick riff on the toms, he starts a beat on the snare, leading the band into something happier and louder to end tonight's performance.

Adrian kisses me sweetly and then nods offstage—he knows I can't sing another word. He follows me just to set the stool aside, picks up his own guitar, and handles the vocals to sing Scuttlebutt through the end of the show.

I wait behind the side curtain, Andy swaying awkwardly next to me as I try to catch my breath, blackening Adrian's formerly white handkerchief with what's left of my eye makeup.

Andy leans close. "That was beautiful, Marina. Calla would be so proud." He pats my shoulder, bobs his head once, and makes himself scarce.

Scuttlebutt finishes the song, and the exhausted crowd shares their noisy gratitude, screaming "Marina!" and "Darcie!" I sniff and scan the backstage area behind me, looking for Darcie, but then Adrian is beckoning me onstage. I join the band; we clasp hands and bow, clapping for one another as well as offering our applause to tonight's forgiving audience.

This has been the most incredible night of my entire life.

And just like that, it's over.

The band filters out, noisy and excited and amped on adrenaline as we pour through the backstage door, Adrian's arm tight around my shoulders. I could melt into him.

As our small blob of musical humanity makes its way toward the green room, I stop and move to the side, pulling Adrian with me.

"You guys comin'?" Tyler asks over his shoulder.

"In a sec," Adrian says.

I lean against the papered wall and wait until they've all disappeared into the post-show cavern. "So …"

"So …"

"Thank you," I say.

"Are you kidding? Thank YOU. You saved us! Plus, you sound absolutely incredible. Like, honestly, so, so good."

I'd blush, but my face is already sweaty and reddened from the physical and emotional toll of the last ninety minutes.

"Your dad's waiting," Adrian says.

I nod, willing the tears to stay put. "I guess it's time for Ariel to go back to the sea." I shrug, eyes burning, but then I look up at Adrian, and his face breaks my heart all over again. He pulls me against him, his arms so tight around me, I don't ever want him to let go. Not ever.

"I won't leave you alone to fight Triton. I promise." He

squeezes harder, and then pulls back just enough to kiss me, a fairy-tale kiss for the beautiful books with ribbon bookmarks that decorate our bedroom shelves.

The backstage door opens behind us, and Andy Drayer sticks his head through the gap. "Marina … your dad …" I nod once and turn back to Adrian.

He cups my face in his huge hands. "This is not the end. I'm not going anywhere. And if Trent Andersen thinks he can keep me from seeing you, then he doesn't know much about love."

I laugh and cry in the same breath, the sound echoing off the narrow walls making us both crack up.

He said love.

On tiptoes, I stretch and kiss Adrian once more before hurrying toward Andy and the open door, toward my father and his wrath.

I don't look back. I can't look back.

Only forward.

Andy opens the door wider so I can squeeze through. The venue has mostly emptied in my brief absence, just the Beanery staff talking animatedly amongst themselves as they clean up. This hiss of the steam wand on the espresso machine makes me jump.

Sierra and Lily wait way over by the hall that leads to the main exit. I wave, but then give them a subtle shake of the head that says *I can't talk to you right now. Gotta deal with my dad.* They get it, offering the *I Love You* sign, and then the narrow hall swallows them up.

My father and Tim stand near the wall out of the way of Beanery staff, not talking to one another, both looking like they're on a break to reload during yet another fierce battle.

I slide up in front of them. "Hey."

Uncle Tim's face cracks and he wraps me in a hug. "Oh, kiddo, that was something else. Really, really fantastic." He releases me and pushes back. "I loved hearing you sing *and* play—you're such a natural up there!" He pats the side of my arm. "Wasn't she phenomenal, Trent?"

When my father finally looks at me, something in his eyes, in his face, has changed. He looks older, his face pale and unshaved and his usually bright eyes red, the bags under them more purple than I remember. His shoulders are slumped, the corners of his mouth downturned.

"Dad ..."

He shakes his head. "We're not doing this here." And then he pushes off the wall, walking away from Tim and me.

I want to beg Tim to stay right here, to not follow my father. But when he pauses and looks back at us, watching him, I know the only way through this race is going to be to jump into the shark-infested waters and swim as fast as I can.

CHAPTER 38

BEHOLD THE FLOOD

When Uncle Tim follows us into the house, my dad doesn't protest. Doesn't tell him to mind his own business or that this is "between me and Marina." The look on Dad's face, the way he carries himself as he plods up the front stairs, not even bothering to wait for the lazy door to pull the car into the garage, tells me something big has happened tonight.

I think I am the straw that broke my father's back.

He punches in the alarm code, throws off his coat, slides out of his shoes. "Anyone want coffee? Tea?"

Uncle Tim and I share a look. "Dad, you sit. I'll make us something."

He doesn't argue. Doesn't storm past me and slam things around in the kitchen like he normally would. His lips aren't slightly parted, the words from yet another of his reprimands or speeches ready to fire.

As the kettle heats up, I prepare cups with the organic tea Dad prefers, throwing a regular, store-bought English breakfast tea bag into Uncle Tim's mug, a sachet of peppermint into mine. My dad has slid into his spot at the head of the table, my uncle in the second chair to my father's left. The quiet is louder than the Beanery concert.

When the kettle whistles, I exhale with relief that something other than my father's anger has punctured the veil of silence.

One at a time, I fill the mugs with boiling water, quickly pouring fresh organic cream into a tiny pitcher and grabbing the antique china sugar bowl from the baking cupboard. Dad doesn't use sugar, but Uncle Tim does. I slide everything onto a serving tray, alongside three silver teaspoons, and take it to the table, realizing in that moment that my body, now cooled from the day's swim events and the evening's energetic performance, is exhausted and sore.

And I still have a day of races left, hurtling toward me in just seven short hours.

"Thanks, Mari," Uncle Tim says, passing out the tea.

Spoons tink against the sides of our cups as milk and sugar are added. Uncle Tim fusses with his tea bag. I scoop in more sugar than I need, simply because I can't just sit here and wait for the bomb to detonate.

"You were really something out there tonight," my father finally says, his stare drowning in his tea.

"Thank you. Dad … I'm sorry I lied—"

He puts a hand up to stop me. Oh boy, here we go.

"That song … you wrote that for me? For your mom?" His eyes finally meet mine; a tear slides down his cheek. It takes my breath away—I haven't seen my father cry since my mom's funeral. I haven't seen him show any emotion other than anger and frustration since the day we handed over the keys to our old house to the real estate agent and drove away from our old life, a life where my mother played such a big role.

I move from my chair to the one right next to Dad's. "I did. I wrote it for you."

He smiles, another tear chasing the first one. He swipes at

it and then rests his closed fist on the table. "It was beautiful, Marina. Your mom would've loved it." I wrap my shaking hands around his.

And then I'm out of my chair so I can climb onto his lap and wrap him in all the love I have to give, all the love I've wanted to give him over the last eight years. "Daddy, I'm right here. Don't shut me out. We're a team, remember? Dad and Marina against the world?"

He hugs me back, rocking me against him like he used to do with three-year-old Marina after a nightmare. We're both crying, my dad apologizing for what he's become, for what he's done to our family. I push back and rest my hands on his pale, stubbled cheeks. His eyes look like a Bassett hound's.

"You've done everything you knew how to do," I say. "But you need to take care of yourself too. Mom would be so sad if she saw you like this."

He takes the tissue box Uncle Tim offers and plucks a few sheets. "I'm so sorry, Marina."

"Dad, I love you. I love you so much," I say, wrapping myself around him again in a tight squeeze. "I don't need you to apologize for anything. I just want my dad back."

"I know. I know." He rubs my arms. I stand and slide back into my chair, worried I might be crushing him. He feels too thin. "It's just been so hard, ya know? I miss her so much."

Tim and I scoot our chairs alongside Dad's, each taking one of his hands while he talks. It pours out of him in a great flood, his grief, how he wanted to be strong for me, his worries about screwing me up, how pushing me to be the best meant that he was a good parent, how I'd already lost my mom so he had to protect me from losing anything precious ever again.

"Seeing you up there tonight ... I can't quiet the music that flows through you. I know that now." He clears his throat. "I think I've known it all along. It's just ... I can't lose you too."

Hope burns like a sunrise in my chest. "Dad, you won't! You're stuck with me. I'm not going anywhere."

"That doesn't mean you're running off to join the band, though, kid," he says. We laugh quietly through fresh tears. The air in this room has never felt so light.

Dad talks until he's hoarse and our unfinished tea is long cold. He's folded a tissue into an origami dragon while Uncle Tim and I listened to every word.

At 3:00 a.m., as Dad's saying good night to his brother at the front door, I tuck this tiny dragon into my pocket for my treasure box. Something to remember the night Trent Andersen finally broke apart, just so he could be made whole again.

I make sure he gets to bed okay, doing a final sweep of the house to lock up for the night. We have to be up and at the pool in four hours—just because we had an emotional break-through tonight doesn't mean I can let my swim team down at the meet. I hoist my swim bag over my shoulder and slide my small purse off the dining table, eager to check my phone.

Eager to check in with Adrian, to thank him for what has literally been a life-changing night.

With my gear handled and my competition suit rinsed and hanging to dry in the bathroom, I wash my face—which, by the way, is a disaster of cosmetics and dried tears—brush teeth, feed Neptune, and slide into bed, my ratty stuffed gold-fish shoved under my head so I can see my phone in the dark-ened room.

A string of texts from Adrian:

Worried about you. Is everything OK? Are you grounded forever?

Please talk to me as soon as you can.

Just a reminder about how awesome you were tonight. Remind your dad how incredible you are.

If I don't hear from you soon, I'm showing up at the pool tomorrow. I'll be on your porch tomorrow night.

Gahhhh, Marina, PLEASE TEXT ME. Worried!!!

I smile with the last of my energy, my thumbs clumsy across the phone's screen:

Everything is on its way to being OK. Better than OK. Thanks to the cosmic forces that brought you and me together, tonight, I shall count the stars.

CHAPTER 39

TIME HEALS (MOST) WOUNDS

I swam on Sunday of the regional meet, the day after that first Scuttlebutt concert. I didn't do as well as everyone had hoped, but that's what happens when you've had three hours of sleep after likely the most emotional and exhausting eighteen hours ever.

Trent Andersen and I have reached a tentative peace, one that feels every day like it could become more solid. Uncle Tim and Auntie Shelly are back to coming over every Sunday for dinner. Dad is going to actual therapy with a registered professional and has given up the self-help podcasts. He adopted a Lab/Siberian husky mix puppy from a local rescue, on the advice of his therapist, that he named Turbo, because she never stops running, so he has someone to fuss over other than me. He's even put on some weight and is back to eating the cookies that Lily, Sierra, and I bake on the Saturday afternoons I'm not at the pool.

Because, thankfully, I'm not at the swim club seven days a week anymore. I can't swim every weeknight—it conflicts with my sessions with my amazing new vocal coach, referred to us by the awesome Ms. Amberly. I'm attending normal school—no more tutor or threats of homeschooling. And when Coach Tosto put up a fuss about futures and scholarships and commitment, my dad didn't raise his voice, didn't break under her iron fist. He stayed the course—he kept his promise, the one he made to me.

That he would let me breathe.

If I swim three days a week and keep up my grades, I can perform with Mr. Malcolm and the rock school kids. I can have a life with my friends on the weekends. I can rehearse and perform with Scuttlebutt, at least until Darcie's voice heals. Because she did have to have the surgery after all. Luckily for her, she had a way better surgeon than my beloved choir teacher.

Even Darcie and I have come to an agreement that we are better off friends. Ursula and Ariel, together at last!

And when Red Jones from Big Town Records comes calling, my father lets him into the house for a sit-down about Marina Andersen's future plans in the music industry, a discussion my father entertains but won't allow to develop any further until I graduate from high school and pick a university.

Fair enough.

But right now? I'm in my room with Lily and Sierra, trying to figure out what to wear. The windows are open, allowing in the fresh, unseasonably warm spring air. Sierra is fighting with her hot rollers; Lily, her own blond coif already perfect, is braiding the sides of my hair so it stays out of my face during tonight's performance. It's Andy Drayer's sixtieth birthday party, and his wife has gone all out, including renting our house to host all their family and friends.

As we speak, the Andersen hive buzzes with caterers and waitstaff and tech guys putting up lights and a stage in our recently refreshed, bursting-with-spring-colors backyard, the stage on which Scuttlebutt, featuring Marina Andersen on vocals, will be performing. They've had to get permits from the city for the noise, and the neighbors were more than eager to accept an invitation to the home of formerly mysterious recluse rocker's home for a free concert, made even sweeter by free food and a champagne fountain.

Someone knocks on my door. "Come in," I say, figuring it's my dad or Uncle Tim or Auntie Shelly. The stairs are taped off to keep nosy folks out of our upper living space. Just what my dad needs is some idiot fanboy sneaking into his bedroom to steal hair from his brush.

The door opens, and a face that speeds my heart peeks around. "Am I interrupting?"

"Cousin! Enter at once!" Lily gestures with the comb in her hand.

Adrian smiles. Sierra shrieks and her eyes about pop out of her head—her hair is a tangled mess—so she hops into the bathroom and quickly closes the door.

Lily finishes wrapping the band around the last braid, tucking it into the clip that holds the other one on the back of my head. "I'm going downstairs for a soda. Anyone want anything?"

"Nah, I'm good," Adrian says. I hoist my travel mug filled with honey-lemon tea, a preperformance necessity.

Lily winks and slides out of my room. Adrian reaches out a hand where I'm sitting in my desk chair, temporarily repurposed for beauty purposes, and pulls me to standing.

"You look beautiful," he says, kissing the tip of my nose.

I lean back. "You don't look too shabby yourself." He kisses me again, on the lips this time, longer and sweeter.

"I had to sneak past your dad to get up here," he says, smiling.

"Yeah, and if he finds you in my room, he'll turn you into kibble for Turbo."

"That dog is nuts—she's downstairs sniffing everyone's crotches."

"Sounds about right. This is her house, after all, and my dad is her human. She's very protective," I say.

"I'm glad he has someone—something—else to focus on for a while."

I chuckle. It's true. Turbo won't even let me sit next to Dad on the couch during our shows unless she gets to lie across both our laps. He used to be so protective of me, so demanding of my time and who I talked to, where I went, what I did. I'm forever grateful to that therapist whose suggestion led us to the adoption center. My dad needed Turbo as much as she needed him.

"So, you ready for tonight?" Adrian asks, letting go of me to sit on the end of my bed.

I turn back to my desk, the surface covered in makeup, and pluck my lip gloss from the pile to replace what he just kissed off. "I am. Are the guys here yet?"

"On their way. I just wanted to check on you." He smiles.

"Liar. You just wanted a smooch."

"That too."

The bathroom door opens, breaking the spell of our eyes locked on one another. "I'm sorry to intrude, but Marina, I desperately need your help." Sierra's usually lush brown hair looks like she got it tangled in a lawnmower.

"That's my cue." Adrian stands and kisses my cheek quickly before waving at Sierra, now close to tears.

I pick up Lily's abandoned comb and turn to my poor friend. "C'mere, Sebastian. Let's get you sorted out."

CHAPTER 40

MARTIN COMES HOME

Just because the concert is happening in the backyard of a nice residential neighborhood doesn't mean it's any less raucous or crazy than it would be if it were held at a proper performance venue.

Over the last six months, I've performed in five shows with Scuttlebutt, four at the Beanery and one night at the Orpheum in the downtown core for a Battle of the Bands gig—and even with every ticket sold and a thousand people in that Battle audience, we might have a rowdier crowd here today.

We play a set of two or three songs, and then someone comes up to give a speech or toast for Andy Drayer. Our yard is filled to the brim with his family and friends, industry professionals, more than a few famous rockers (which explains the earpiece-wearing security around the yard's flank and outside the front of the house). Andy's wife shares an emotional story about how they first met; his three kids take turns telling stories about growing up with the "coolest dad ever," even though none of them are rockers themselves, much to their dad's shock and dismay; Darcie gives a quiet, scratchy-voiced anecdote about how much he has influenced her life, how he was more dad than uncle to her, even if he embarrasses her by calling her "Little Deedee." Even my dad shares a story about the "old days" when Andy produced some never-released solo work he and my mom did.

Andy Drayer is well loved. He finally comes on stage and thanks everyone, says a few tear-jerking words of his own, reminds the few producers in the crowd that Scuttlebutt is "the next big thing" and they'd better pay attention, and then he insists that we stop with the "mushy crap" and get back to why we're all here: to worship at the altar of rock 'n' roll.

So we do.

We burn through the playlist, the flames licking the faces of everyone in the crowd, until we're all drenched with euphoria and exhaustion. Ms. Amberly, outfitted in another outstanding custom dress, this one with galaxies on it, and her boyfriend get people dancing. Coach Tosto stands off to the side, dressed in her standard Adidas tracksuit, bobbing her helmet of officious gray curls, the slight smile suggesting she *might* be having a good time.

During a brief break, I turn my back to the crowd to take a quick drink and mop the sweat off my forehead. The mic clicks behind me, like someone has grabbed it, and then applause breaks out.

"One more quick thing I wanted to say ..." It's my dad. I spin around, immediately noticing that clutched in his right hand is my mom's guitar.

And the strings are fixed.

He pulls it in front of him, fumbling with the tuning keys as he talks. "What a show, hey? Let's hear it for the phenomenal musical stylings of Scuttlebutt, fronted by my very awesome daughter, Marina Andersen ..." The crowd erupts in rowdy hoots and applause.

When they quiet, he talks again. "This guitar"—he hoists it in front of him—"it was Calla's, a Martin HD-35 Nancy Wilson Dreadnought acoustic. I gave it to Marina after Calla died, and she used it to write a song that is one of the reasons we're here tonight." He sniffs. "Sure, Andy, you're great and all that, but without my amazingly talented, brave, *rebellious* daughter"—he waits for the ripple of laughter to quiet—"we wouldn't be here on this beautiful spring night, under this breathtaking blanket of stars, among friends and loved ones.

"I tried to keep Marina away from the music. I tried to protect her from this industry that will chew her up and spit her out." Heads nod knowingly amongst the crowd; I'm still holding my breath, unsure of what's coming next. "But, like my therapist says," (nervous chuckle), "a child's will is like a river over stones. You can redirect it; you can try to dam it; but eventually it will wear down the stone to a smooth finish to reach where it needs to be. Marina's will knew where she needed to be." He looks over at Adrian, standing stage right. "Even if it means she risks her heart."

A collective *awwww* murmurs through the partygoers. Adrian's face turns a shade of red I didn't know was possible in human skin.

"So, not to hijack Andy's big night, but I want to thank my daughter, and thank you for protecting and nurturing her, for showing her that music can also mean love. Because this yard is filled with love for a guy who has shaped our music for decades. And speaking of the music, I'd like to see if maybe Marina would play with her old-fart rocker dad, maybe sing her song for Calla, with me, tonight." He stretches the Martin toward me.

I walk across the stage, take the restored guitar, and wrap an arm around my dad, letting the warm applause wash over us. I kiss his cheek and wipe off a tear he is no longer ashamed to shed. "I'd love to sing with you."

"Good thing, or else I'm gonna look like a turd." We share a quick laugh as Adrian and Damon slide a couple of stools center stage and adjust the mics for us.

Adrian offers his acoustic to my dad and then shakes his hand. I hear him mutter under his breath, "Thank you, sir."

My dad nods, climbs onto his stool, and looks to me. "On your count, Marina."

I nod once at my dad and tap my foot where it hangs over the stool's foot bar, hugging my mother's guitar against me as the first notes dance into the night air.

CHAPTER 41

OPEN DOORS, OPEN HEARTS

With every party, there are those who stay just long enough to eat some food, shake some hands, and share good wishes with the guest of honor. Tonight was a little different, the live music and the chance to reconnect with old friends enticing folks to stay longer than they might have otherwise. But once the music stopped, the crowd thinned. Even old rock stars need their beauty sleep.

This is good for those of us who are *not* old rock stars, because there is a huge spread of sushi, fancy hors d'oeuvres, and birthday cake left to feed an army of teenagers. Which we basically are. My dad told me last week it would be okay to invite the rock school and choir kids to come over at the midpoint of the party, once the Drayer family had their chance to spoil Andy. And it's an incredible step forward in our ongoing efforts to communicate, and cohabitate, better.

I certainly wasn't going to say no to my dad opening our home to my friends.

The backyard stage is quiet and dark—the noise ordinance *does* have to be obeyed—but all my musical friends, even the Scuttlebutt guys *and* Darcie Drayer, sit in chairs and on benches clustered around the giant gas-fueled fire pit. A few people have guitars. My Martin HD-35 sits in her case against the chair I recently abandoned.

But it's so awesome to see the fire pit lighting up the night again. Not unlike my dad, it's been quiet for too long, as if it was too sad to share its warmth.

Turbo is the belle of the ball, flopped on the sneakered feet of some of my rock school buddies, now that she's had her fill of snacks off everyone's plates. My dad has retired to the kitchen with Uncle Tim, Auntie Shelly, Andy Drayer and his wife, and a dozen or so of their old-timer friends. From the laughs echoing across the yard through the open windows and sliding doors, I'm confident that this evening was exactly what my father needed.

I feel like I'm floating every time I hear his laugh. I've lived for so long with that cold rock of anxiety in my stomach, I'd forgotten what it was like to feel light again, to not be weighed down by my dad's misery.

And at this very second, I am the opposite of weighed down. Adrian and I are wrapped up in each other, nestled by the quiet rectangular pool, the underwater bulbs painting shadows along the tiled bottom as a light wind ruffles the water, its surface decorated with twinkling votive candles floating on actual lily pads. We're sharing a quiet, playful conversation, enjoying every moment we get to be in each other's company to talk about music and life and our favorite songs and our futures and dumb jokes we've heard and yes, even tidal marsh creation and coastal wetlands.

When we run out of things to say, we sit together, watching the water. Adrian then stands and wraps his arms loosely around my back. We press our foreheads together, and he sings to me, his smile inviting me to join in, swaying softly as we sing low enough so no one else can hear.

When it gets to the line where the verse includes the words "I love you," Adrian lifts his head from mine and looks me right in the eye, the words sliding across his lips. He stops singing and bends his head to kiss me.

I let him. I will always let him kiss me. Because I'm not Ariel, and he's not Eric.

We're Marina and Adrian, and the music has repaired our hearts.

And then all of a sudden, we're flying, the two of us hitting the water, gulping under the water for the brief second it takes to realize what has just happened. Adrian reaches for me, and I reach for him, our laughs exploding huge bubbles out of our chests that race us to the surface.

Sierra and Lily and the other members of Scuttlebutt stand poolside, laughing and whooping.

I skate my arm across the water to throw a wave at my obnoxious friends. They squeal and try to hop out of the way, nearly ending up in the pool themselves.

"Kiss the girl!" Sierra yells, in the accented voice from that silly Disney crab.

"I should probably do what she says." Adrian grins wickedly. We're treading water with one arm each, legs kicking to keep afloat, but he pulls me to him, and with his free hand, he kisses me solidly, the hoots and hollers of our posse serving as background music.

We break for a breath, and I laugh, embarrassed that we're creating a spectacle. Adrian kicks and moves us toward the shallow end so our feet can touch. "To avoid drowning," he says. "You've had a good night?"

"I have. The best night. You?"

"Definitely the best night."

And then there's a scream as Sierra shoves Lily into the water, which starts a chain reaction where everyone else cannonballs into the pool, fully clothed. I cannot imagine how many cell phones are meeting their untimely deaths right at this moment.

People near the outdoor fire pit take notice. It's about to get very crowded in here.

But before it does, before the moment slips away like a wisp of campfire smoke into the sky, I flatten my hand against Adrian's cheek so he can look only at me. "As a wise mermaid once said, 'You're the one that I've been looking for.'"

Adrian grins, locks his lips against mine, and pulls me beneath the water's edge as the tempest of our friends rages around us.

ACKNOWLEDGMENTS

Wow, what fun this has been! Right? Did you guys love it?

First off, I must offer my applause and wild thanks to Robert Randall of the Young Actors Project for inviting me to collaborate on this undertaking. As a long-time fan of the YAP films and acting program, the invitation to write Marina's story was a lot like Darcie Drayer showing up at the swim club, or Ursula offering my voice in trade for the prince. I am grateful, however, for all our sakes, to have been allowed to leave the singing to Marina.

Thanks, of course, go to Catherine Randall for the ongoing support as we worked through the project, as well as to Olivia Randall for the terrific research help with all things swim related. Any mistakes in Marina's world of elite swimming are solidly my own.

A heartfelt thanks to my songwriting friend, poet Edi Nightingale, for her stellar assistance writing the songs for Marina and Adrian to perform. Here's a challenge: I'd love to hear some YAP fans write the music to go along with our lyrics! Record them, upload, and tag me on Instagram.

Thanks to the 2015 Juno MusiCounts Teacher of the Year, blues musician, and actual rock school god, Steve Sainas, and his musician daughter, Elsa, for their help with painting Mr. Malcolm and the rock school kids into the story. What I would give to have some musical talent!

Heartfelt thanks also to my wildly talented musical friends, Chris Ho and Elizabeth (Beth) Isaacs, who generously helped with my musical research when I put out the call.

Thank you to Laine Taylor and Shea Smeltzer for doing such a terrific job bringing Lily Bennet and Sierra Schmidt to life on the YAP screen. Your performances made my job so much easier as I stitched you both into Marina's hectic life.

Thanks to my daughter, Yaunna, for listening and helping me work out story stuff as I built Marina's world. Some of you may remember YAP's film, *Thirteen*, from a few years back—the actress who played Caroline? Yeah, that's my Yaunna, and without her love of screen and stage, YAP and the Randall family would not have waltzed into our lives.

Lastly, I want to thank the unbelievably cool and passionate fans of YAP's films and acting programs. Thank you for giving us an audience with whom we can share our work. I hope that watching the YAP films (and reading Marina's story) inspires you all to go out and express yourselves, whether with singing or writing or making films with your friends or painting or dancing or drawing or spoken-word poetry or whatever.

In the famous words of legendary author and creator Neil Gaiman, who encourages us to "make good art":

"The one thing that you have that nobody else has is you. Your voice, your mind, your story, your vision. So write and draw and build and play and dance and live as only you can."

Now, get busy.

YAP PRODUCER'S NOTE

FROM ROB RANDALL

Thanks to all the fans who love *The Girl Without a Phone* as much as my family and I do—and who have watched our movies on YouTube. Allowing Lily and Sierra's fairy-tale-inspired world to expand into books has been an exciting adventure.

There are many limitations to the stories we tell in our movies because, well, they're movies—but in a book, the only limitation is the writer's imagination. The characters can go anywhere, do anything. The stories can be bigger!

I hope you enjoyed our first book, *Fish Out of Water: A Little Mermaid Story*. More exciting—and big—adventures await, so stay tuned!

Subscribe to us on YouTube and social media to stay up to date. Just search "Young Actors Project" or YAP.

~

ABOUT THE AUTHOR

Jennifer Sommersby writes young adult and middle grade fiction for kids. When not writing, she works as a freelance editor for writers of fiction and nonfiction.

Her young adult novel, *Sleight*, from HarperCollins Canada and Sky Pony (US), was a Canadian Children's Book Centre Best Book for Kids and Teens, Fall 2018; its sequel, *The Undoing**, will be released on March 31, 2020. (*This sequel is called *Scheme* in the US and releases April 21, 2020. Both books are also available for Polish readers from Prószyński i S-ka.)

As a recipient of a 2019 British Columbia Arts Council Creative Writers Grant, Jenn is looking forward to her next young adult project, a story about a teenage water diviner living in a waterless world, set in British Columbia, called *The Bright Day Is Done*.

Jenn is mom to three kids and two very spoiled tuxedo cats, a lover of books, and a Superman freak. She also writes romantic comedies for adults under the pen name, Eliza Gordon. If she's not at home writing, look for her hiding in the aisles of the nearest bookstore or stuffing her face with popcorn in front of her favorite movie.

YAP: YOUNG ACTORS PROJECT

Short films, web series, and more brought to you from award-winning filmmaker Robert Randall. Click on the logo above to visit and subscribe to the YAP Channel on YouTube.

Visit our merch store online! And follow us on social media—Instagram, Facebook, and Twitter.

Subscribe, share, enjoy!

SLEIGHT: BOOK ONE OF THE AVRAKEDAVRA

ALSO BY JENNIFER SOMMERSBY, A YA FANTASY ADVENTURE SURE TO ENCHANT!

Delia smiles at the shadow only she sees—

Something slams into her. The lyra whirls like a half-dollar spinning on its edge.

My mother is thrown backward.

And she falls.

Growing up in the Cinzio Traveling Players Company, Genevieve Flannery is accustomed to a life most teenagers could never imagine: daily workouts of extravagant acrobatics; an extended family of clowns; wild animals for pets; and her mother, Delia, whose mind has always been tortured by visions—but whose love Geni never questions. In a world of performers who astonish and amaze on a daily basis, Delia's ghostly hallucinations never seemed all that strange . . . until the evening Geni and her mother are performing an aerial routine they've done hundreds of times, and Delia falls to her death.

That night, a dark curtain in Geni's life opens. Everything has changed.

Still reeling from the tragedy, the Cinzio Traveling Players are also adjusting to the circus's new owner: a generous, mysterious man whose connection to the circus—Geni suspects—has a dark and dangerous history. And suddenly Geni is stumbling into a new reality of her own, her life interrupted daily by the terrors only Delia used to be able to see.

As the visions around her grow stronger, Geni isn't sure who she can trust. Even worse, she's starting to question whether she can trust her own mind.

Visit www.jennsommersby.com for more information and buy links. Available in Canada from HarperCollins, in the US from Sky Pony, and in Poland from Prószyński i S-ka!

THE UNDOING/SCHEME: BOOK
TWO OF THE AVRAKEDAVRA

*The sequel to **SLEIGHT**,*
available March 2020!

The most dangerous magic must be destroyed.

Genevieve Flannery's family inheritance is both an invaluable gift and an unspeakable curse: she is one the heirs of the *AVRAKEDAVRA*, a trio of ancient texts capable of preserving everlasting life, or eroding it completely. Burdened with the power of untold magic and tormented by those who would seek to exploit it, the three *AVRAKEDAVRA* texts must be destroyed.

If only the road ahead were easy. Genevieve is grateful to have her fellow heir, the irresistible Henry, by her side, but when the father she never knew she had becomes their guide, all bets are off. Together, this new team must rely on unexpected allies as they embark on a harrowing global search to acquire the pieces necessary to destroy an ancient magic and complete The Undoing.

But loyalties among the magical community are fragile. Genevieve, grieving the loss of her mother, struggles to control her new *AVRAKEDAVRA*-bestowed gifts, and with mounting threats to her psyche and body, she clings mightily to the promise of a brighter future once this is over—if they can survive it. And Henry, broken by his father's treachery but entranced by the heartwarming connection his family's text has granted him, grapples with the fact that once they succeed in destroying the books, he'll lose the only family he has left.

Forced to question all they hold dear, the young heirs must remember Genevieve's mother's greatest lesson:

The key to good is found in truth.

Visit www.jennsommersby.com for more information and to preorder *The Undoing* (Canadian title)/*Scheme* (US title). Also available in Poland from Prószyński i S-ka!

9 781999 051662